PENGUIN B

MONKEY-N

Usha K.R. is the author of the novels *Sojourn*, *The Chosen* and *A Girl and a River*. *A Girl and a River* was shortlisted for the Commonwealth Writers' Prize, 2008, and won the Vodafone Crossword Award, 2007. She lives and works in Bangalore.

Monkey-man

USHA K.R.

PENGUIN BOOKS

PENGUIN BOOKS

Published by the Penguin Group

Penguin Books India Pvt. Ltd, 11 Community Centre, Panchsheel Park, New Delhi 110 017, India

Penguin Group (USA) Inc., 375 Hudson Street, New York, New York 10014, USA

Penguin Group (Canada), 90 Eglinton Avenue East, Suite 700, Toronto, Ontario, M4P 2Y3, Canada (a division of Pearson Penguin Canada Inc.)

Penguin Books Ltd, 80 Strand, London WC2R 0RL, England

Penguin Ireland, 25 St Stephen's Green, Dublin 2, Ireland (a division of Penguin Books Ltd)

Penguin Group (Australia), 250 Camberwell Road, Camberwell, Victoria 3124, Australia (a division of Pearson Australia Group Pty Ltd)

Penguin Group (NZ), 67 Apollo Drive, Rosedale, North Shore 0632, New Zealand (a division of Pearson New Zealand Ltd)

Penguin Group (South Africa) (Pty) Ltd, 24 Sturdee Avenue, Rosebank, Johannesburg 2196, South Africa

Penguin Books Ltd, Registered Offices: 80 Strand, London WC2R 0RL, England

First published by Penguin Books India 2010

Copyright © Usha K.R. 2010

ISBN 9780143068563

For sale in the Indian Subcontinent and Singapore only

Typeset in Sabon by InoSoft Systems, Noida

Printed at Replika Press Pvt. Ltd, Sonipat

For Bharat

PART I

Prologue

~

Monday, 3 January 2000

In the first week of the new millennium, the strange creature was spotted for the first time. Half man–half beast, it made its appearance in Ammanagudi Street in the south-eastern part of the city, an area that would once be described as a middle-class residential locality but now hovered between house, office, market and slum. It was late evening and twilight had faded into darkness. There were no lights as there was an unscheduled power cut. It would be pertinent to add that Ammanagudi Street had recently been declared a one-way, that is, traffic was allowed to move only in one direction on it, and its footpaths had been dug up by the maintenance cell of the public works department.

A local eveninger, hesitant, unbelieving of its own skill and good fortune, broke the news but soon the national dailies and news channels had elbowed it out of the way. What did the creature look like?

'Nasty, brutish and short,' said Shrinivas Moorty, reader in history at the National Trust First Grade College, allegedly the first person to get a good look at the creature.

A long-time resident of Ammanagudi Street, Mr Moorty was in the act of parking his scooter on the ground floor of his block of flats when the creature almost fell on him from the balcony above, before making off swiftly down the road. It appeared that the creature had first alighted on the terrace of the building, made its way down the drainpipe to the balcony of Mr Moorty's second floor flat, where it mangled a litter of newly born kittens, before raking a casual paw through his wife's forearm when she came out into the balcony to see what the noise was about, then swung itself down to the balcony of the beauty parlour on the first floor, where it destroyed a potted plant garden, before finally dropping down to the ground floor and fleeting past the alert and resourceful Mr Moorty. (Mrs Shrinivas Moorty was prostrate and unavailable for comment. The beauty parlour had closed for the day.)

Next to identify it were two employees of the city's premier research institute in the social sciences, the Centre for Socio-Economic Studies, CSES, who had just been dropped off by the Centre's van.

'It missed me by a hair's breadth. If I had been one step ahead . . . who knows . . . Arokya Mata alone saved me,' shuddered Miss Neela Mary Gopalrao, executive assistant at CSES. 'I first thought it was a bat, a giant vampire bat,' she added as an afterthought.

'It was huge and black, like a rakshas, with red fire coming out of its eyes—' volunteered Sukhiya Ram, Class Four staff on contract at the Centre, clearly enjoying the attention he was getting.

A software engineer encountered the beast as he emerged from his office in Bhimaiah Plaza at the end of Ammanagudi Street. Expressing a desire to remain unidentified, he said, 'It was like running into a rock. My chest is still hurting . . .' So great was the impact that he was knocked over and the creature escaped before he could see it properly.

Miss Pushpa Rani, an employee in a call centre, who was making her way home to a gully off Ammanagudi Street, was still a little disoriented when she clutched the reporter from the leading English-language newspaper by the hand and said, 'It was Yama, the God of Death himself, I know it . . .'

A flower seller thought the creature was wearing striped Hindustani drawers but since it was only the local eveninger that reported it, and with many a disclaimer, that bit was disregarded.

Over the next month, 'sightings' were reported from other parts of the city, always after dark. Successive encounters with the

USHA K.R.

creature revealed it to be stealthy, violent and even sadistic, as it freely scratched its victims—five people were treated for identical puncture wounds in hospitals in different parts of the city—bit a shopkeeper's ear off, and so frightened a couple stealing a few quiet moments on the terrace of a building, that the young man lost his balance on the parapet wall and fell to his death. The creature also proved elusive for though it was confirmed to be a short, dark, hairy, man-like, light-emitting beast, no one could snatch a bit of its hair or a piece of its skin for the DNA tests that the scientists so eagerly wanted to conduct. The city grew understandably nervous. Even as they organized vigilante squads, people protested against the inadequate policing of their streets after dark and mobs gheraoed the state electricity board office and the local payment counters, demanding better lighting. The chief commissioner of police issued a statement warning against a 'fear psychosis syndrome' and urged people to remain calm.

Meanwhile zoologists, anthropologists, sociologists, talk-show hosts, astrologers, rationalists, fashion designers and others debated on the 'monkey-man', as the creature came to be known, in various fora. In inter-college festivals, it became the darling of extempore speech makers and 'If I were to encounter the monkey-man' became the topic most often pulled out of the hat. The Letters to the Editor column of every newspaper was choked with readers' views on the creature, displacing burning issues of national and international importance. A reader with a scientific bent of mind suggested that it could be a cloning experiment in a biotechnology lab gone wrong—a pharma giant, an MNC, had recently set up a captive lab in the city with much fanfare. Another felt that the creature could be a secret agent planted on the streets of the country's fastest growing city by a hostile foreign power to create panic and chaos and demoralize the people, right in the beginning of the new year, of the new millennium. A prominent local godman pronounced that this was a sign that god was angry and had sent down a malevolent avatar to warn man against his growing greed and avarice. Not to be outdone, alert cultural scientists filed away every snippet of information on the creature, grooming it to become an urban legend.

But coming back to day one, it was Balaji Brahmendra—Bali Brums to his fans—the charismatic and hugely popular radio jockey of the city's brand new and only FM channel, Voices from Heaven, who stole the show by getting the three people who had first seen it—Shrinivas Moorty, Neela Mary Gopalrao and Sukhiya Ram—on his radio show the day after they sighted the monkey-man.

PART II

one

~

1

Monday, 3 January 2000

On the morning of that fateful day when Shrinivas Moorty set
off as usual at 8 a.m. for National Trust College where he
taught history, there was nothing to indicate it would be different
from any other day, that in ten hours a brief half-registered meeting,
a brush with a strange creature, would change his life forever.

He breakfasted at 7, alone, on cornflakes and milk. After
blundering about in the kitchen he pulled out the wrong container,
a cooking utensil instead of a bowl and, as the stream of crisp
brown flakes poured into the vessel—pretenders all for he knew
that they would turn into soggy pieces of cardboard as soon as
he wet them with cold milk, and gritty too, once he added the
sugar—he eyed the rooster on the box resentfully. When he was
young cornflakes and milk was considered fever food, given only to
children who were ill. And the flakes had come in plastic packets,
manufactured by the same people who ran the distilleries for the
local liquor company. Usually, his wife served him a full south
Indian cooked breakfast, hot off the stove. But it was a Monday
and she had the nurse in early for her massage. Everything that
Lily did was high ceremony, so also this morning ritual involving
mysterious, strong-smelling unguents for the many, imprecise aches
and pains that had beset her of late. She had coaxed a nurse
out of retirement to come thrice a week to give her the massage
and now the woman quite doted on her. Lily could command a
winning manner when she wanted and she was particularly adept
at binding the loyalties of those who served her. There had been

an old woman, a family retainer, part of Lily's 'dowry', who was so devoted that she would quite hiss at him when he tried to come near Lily in the early days of their marriage.

'I'll see you then, in the evening. I'll be late, don't wait up for me,' he called out his usual morning departure, and as always there was no reply.

As Shrinivas Moorty turned to shut the front door of his flat, the drawing room suddenly turned bright in the morning light, as if the sun, in a momentary act of kindness, had shifted its position slightly to accommodate him. The battle against the gloom, the smallness of the place and his wife's contrary tastes had been hard-won. The hand-woven woollen durrie glowed blood-red in the sun—a decoy for the ugly mosaic floor, the implacable mild-steel window frames were covered by the double lace-and-linen curtains—here, full marks to her, and the cane chairs he had wrested now stood on the sides of the room—pale, ascetic and proud. Right in the beginning he had thrown out the soft, oversize sofas she had tried to stuff into the small room, likening their feel to the hot fleshy embrace of a woman one has ceased to love. But sometimes, on a morning like this, when the straight-laced sticks of cane cast striated shadows off the easterly sun, he wondered whether theirs was not the reluctant, bony clutch of one who had ceased to love him.

He started climbing down the two flights of stairs—there was no lift, the builder having run out of money by the time the lift came to being installed and the flat owners refusing to pay more for it. Moreover, this was one of the earliest blocks of flats to come up in the city, and so, rudimentary in many ways. To think that at one time a balcony in each bedroom and a 'utility unit' with a gleaming steel sink was considered almost revolutionary . . .

He hoped for a glimpse of the Chinese girls who worked in the beauty parlour on the first floor but it was too early. They were not open yet. No one else was about, only the resident tom cat—fat, grey and so blasé that it loped past, disregarding Shrinivas Moorty completely. He chased after it dutifully and, after scuttling a few paces, it stood and stared at him. As a boy, he had liked chasing cats. And there had been several around then, when, instead of these flats, there had been a house—*his* large, damp, uncomfortable, litigation-ridden house. He considered going up to warn his wife about the lurking tom, but baulked at the thought of climbing up two flights of stairs again.

He lost his temper when he reached the basement. His neighbour's large red car was blocking the way to his scooter, parked in the row behind. He had suggested so many times to the Singhania slug that they exchange parking spaces, but the man would not agree; he wanted to have his cake and eat it too—prime first row parking *and* a large car. The sight always made him happy—the cars crouching between their designated yellow lines while his scooter stood in the middle of its allotted space, breathing the air as a free man. No need for him to mince around either, worrying about the paint scraping off the sides, for the parking basement too, like the flats, was before its time, pre-dating the large cars and the SUVs, when the smaller Santro and Matiz, and even the humble Maruti, had been cause for delight. But that was no excuse; a clever builder was supposed to see into the future and anticipate such things.

He jerked his scooter off its stand and felt again, for the second time that morning, that dyspeptic twinge, reminding him to get the Milk of Magnesia from the chemist's on his way back home. He squeezed past the supporting beam of the basement, gleeful of the neat stripe of paint that the handle of his scooter ploughed out of the side of Singhania's car but acquiring at the same time, a band of whitewash across his elegant, vegetable-dye printed bush-shirt.

He roared up the ramp and at the gate, he stopped. There was no way of getting to the street. The footpath outside his gate was completely dug up. Overnight, the stretch of tightly packed mud that had served as a footpath outside his building seemed to have shuddered convulsively, and broken up into giant clods. Out of its depths two snakes had emerged, one blue and one orange, which now rested, entwined, at the end of the mud stretch. It was not as if the footpaths had never been dug up before—the drains were always being repaired and it was preferable that they be disturbed in the promise of a better future than to salvage a flawed past. For the twisted coils of orange and blue plastic carried fibre optic cable—veins of glass through which signals from his telephone pulsed in the form of light waves, travelling far more efficiently than through the usual metal wires, he was given to understand. They made for better 'bandwidth', which seemed to be the operative word these days. But these creatures seemed not to know their place. Instead of being inert conduits of 'good', they were too bright, too loud, too brazen, challenging the very sun as they lay casually coupled in orange and blue—colours that should have clashed but now proclaimed a new harmony. Not that he had anything against technology, he was far from being a Luddite. Moreover, his father had foreseen many of these changes and spoken of them approvingly. For thirty years, his father, in regulation brown trousers and cream-yellow shirt, briefcase in hand with a steel dabba in it, had caught a bus at the end of the street and ridden to the outskirts of the city to his job in the Indian Telephone Industries. Connectivity had been his business and his hobby horse. But still, he would not have approved of his footpath being dug up so savagely.

As Shrinivas Moorty stood at the gate, looking at the chasm before him, he contemplated going back, roaring down the ramp, sloughing another ribbon off Singhania's car, this time on the other side, and taking a bus to college instead. But just then he spotted a strip of connecting land, an isthmus of mud that would get him safe passage across the chasm, to the street. It involved a tricky bit of manoeuvring though, but except for a brief moment when the yellow plastic box advertising the STD/ISD phone booth, hanging from the branches of a prolapsed honge tree scraped his face and dislodged his spectacles, he made it across safely.

Ideally, he should have turned right, but a flyover was being constructed on the main road and all the traffic was being re-routed through Ammanagudi Street. The disruption was supposed to be temporary and the flyover was eventually supposed to ease the congestion, but it was getting on to two years and it showed no signs yet of being finished. In the larger interests of the city, to accommodate the people and the vehicles that swilled into it each day, Ammanagudi Street had embraced it all—the noise, the traffic, even the sludge of brown mud that flowed in from the excavations on the main road, silting its monsoon drains. Shrinivas Moorty didn't know which phrase he disliked more—his father's nostalgic cliché, 'Pensioner's Paradise', which suggested a cityful of toothless ex-public servants taking the balmy evening air together as they traded notes on their respective ailments, or the currently aspirational 'Silicon Valley' harking to a place that ninety-nine per cent of the populace had not even heard of. In the four hundred years since its founding, the city had forgotten its mud fort origins and far outgrown the four tower outposts which its founder had built to mark the limits of its healthy growth. Those towers now formed the heart of the city; the one on the hillock in Lal Bagh was a favourite picnic spot, and he himself had eaten many memorable meals there with his cousins.

The Ammanagudi Street of his boyhood was a nice mix of cows and men, and of course, the goddess after whom the street was named. Of the old shops, only two remained—a cycle-repair shop and a flour mill, going about their business for more than thirty years—till they were shown up by a fast food 'palace' selling hot tomato soup at five rupees per cup and a cyber cafe with twenty-four-hour Internet access that had come up on either side. Shrinivas Moorty wondered which of the two would go first, for few people in the area travelled by cycle these days and as for the flour mill —he knew his wife had long given up sending rice and wheat to be ground; he suspected she even bought the idli batter readymade now. Instead of going to the kirana shop next door with a list of things she had run out of, she took the trouble to go further up the street to the new super market, where there was no counter separating the customer from the goods, and she walked down the aisles, slinging things that took her fancy into a trolley, often forgetting to buy the things she needed most.

Ammanagudi Street had always smelt of cow dung, for a little beyond their houses, just before the road narrowed, there were many Golla households with their cows penned in rows in their compounds. As a boy he had gone there each morning with a pail to fetch the milk, fresh and frothy, for his mother had had a horror of milk that came in bottles and later, plastic packets. Two of those houses were being fought over now in the munsiff's court as the illiterate black lettering on the freshly whitewashed walls informed passers-by; a couple of forlorn cows sat in their dung in the large yard of one of the houses, the other was empty. One of the Golla brothers, Bhimaiah, had sold his cows and cow pens at the right time—just when the IT boom had hit the city. He had put up a building to specification and now the many-paned, glass fronted façade of I-Soft Global Technologies glinted in the morning sun. With true neophyte brashness he had named the building after himself—Bhimaiah Plaza—instead of a more neutral and stylish Deluxe or Pearl Plaza, but, in complete disregard of the gleaming 'software' windows the cycle-shop owner still called it Bhimaiah's kottige, implying that a cow pen it still was, even if the cows had been replaced by programers and writers of code.

If Shrinivas Moorty's father, Vasudev Moorty had embodied the spirit of the sixties—the burgeoning, self-righteous enthusiasm of a city in a newly independent nation, preening on the largesse of its prime minister, whose protective socialistic zeal had gifted it with four large government-owned factories manufacturing aeroplanes, telephones, machine tools and electronic goods, all that was needed for the nation to march ahead—Bhimaiah was the brash face of the liberalized nineties, when the doors of the economy had been opened to the private sector and the foreign investor, when the old system of import restrictions, quotas and licenses and, hopefully, shortages, was over, and the government was beginning to roll back its overweening presence. It was time for the country to stop thinking of itself as a frugal middle-class housewife and behave like a memsahib. It was time also for small men to think big and be nimble. Quick to seize the advantage, impatient with the old and ready to let it go, Bhimaiah had broken the time-honoured distance between office and home and built an office complex in place of his cow pens. And the city that had been so careful to mark separate zones for the two had looked on indulgently at first and then joined in the scrum. Men would no longer wear a uniform and go to work in a bus, the city seemed to have decreed. They would roar in on their red Hero Hondas or in spanking new cars, into houses-turned-hastily-into-offices to work late into the night behind dazzling one-way shutters of glass.

It would be unfair to blame Bhimaiah entirely, Shrinivas Moorty acknowledged, for in truth his own father had shown the way. Theirs had been the first 'bungalow' to make way for flats on Ammanagudi Street. He thought of the relief, and the disbelief, with which his father had received the builder's proposal twenty years ago. They had grown tired of the house his grandfather had built, despite the large compound and the full grown mango and sapota trees that yielded fruit year after year, for it was now crumbly and beyond repair; thick nests of caterpillars bred in every damp nook and fungus-ridden cranny, and colonies of huge black ants seeped out of the floors when the weather turned warm. What was more, his father's brother was demanding an immediate share in the property and they had erected a shaky partition in the middle of the house, dividing it into two equal portions and coming up with ridiculous living arrangements. In the kitchen they had lost the cooking platform and the grinding stone and while they kept the taps in the bathroom, the commode went over to the other side. The dimensions of the property had been a little too small for a multi-storeyed building but the developer had said that he would 'adjust' things with the authorities. Of course they would have to settle for a lower price. His father and uncle had got two flats a piece, and his father, too timid to own more than one of anything, had immediately sold the second one. In a way Shrinivas Moorty was glad that his father had not survived to live in the flat; he had died just before the 'flat warming' ceremony. His mother had lived with him in the flat for a few years, bewildered, ill-at-ease in the confined space, before moving to Mysore to live with his sister in a house with a garden; she said her daughter needed help with her three small children.

Shrinivas Moorty slowed down and allowed the SUV to overtake him, knowing that this must be its first time on Ammanagudi

Street. As he expected, the large car braked in panic as it took the curve and the temple jutted out into its path—the Mother was taking her ease. 'India's No 1 Car,' he read the sticker on its humped back, 'And You're Behind It!' You had to be patient at this point in Ammanagudi Street, and go past with care. For this was Mother Land, No Man's Land, for here the Mother reigned. They had never had cause to venture past this bottleneck on the road before the work on the flyover began and the natural exit from the street got blocked. The temple and its slummy netherworld had not been their concern. Shrinivas Moorty knew it only as the place where his servant lived. But now that he had had to go past the temple every day for the past two years, past the potholes filled with the over-runs from the manholes and the plastic bags that floated on the scum and got caught in the foot rests of his scooter every now and then, he had seen for himself how the Mother lived and even become familiar with Her routine. Every morning he did what every other passer-by did—turn right to have a glimpse of her face—black stone, freshly anointed with oil, her nose, eyes and mouth outlined in silver, calmly accepting of all that her devotees did to her. A trishula was planted in front of her, lemons impaled fresh every morning on each of the three prongs—marking the bounds of direct access. No one could venture beyond except her priest—an unsmiling young man with a crew cut, the razor-trimmed arc of hair clean and precise against the skin on his neck. Late one morning Shrinivas Moorty had been witness to the priest lighting up a beedi and having a quiet smoke after closing the temple, and then making his way to the self-service joint up Ammanagudi Street, presumably for an idli-vada.

The Mother lived a busy life. Much of her morning was spent on her toilet. Sometimes she wore a crown of turmeric and vermilion powder, and sometimes a mask of white butter with a golden crown. And when she was not ready to face the world she hid behind a screen of marigolds. But on the nine days of the Dasara festival, she came into her own; her face dressed each day with a compact of different coloured powders, illuminated with lamps; on one of the days she even wore a full face mask made of silver.

She reminded him of his wife—the same mysterious rituals with unguents and the stoic acceptance of worship. He remembered his mother and sister, who were easier than Lily and the Mother, and whose ablutions too were not as complicated, rubbing on their faces something called Afghan Snow, that came in an icy white glass jar and had a picture of melting snow-covered peaks on the outside.

After Dasara was over, there was an auction of the saris the Mother's devotees had offered her, saris She had worn just once. His wife had managed to get several of them, even some silk ones, at throwaway rates, to be gifted to the servants. She had given his mother one of the saris once, a silk one and very pretty, but for some reason his mother had been offended.

On the morning of the Ooru Habba, the local festival, the crowd was thick outside Her door. Once he had seen reflected in the water collected just in front of the trishula, a man caressing the crop of a rooster he held firmly in one hand, and feeling the edge of a knife in the other. A drying red pool was all that remained when he drove back in the evening. There must have been a feast that day for even the urchins had ignored the smashed-open pumpkins, their vermilion-smeared insides spilt on the street.

The evenings were always festive in Mother Land, where amidst the thronging crowds, the smell of frying bhajjis and ambodes wafted from the open carts. There were boiled groundnuts in winter, in large aluminium vessels, trailing wisps of smoke, sold by the pav, the measures resting on their sides on the pile.

It embarrassed him even to think of it now but when Shrinivas Moorty was in college he had been part of a public interest litigation to declare Ammanagudi an encroachment upon public land, upon the road, till it was pointed out that the Mother couldn't possibly have encroached upon a road that was named after her. There was no khata to her name, possibly, but she was there first, long before their houses were built, before even the cows in their kottiges had come up, when there was just her and the paddy fields. Besides, there was the eighteenth century sketch, 'Pagoda of the Amma' by James Hunter, a lieutenant in the British Artillery, who witnessed the British capture the city from Tipu Sultan, and who sketched the fort and other prospects of the city. Hunter's 'Pagoda of the Amma' and Ammanagudi, it was more or less agreed, were the same. Although Hunter's temple stood at the edge of a lake with steps leading down from an outer courtyard—all of which had disappeared since—the outline of the temple was unmistakable. Ammanagudi had acquired red and white stripes now and seemed to have shrunk in size or maybe it was just dwarfed by the life that had sprung up round it.

High in the sky behind the Mother's temple, Shrinivas Moorty saw a hoarding had come up, one that he had not noticed before. 'This Ugadi,' a jeweller of renown invited, 'display your family jewels . . .' They meant, of course, the gold and diamonds and rubies that were usually kept safe in bank lockers. He hoped no one would take the invitation seriously for it would not do to be so brazen these days. As far as he knew, women had never bought jewellery; all the ornaments they possessed were given to them on special occasions—marriage, the birth of children, or festivals—by their mothers and grandmothers and other members of their family. But now, even Lily had started doing the rounds of the jewellers, with her two ever-obliging cousins. Thankfully, she neither asked him to accompany her nor pay for her trinkets. She paid for them herself, or perhaps her father did; he made it a point not to ask. He was still musing over whether to get her jewellery for her birthday, a pair of earrings perhaps, that she could go with her cousins and buy, when he came out of Ammanagudi Street and joined the stream of traffic headed towards the heart of the city. And just as he thought he had cleared the bottleneck and made it into the widening swell of the road, he had to brake sharply. This time it was not an SUV or even a hoarding but a young woman who had cut across his path.

'Careful!' he called out, breathless, for the acidic twinge had seized him again.

She took her own time to cross the road and he noted sourly the colour of her clothes—a saffron orange sari and blue blouse—rivalling the Mother's taste or equally, the plastic bucket and mug in his bathroom. It was only when he reached college that he managed to place her—she strongly resembled the nurse who came to give his wife her tri-weekly massage, the same broad-boned face and gleaming dark skin; they could well be mother and daughter.

2

Neela hated walking through the slum to reach the bus stop on the main road. It was not just the slush that wet the edges of her sari or the smells—these she could take in her stride. It was the throng in the temple, the flower sellers and the beggars, the unavoidable mass of humanity that pressed upon her, so close, so early in the morning, that she could not stand. And that morning, to add to it all, she had almost been run over by a scooter and the fat balding rider had shouted at her.

She lifted the pleats of her sari delicately, baring her three inch heels, and hurried past the temple, drawn quite against her will to look at the face within—shorn of all adornment this morning. She touched the pendant that lay on her chest, breathed a quick prayer and walked on.

She had always gone to work on her moped, but ever since the digging for the flyover began, the traffic had grown too heavy and the road too bad for her two-wheeler. Moreover, the fine cement dust settled into her hair and skin and lungs and brought on her allergies, so she took the office bus—safer on all counts.

At the bus stop she stood a little apart from the others—canteen and Class Four staff mostly, no others from the officer grade came to this stop—tapping her silver-sandalled foot impatiently, ignoring the hesitant smiles of the temporary library trainees. Another thing she lived in dread of was that Sukhiya Ram, her office boy, would try to give her a lift. Once, just once, she had made the mistake of getting into his autorickshaw for the bus had come early that day and she had missed it, and since then he'd stop every morning.

'Madam, madam! Come, come! We go auto!' he'd call in English, with irritating good cheer, while she ignored him fiercely and the library girls giggled.

It was all because of the flyover. If she did not have to walk through the market, she would not have caught sight of Sukhiya Ram one day, emerging like a rat from his hole, somewhere in the slum behind the temple, nor greeted by his raucous cries of welcome and told that they were practically neighbours. She would not have had to endure the stares of his entire biradri, who had been brought down by a contractor to work as labourers on a construction site, who lived together in the same crowded tenement, and had jostled to take a look at her while Sukhiya Ram greeted her fervently.

It was a relief to see the bus, for within it, order was restored. As per its unwritten rules, she sat in the first seat while the library girls made their jerking, lurching way down the aisle, banging against the seat handles, to the back of the bus which was their designated place. No one ever had to spell it out, but everyone knew who sat where, who had the right to first seating and who would stand when the bus was full.

By the time Neela's jangled nerves settled, the Raghavendra Swamy Matha usually came up on the right and here the passengers—all except the sleeping, the secularists, the other-religionists and by-the-grace-of-god, the driver—would turn as one man to the right, with a variety of pious signs and sounds, to catch a glimpse of the idol of the saint Raghavendra Swamy that stood in the open doorway. Neela would then take out her pocket radio and plug in her earphones. And Kamala, who sat in the second row, would take out her mobile phone.

'Hello! I'm on the bus . . . can't hear you . . .' Kamala would say, but for Neela, the next hour was pure bliss. For nothing came between her and Balaji Brahmendra, the RJ of the breakfast show of the city's only FM radio station, a man with a voice that sent her shivery with anticipation every time she heard it.

The bus turned into the gates and there was Sukhiya Ram, in his pre-peon avatar of blue and gold—he was a handsome lad, no doubt about it—waving the bus on past the grey stone buildings of the Centre for Socio-Economic Studies, to the depot where it would disgorge its passengers.

USHA K.R.

The previous year, half the permanent staff in the quasi-government Centre had been let go after a golden handshake, and a 'head hunting' agency had been recruited to hire a skeletal staff on annual renewable contracts. And since the rules for contract staff were flexible, from 9 a.m. to 10 a.m., Sukhiya Ram, dressed in gum boots and a uniform with epaulettes, was stationed at the entrance, smartly guiding the buses and cars and autos from the gates to the reception, after which he cast off his splendid ensemble and slipping into modest khaki, became the Class Four staff he would be for the rest of the day in Neela's office. But to make sure that he was not late, he was given autorickshaw fare to come to work, and innocent that he was, he actually took an auto to work, instead of pocketing the fare and taking the office bus.

Neela Gopalrao was one of the first to get down from the bus and she walked away quickly, not waiting for Daisy, knowing she would run and catch up with her. There were two components to the part-government, part-autonomous CSES—a centre for higher education and one for research. Neela was the right hand to the head of research—all applications for the funding of projects were first opened by her, and then forwarded to the head, a fact she never forgot.

'I have to go to Accounts . . . half an hour's work . . . see that Dr S's room is cleaned,' she told a panting Daisy as soon as she caught up with her.

When she arrived, after her detour to Accounts, she found her department in a furore. Sukhiya Ram was standing in the corridor, banging a stick repeatedly on the ground while Daisy stood by, wringing her hands, her eyes alight with excitement. The door leading to Dr Subramanyam's room was open and she could hear sounds within. A couple of uniformed security men stood outside in the landing, well out of the way.

'Snake, madam,' Sukhiya announced happily. 'In boss's room, behind the computer.'

The snake catcher from the nearby village had been sent for and was in the room, looking for the snake. Their in-house snake catcher, a peon in the higher education department had refused to come as it was a Monday. It was Sukhiya Ram who had first sensed the snake, for when he unlocked the door in the morning, the room smelt of cold boiled potatoes.

Neela walked past Daisy and Sukhiya Ram into Dr Subramanyam's room. The two security men who stood hesitantly at the door, ready to bolt, had the presence of mind to salaam her. At the far end of the room crouched the snake man from the village, a familiar figure on the campus, his face wizened, even a little dissolute, but whose gold necklaces and many-stoned finger rings and vermilion smeared forehead dazzled the eye. One had to show the right respect to the enemy and every battle had its own armour.

The snake was spotted. The security men fled. Neela alone stood her ground. The snake man plunged behind the computer with his rudimentary equipment—a loop at the end of a stick, which he slipped over the snake's head and tightened—and pulled it out. There were screams from the corridor, Daisy's high-pitched squeal ringing out above every other noise. The creature seemed barely sentient. Even as they noted the tell-tale white markings on the hood, the snake man threw it into the sack he was carrying and held its mouth fast. By the time he made his way out, the snake had started struggling inside.

'A king cobra—must be fifteen feet at least,' one of the security men said.

'Fifteen! Not more than eight I'd say . . .'

'Did you notice the bulge in its middle? The snake must have just eaten. If not . . .'

'What will he do with it?'

'Release it within the grounds so that he'll be called again to catch the same snake. Maybe the two of them will set up an act together,' one of the security men dug the other in the ribs.

'He might sell it for its skin—'

'Today every crow and brahminy kite nesting on the trees in the Centre will have a feast.'

'I thought they were a tribe of snake worshippers—'

That was a new voice. Alka Gupta, one of the research scholars was frowning over the perfidy of the snake catcher.

USHA K.R.

'People will do anything for money these days, even sell their dharma . . .' Sukhiya Ram was unctuously grave.

Alka looked up at him, smiling. 'You are wise, Sukhiya, you know everything,' she said in the indulgent tone that everybody used for Sukhiya Ram. Everybody except Neela, that is. Sukhiya Ram, everyone seemed to have decided, was the mascot of the Centre. His romantic tale of how he had fled his village of cowherds in north India from a blight which had carried off the livestock of the entire village, made his way to the south with a group of fellow villagers and once in Bangalore slipped out of the clutches of the contractor and struck out on his own as peon cum security guard at the Centre, had warmed everybody's heart, including Dr Subramanyam's. Neela alone found nothing to be charmed by in the fresh-faced youth.

'Get on with your work!' Neela said sharply, looking at her watch. 'This department has been turned into a tamasha since morning. Any excuse to stop working. Get going now.'

Part of her bearing came from being associated with Dr Subramanyam, who was clearly the star of the place—a man of impeccable academic and research credentials, a PhD in a rarefied branch of economics from the Brinkelmeyer School at Columbia, who had gone on to occupy the M.T. Friedman Chair in developmental economics thrice in succession (a feat unheard of in the history of the department), a consultant with prestigious international organizations and advisor on matters of policy to national governments. Dr Subramanyam had confessed once that at one point in his life, he had begun to feel most at home in the lounge of an international airport. The Centre had been lucky to get him to shape their research policy and to garner funds for them, and it was here that he outdid his homespun, disgruntled counterpart, the head of higher education at CSES. It was he too who had streamlined the administration of the Centre, which had grown into a juggernaut over the years. He had conceived of a policy to retire those whom he perceived as adding to the flab, 'counselled' them into accepting the terms of offer—which, on the face of it were more than generous—and bedazzled the uncertain board of governors into passing what he described as 'the economic imperative of our times'.

Dr Subramanyam had accepted to head CSES Research, which everyone knew was a little obscure for a man like him, to be with his ailing father. He had also foregone his splendid bungalow on the campus to live with his parents in their modest Malleshwaram home where he had been brought up—a fact that was highlighted in the many interviews he gave to the press who sought him out for they found him knowledgeable, photogenic and always forthcoming. He was a handy man to have on the TV business channels for he could be relied upon for impressive soundbytes on matters of policy and practice. Rumour had it that he had been recommended for the Padma Bhushan, the highest civilian honour in the country.

Currently, he was travelling; a two-month series of lectures in Columbia, and then flitting between universities, multinationals and state capitals, trying to pull off a collaboration of mammoth proportions and funding, which Neela, being privy to the information, knew that jealous rivals were trying to scuttle. Like the rest of the Centre, Neela adored him largely because he was such a high flier—his name evoked instant recognition and respect; moreover, he wore a suit well and smoked a pipe. Sometimes, on the rare occasions when he was not travelling, at the end of the day they would have coffee together, just the two of them, and he would let fly at people, talk about his projects and his aspirations, 'the work ahead of me', as he called it. It pleased her that he was vain and catty—Oh that man, he'd say dismissing a scion of industry with a snort, let me tell you what he was doing when I bumped into him in the prime minister's office . . . She thrilled to his casual access of high places, his dismissal of hallowed icons and the fact that she alone was witness to his candid self. With him she adopted a respectfully arch manner, throwing out a teasing possibility, the promise of something more, while staying within the bounds of propriety; relying on her basic feminine common sense, she knew she should always be well groomed and pleasing to look at. But this also Neela knew—she might try hard to please Dr

Subramanyam and he might be imperious, even dismissive at times, but he would last one term as director, maybe two or even three, while she would be executive assistant to the director forever.

The morning was almost gone by the time Neela began hers. As usual there was a slew of e-mails—she deleted the queries for the funding of projects, most of them preposterous, without reading and without remorse. People who could not follow instructions given on the website deserved neither funds nor consideration. Then, impatiently, she switched accounts: from her CSES one to Hotmail and the next ten minutes were spent composing her two-liner to Balaji Brahmendra, the RJ, and right then, her counsel. The next morning or perhaps on the evening show, he'd make a reference to her e-mail. Sometimes, it was a game between just the two of them—he'd use the words that she had used in her letter, scattering them throughout the programme—a sign for her alone, a special secret. He was pithy, spoke in riddles almost. She had come to understand that he would not say more. It was up to her to read between the lines, unravel his riddles, winkle the nugget of advice from his cryptic sentences—and she never failed to do it. And almost as much as his clairvoyant mind, she loved his rudeness; the way he mocked all the big shots on his programme, without their being able to do anything about it—it was after her own insulting heart.

Neela was always in a good mood after having written to Balaji Brahmendra, and so she looked on Alka Gupta almost kindly when her shadow fell across the desk.

'My cheque . . .' Alka said with what Neela considered becoming hesitation.

Making much of it, Neela pulled out a bunch of keys—the master keys to all the locks in the department, and after much deliberation, selected one. She unlocked one of the drawers and pulled it out a little. Alka, standing across the broad desk, could not see.

There it was—the cheque. And the other thing. The letter.

'No,' Neela shook her head, 'not yet.'

Sukhiya Ram, who was wiping her computer with a soft damp

cloth, turned round in a gesture of protest, but she quelled him with a look.

'Next week, perhaps.'

'But it's already the third. My cheque should have come in by the fifteenth of last month . . .'

Neela shrugged. 'You want to come and go as you please, a free and easy contract, not be shackled to your job like me . . . What do you call it? Yes, flexitime. You can't complain that you have no hold over the accounts department. Someone must be on leave there. They will send the cheque when it is ready.' She fixed her level gaze on Alka, till the other dropped her eyes and turned to go.

Each day Neela tried to unravel a bit more of the Alka Gupta enigma—from the dusting of talcum powder on her feet, the after-bath overspill, no doubt, from her armpits and her cleavage, to her scabrous lips, now twitching uncertainly; a girl younger than she was by several years, who had lived in places that Neela could not identify on the map, studied in colleges and worked in offices that were just big names to Neela, but who had not the gumption or the power to demand a cheque that was rightfully hers. As soon as Neela had finished her graduation in commerce, she had enrolled in a secretarial course, and then sought a safe job. Is it a government job, her mother asked when she was applying to the newly created Centre for Socio-Economic Studies. Yes, she replied. Once I'm confirmed they can't throw me out for the next thirty years.

At thirty-two, Neela lived with her parents, their only child, in one of the lanes behind Ammanagudi Street, in a two-bedroom flat that would be hers eventually. She had two almirahs full of hand-picked saris, her salwar-kameez collection was still building up in a third and she had enough gold not to repeat her earrings for a whole month. Try as she might, she could not understand the logic of Alka's life, how she could be who she was. Alka shared a flat with two other research scholars who worked at the Centre—the three of them had had a tough time finding the flat since nobody wanted three single women as tenants. There was no one to cook or care for Alka, which showed in her thin bony frame. She seemed to subsist on coffee and Marie biscuits and dressed with ragamuffinly uncare but, Neela supposed, when one wore jeans it did not matter. Nevertheless, she smelt clean, trailing the light fragrance of lavender and her teeth were large and white.

Alka would fumble with embarrassment and elaborate courtesy when giving instructions to the sweeper, whom Neela addressed with instinctive authority, yet she hesitated not a bit to slip into first-name familiarity with Dr Subramanyam and various other visitors, whom Neela addressed as 'sir'. Periodically, she would disappear into the rural interiors, travelling by red-board mofussil buses, as part of the field work for her projects and when she returned she'd work late into the night, the door of her office locked, one of the few still working in the Centre. She was known once to have slept the night on her capacious desk; Dr Subramanyam had asked her to use the sofa in his office if she ever needed it. Her father was in the diplomatic corps and was stationed at Washington, D.C., her mother she rarely mentioned. There was little chatter of any sort from Alka—no inconvenient family, or embarrassing parents, or interfering, match-making aunts. She appeared open and candid and friendly, even a little stupid, yet it seemed almost an offence to bring up anything personal with her. To Neela, Alka Gupta represented arcane and frightening possibilities; she could only react by needling her.

To cope with the vagaries of such encounters, with the flow of people of uncertain status through the Centre, Neela had devised her own tool of assessment. She instinctively measured every person she met on a five point scale. Ignoring/Disregarding/Being mean to this person would/may: 1) be bad for my career and well being; 2) cause problems in the short run; 3) not matter either way; 4) uplift my spirits momentarily; 5) add spice to my life.

Alka stood at number five, Sukhiya and Daisy at three—she snubbed them out of habit and because they expected it. Dr Subramanyam was the only one who merited a number one. The other project heads who trailed through the Centre periodically, like Antonia Larson, were at number two.

But sometimes her finely tuned system did not work. One encounter in the recent past had left her completely disarmed and defenceless. What should have been a number five had turned into a number one, and then inexplicably escaped her scale altogether; it had become a matter of the heart. It had to do with the letter that lay at the bottom of her drawer, which, like Alka's cheque, could incriminate her. The only other person who knew about it, she suspected, was Sukhiya Ram and he was a number three, so he did not count. In this matter, the advice columns of the magazines and newspapers that were her unfailing guide to behaviour, and to morality even, had failed her. Thankfully, she had Balaji Brahmendra to turn to.

3

'Hey, hey, hey! Good morning, good morning, *good morning*! Hope you've all slept well through the rather cold night . . .'

Balaji Brahmendra was used to being complimented on his muscular voice, the richness of its timbre and its perfect pitch—it was not for nothing that he gargled in warm saline water and did his voice modulation exercises every morning. '. . . get ready to spend the next three hours with me . . . your very own Bali Brums . . . a voice from heaven!'

'Hey, do you ever think before you say good morning to your friends and family first thing in the morning? Well, you had better . . . The first SMS of the day is from our regular listener Pushpa Rani—Hi P. Rani, my Prani—who says, Bali, today I learnt what good morning really means . . . I saw the sun today in the morning after a whole month! No, she doesn't stay in the Arctic but in our very own Bangalore. It just happens that she was on the eight-to-four night shift till yesterday. Believe me, she says, it's the most glorious sight in the world to see the sun rise. We believe you, Flower Queen . . . thanks for the message . . .'

'Can you smell my coffee, Bangalore? The steam is curling out from the top and I am sending its aroma across the air waves to you . . . You are not a true Bangalorean if you don't begin your day with kapi. By the way Sheetal, thanks for the first rhyming SMS of the day. Here it goes guys 'n' gals—I listen to your voice, first thing by choice . . . Wish me good morning, every day Prince Charming! Hey that's nice of you Sheetal, as cheering as my cup of Barista's kapi . . . A happy new year to you, though it's three days old already. The first question of the morning: Who introduced coffee—yes, this morning cup that five million of us cannot do without—to our state? I repeat . . . SMS me with the right answer on . . . Take it away Lataji—'

He had received sixty messages since morning and had had his fix of adulation along with his coffee—an invitation from a schoolgirl to come home for dinner and meet her dog, another asking him to guess her birthday, appeals to enlist his support for a series of causes, a heart-rending plea for money, compliments and more compliments, one from the incorrigible Nelly telling him how much she loved his voice. I love your name, she had said earlier, Bali Brums, a nice, crisp tit-bit that you can crunch up in your mouth. And so close to balls 'n' bums, his girlfriend Chantal, short for Shanta Lakshmi, had wickedly added. Insha Allah, we will meet some day Nelly, he had promised.

He loved to banter with the regulars, especially when they fell in step with the rhythm and the mood of the programme and helped him froth up the conversation. Like this girl, Pushpa Rani, who had seen the sun rise after a month. She signed her messages P. Rani sometimes and he had turned it into 'Prani' and she had taken the cue and started identifying herself in different ways, so ingeniously that it managed to surprise even him. 'Flower Queen' she would call herself or 'The One with the Life Force' and sometimes 'Animal', playing on the different meanings and forms of her name. He could tell that chatting with him in the morning made all the difference to their day.

'Hey, hey Nelly girl, come you can't be miserable, the new year's just begun. I told you to make that resolution, didn't I? Drop that baggage from your life, float as free as a bird, a kite in the sky. Drop all the old petty hatreds and resentments, the bad bad things that keep you from feeling good. Tell you what, here's just the thing for you . . . a pick-me-up from the velvet-voiced wonder . . .'

'For those of you driving to work, I'm happy to say that we are free of traffic jams at the moment . . . oh, oh, what's this . . . Mohan has just SMS'd to say that traffic's piling up on Hosur Road, so all those on the way to Electronic City watch out, and remember please, no road rage, whatever the provocation. Bali Brums says keep your cool. Did you know that road rage accounted for fifteen per cent of traffic related offences last year? I had a run in with a motorcyclist myself this morning. Yes folks, I don't lead the kind of charmed life you people out there imagine I do. I'm just like any one of you. But I didn't lose my cool and start a fight . . . I had to keep the smile in my voice for you—'

A two-wheeler banged into him just as he backed out of his driveway that morning, and the rider fell off. And even though it was his fault, the man started hollering. He would, of course, since the unwritten rule of the road was that the bigger vehicle was always the offender and Balaji's silver Lancer was quite the king of the road. He pacified the man and sent him off quickly with some cash. If the motorcyclist had discovered who he was, he'd have tried to extract more money, perhaps even come to the radio station and made a scene. Besides, the Lancer was not quite his, not yet in any case. He was still in the process of taking it over from his father, who had given away a young car to his son to please his wife, and had gone in for an older model himself. Balaji was sure his father had parted with the Lancer to save on taxes, but the way he behaved, anyone would think he was doing his son a favour.

'Thank you, Jijo and Sumati, for responding so promptly to our call for B+ blood donors. The director of the Heart Foundation sends you his grateful thanks. And speaking of hearts, let me play you a song from the current smash hit—smash it *Dil hai badshah*!'

A quick look at the left hand column of the log editor showed that he had less time between songs; he'd have to speed up the mellifluous pace. But he had become an expert at folding his voice into a song that had already begun playing.

'And thanks dudes, for all those compliments . . . tell me more, tell me more, I love to hear nice things about myself from all my fans, I mean, listeners, though you know what, I might get a swollen head . . . Before I go, let me announce the winner of yesterday's Know-your-City quiz where you had to get both questions, the easy and the tough one, correct. Congratulations, Savita, you were bang on and yours was the first SMS to come in. To my first question, who was the founder of Bangalore, I got hundreds of right answers. That was easy—Mr Kempe Gowda. But the other one—how much has the city grown since the country became independent?—was tough. And to answer that we have in our studios today the renowned demographic historian Dr Suryanarayana Rao. Welcome Dr Rao . . . Tell us, tell us how much the city has grown . . .'

'Thank you . . . er . . . Bali Brums . . . My daughter sent me with strict instructions not to call you Mr Balaji . . . Well, to tell you about the growth of Bangalore city . . . today, in the year two thousand, we have crossed five million, five and a half to be more precise, but when we started in nineteen forty-seven, there were just about four lakh Bangaloreans. Moreover, the city has expanded eight-fold from a mere sixty-six square kilometres to five hundred and thirty one! And further—'

'Thank you for those revealing vital statistics Dr Rao . . .' Balaji cut him off swiftly. 'Well guys . . . Savita had this interesting bit of information to add. When Kempe Gowda was building the city walls, he found that they kept falling down again and again. The goddess, it was said, was displeased and would be pacified with nothing less than the sacrifice of a pregnant woman. Kempe Gowda was in a fix, and so his daughter-in-law Lakshamma offered to give herself and her unborn child to the goddess. After that, the walls stood firm. Think about that now, when you drive through our fine city . . .'

He had just finished seeing Dr Suryanarayana Rao off—the man would just not go, he insisted on telling him all about his daughters and more trivia about the city than he needed or cared to know—when the programme director sent for him. Three mistakes today. He had mentioned Barista—they were not advertisers and he had no business bringing them up during the show. Why, the PD asked slyly, was he endorsing their chain? And referring to his listeners as fans? But they are my fans, he countered, they love me. But they love Voices from Heaven more, the PD retorted. If they love you, as you claim they do, it is because you are a voice from heaven. Tomorrow, if you were to go, they'd forget you in no time. Okay, slip of the tongue, Balaji shrugged, it won't happen again. The third one, however, was a colossal blunder. Even he admitted that to himself, though not to the programme director. Something as gory as a pregnant woman sacrificing herself ought not to be mentioned at all—that too on a breakfast show! It might put people off their idlis and dosas, or cornflakes, or whatever. He could lose his job for that. This quest for sensationalism was getting out of hand, the PD said. Not sensationalism, he countered, but facts and authenticity. It was difficult, he smiled ruefully to himself, to be articulate and bland at the same time. But his show got the highest listener and advertiser ratings—they could not take that away from him.

two

~

1

Shrinivas Moorty rode in through the gates, as he had been doing for the past twenty-five years—first as a student on a bicycle and now as a teacher on a scooter—except for the hiatus when he had gone to the main university building for his post-graduation. Although, now that the college had been permitted to run its own post-graduate courses there was no need even for that. One could, in a manner of speaking, come in through the gates of the college at sixteen and never get out—like *Hotel California*, the Eagles' song of his college days—'*you can check out any time you like but you can never leave*'—a favourite still of all amateur bands. But that was only in a manner of speaking. His students looked at him in complete bafflement whenever he suggested the idea to them, as if teaching in their alma mater was something that had never crossed their minds, and now that they'd been made aware of it, they'd skirt it respectfully, like one would a vial containing a dangerous culture in the lab.

As he parked his scooter, he frowned at the snatches of the radio programme that came across from the canteen—it did not do his spirits any good to listen to Balaji Brahmendra, Bali Brums as he called himself, at 8.30 in the morning. The Verbal Purge was what he called it instead of the Breakfast Show. What did the canteen boys make of it, he wondered, for they barely understood English. Balaji Brahmendra prattled on in a clever patois, slipping between English and Kannada easily, with Hindi thrown in from time to time, as this was a metropolitan city with a growingly mixed population. They even had a comic act in Kannada in which a woman with a philistine's accent explained Kannada slang in

English. It made Shrinivas Moorty's blood boil but everyone else seemed to love it. He was not a Kannada language chauvinist—far from it, but of late he was beginning to feel that they had a point. Balaji Brahmendra, however, was popular, almost a celebrity. Much to Shrinivas Moorty's displeasure, the college had even invited the RJ to address the students as part of the 'alternative lives' programme, and he had been mobbed by students, teachers and canteen staff alike. But he himself had given the upstart a tough time. Among the many arguments with his colleagues, with Jairam in particular, this had been a fierce one—inviting this RJ as part of the 'alternate lives' series. If Jairam had his way he would invite the RJ to deliver a 'distinguished lecture' too. It's completely against the spirit of the programme, Shrinivas Moorty had held. But a radio jockey is an alternate life, and a viable one too, Jairam said, and we must keep up with the trends. The rural doctor who operated by candlelight, the IAS officer who had set up the largest self-help group in the country, the filmmaker who had made a film on the life and times of a transvestite, the sex worker who was now an AIDS campaigner, would all feature later in the year. In a way Jairam was vindicated. The RJ was such a great hit that they had to shift the venue from the general hall to the newly built auditorium, and that too was packed. Lily too switched on the radio promptly at eight in the morning. He had to call out several times to her to make himself heard above Bali Brums's voice. Even adults were increasingly turning juvenile, he thought. Perhaps they thought it was a sign of how young they were, or maybe, truly, their brains were getting soft.

He felt a hot acidic rush in his throat and almost retched. He had to calm down; he was losing his temper too easily of late. Small things could set off long tirades—against the government, against the young, against one way streets. He wished the state of the world would not make him so angry. Stray plastic packets being blown about the playground made him feel like ordering all the students to tie sacks on their shoulders and go combing the grounds with sticks, like rag pickers. Sometimes he longed for the stand-up-on-the-bench days of his boyhood, when teachers

USHA K.R.

ordered and students obeyed implicitly, where there was order and respect and harmony.

'Good morning, Sir. What film are we watching today?' He did not recognize him but the boy was fresh faced, deferential and enthusiastic, so he put him down as a first year student.

'Tomorrow, not today. We have a staff meeting that may go on late. *Bicycle Thieves*. Italian neo-realism. Tell the others too, will you? The details are up on the board.'

Part of his popularity, a good part of it, Shrinivas Moorty owed to his film club. He had set it up and nurtured it with many a struggle, often in the teeth of opposition from the other teachers who tried to use it as a stick to beat him over other matters, or as a bargaining point if they wanted him to concede things elsewhere. But he had held on and the students had come in large numbers, especially in the early days before the onslaught of DVDs and before cheap pirated editions of the classics became freely available in Burma Bazar. It was his lectures on the film before the screening and the discussion that followed that drew the students to the film club. After a screening, when the lights came on and he rubbed his hands together and said, 'Right . . . so, what did you think?' they blinked in bemused admiration and gratitude, as if he were the maker of the film. The previous week they'd seen Satyajit Ray's *Pather Panchali*. After showing them *Bicycle Thieves* he'd set them his favourite exercise—discuss the similarities between the approaches in the two films.

As he walked the breadth of the grounds to reach the college, his breathing grew normal, his brow unknit itself and he viewed the building almost with affection—that feeling born out of familiarity. It was old and painted over many times, each successive layer cracking open to reveal its predecessor, a different shade of white; the classrooms were roomy but dark, the regulation wooden desks and chairs, even in the staff room, had remained the same since he had been a student and he was sure the legend OE/02/GF/1970 painted on the sides was not just a stores roster number but a mantra that rendered them indestructible. There had been some attempts to 'upgrade' the furniture in the staff room but the new plastic chairs shifted every time you sat on them and the upholstered sofa was indecorously stained—everyone avoided sitting on it. The latticed cement windows in the corridors were thick with dust, but he had learnt that the art of the cement lattice, the waves and lotuses, was now lost. As he scanned the surface of the building, more out of habit than anything else, he was surprised to notice that there was a 'crest' right on top, above the entrance. It seemed to have been painted over in the same colour as the rest of the building, and while it must have stood out at one time, it quite merged with the wall now. He could just about make out the faint outlines—two crossed swords with a flower . . . a lotus . . . or was it a goddess sitting in the middle. But he could not make out the legend, nor could he remember it. Something like 'Satyameva Jayate' he was sure. He made a mental note to ask his colleague Bela if she had ever noticed it.

On the opposite side of the 'impossibly vast grounds' as Jairam had put it, they had begun digging to lay the foundations of the new building. Well, we'll see about that, Shrinivas Moorty thought grimly. He would do his best to prevent another building from coming up on these grounds. It was just another excuse for the management to siphon off large sums of money from the trust funds. Jairam's claims of transparent accounting notwithstanding, there was no cure for itchy hands; it was difficult to give up the habits of a lifetime. There was a committee meeting at three that day and 'facilities' was on the agenda. But there was no denying that it took a good ten minutes to walk across the grounds, from the cycle shed to the main building. The land for the college had been granted to the National Trust in the leisurely, expansive fifties, when nobody could foresee what the city would be in fifty years' time.

The open quadrangle which was usually deserted at this time was bustling with activity. The business management students and their fledgling lecturer were already there, putting up posters for their seminar. Even as he smiled at one of the students whom he recognized as a film club regular, he suppressed a twinge of irritation. The quadrangle was supposed to be out of bounds for such 'publicity'. All posters and announcements were restricted to the student area which was on the other side of the building. But this was another thing that the new lot of teachers was doing—eating into hallowed spaces, not respecting the rules—all in the name of flexibility, of spontaneity even. He studied the hand-made posters as he walked past. What are the five major problems the worker faces today, the poster closest to him demanded. Apparently the problems were VHAST—Violence, HIV-AIDS, Alcohol, Stress and Tobacco. VHAST? He had asked the young lecturer who taught the business management course when he came across her planning the posters with the students. In our days it used to be expropriation of surplus value. And alienation from the fruits of one's labour. This is the Human Resources module, she told him seriously. We aren't so handicapped by theory. We believe in empowering individuals to take charge of their lives, become more inward looking, not blame the system for everything. You're dressed for the part, I see, he had said and regretted it immediately; she was young and only doing her job as she thought best. In an attempt to live up to what she imagined to be the sartorial demands of her course and simultaneously accommodate the conservatism of the college, she had remodelled the 'business suit' to become longer and looser and arrived at something that looked like a raincoat flapping over tube-like trousers. He walked away from the quadrangle without greeting her for she had not seen him and he did not want to go up to her and say hello. She was one person who would not vote with him in the afternoon's meeting, he knew.

'You are an ostrich with its head buried in the ground!' Jairam had accused him.

'And fools rush in where angels fear to tread!' he had retorted, without thinking, adding, 'If we must trade well worn figures of speech.'

Jairam had brushed aside the softener, the olive branch. He changed tack, trying to reason with him, to appeal to his good sense. You have to recognize the changing dynamics of the times, Jairam said, and listen to those who know better. We are ready to put the blueprint of the new Centre up for scrutiny, the syllabus committee and the logistics committee can go through it with a fine-toothed comb, the management is ready to employ educational consultants—he named a leading firm—to help us out . . .

'Don't give me your newspeak,' Shrinivas Moorty had said, brushing Jairam off.

'You have to get beyond literary allusions, Shrinivas. Get real!'

Get real? These days Jairam's language alternated between clichés and Americanisms. 'Changing dynamics' indeed. It was another opportunistic phrase, as far as Shrinivas Moorty could see. And 'consultants' were bandits in new guise, thieves with eye patches. With age, the opportunistic streak in Jairam seemed to have grown stronger. He would even go so far as to say that that was all there was to his old friend now. They rarely met these days except at official meetings, for Jairam had given up both coffee and tea and had stopped coming to the staff room. Moreover, ever since he was designated head of the new Centre for Inter-Disciplinary Studies he had an office of his own, where he preferred to be between classes. And as always, at the thought of Jairam, he slowed down, his mind drifting.

He turned the corner and ran into the man in question himself. So unprepared was he that he almost reached out to touch Jairam: it was difficult to guard against affection that went back twenty-five years.

'You've become thin,' he said.

'Fit,' Jairam said, patting his abs.

Of course. Jairam had taken to playing tennis twice a week. Further, on Friday evenings he could be seen sporting a red tilak on his forehead. And there was the gold ring with a patron saint's emblem in plain sight on his right hand. Shrinivas Moorty also knew that Jairam was mooting an elective on 'Spirituality' in the new post graduate course, along with the part-time Yoga teacher. It saddened him to see a man, whose mystical experiences at one time had been wholly induced by marijuana, come to this. Which led him to say the wrong thing.

'How is Gee?' he asked, using a long-forgotten diminutive, to which he had no right anymore.

'Geeta is fine, thank you,' Jairam said crisply.

Before he could make amends they were joined by Bela Bose, sociology, and Basavaraj, Kannada, who turned the corner whispering to each other.

'Well, well. Namaskara to Arjuna and his sarathy Shri Krishna. Plotting the lines of battle?' Basavaraj said, in the high pitched, faintly mocking tone that at one time had been an affectation but was now his natural manner, especially when he felt threatened in any way.

'Trust you Basavaraj, to turn everything into high drama—' Shrinivas Moorty began but Jairam nodded to them perfunctorily and turned to go.

'Don't forget, Jairamjiki. Today. Three o' clock. Meeting. And by the by, happy new year . . .' Basavaraj called after him. He too could claim the familiarity of twenty-five years with Jairam: all three of them had been classmates together in National Trust College.

'So are we all set to take them on?' Shrinivas Moorty said, and he heard the placatory note in his own voice.

'"We", Shrinivas Moorty? Are you sure?' Basavaraj said, looking for sly confirmation at Bela.

'Of course . . .' Bela said uncertainly.

'What is the matter with the two of you?' he said, not bothering to hide his annoyance. 'You can't have doubts at this stage. I thought we were agreed . . .'

'It is not we who are having doubts mister . . .'

Shrinivas Moorty subsided at that, knowing Basavaraj was playing his usual games and was better off being ignored. But he was angry with him for implying that he and Jairam were conspiring together, when Basavaraj knew that the truth was quite the opposite. It was just like him to miss no opportunity to make mischief. Many years ago, when they had just joined as teachers, Basavaraj had said in tones more angry than mocking, that one day the two of them would be on the same side, and he had laughed at him. His distrust of Basavaraj had not grown any less over the years and he would have liked not to depend on him. But now here they were—unlikely allies. Their interests were securely tied together. Basavaraj was undeniably his first lieutenant; he had to be endured.

As for Bela, he could not understand how she got on so well with Basavaraj, whom she had pronounced a philistine. He was not angry with Bela—how could he be—he was just disappointed. He turned to look at her, and noted with fresh shock the amount of grey in her hair and the thickened line of her neck where it plunged into her fleshy shoulders. She had grown prematurely old—she, who till yesterday had been a youthful sprite; he himself had likened her at one time to a nymph. Shrinivas Moorty's disappointment with Bela Bose too had a fifteen year old history to it, for at one time he had almost been in love with her, not almost, he *had* been in love with her, and all things considered, one could only marvel at the tactility of the human heart. It must be this, its tactility that caused what doctors called the enlarged heart, surely, and it was no small wonder then that matters of the heart could cause medical complications. For Shrinivas Moorty's had been engorged to the full, its valves tripping, its beat skipping at her very thought, at the sight of the crease in her left cheek when she smiled and on hearing her voice, edged with gravel and an accent that he was not familiar with. And just as surely, his heart had shrunk, squeezed like an orange of all its love juice and then had come back to its normal size and assumed its steady chunter.

'By the way . . .'

Shrinivas Moorty looked up. Jairam had come back.

'I came looking for you about something else, something more urgent. Not the meeting,' Jairam said to him, ignoring the other two. 'SVK is not well. Quite ill, in fact. Lenin called. I am going to his place at one. We could go together if you like.'

2

Shrinivas Moorty was just about to go into class when the peon came in. There was a phone call for him in the office. His wife. It was urgent. He checked his impatience and hurried out of the staff room. At times like this he wished he had a mobile phone.

But he'd declared his contempt for it and for the intrusiveness of all modern communication media far too often and too vehemently to change his stand. He was reputed for ejecting 'flashers'—any student who flashed a mobile—from his class. The students accepted his whim with good humour for they had simple ways of getting round it. Besides, they liked such eccentricities in their teachers, it helped to build personality and gave them ready talking material for the canteen.

'My back is aching. You forgot to get my medicine—' petulant, abrupt.

'Lily!' he sighed. 'I was about to go to class . . .'

It would not have occurred to her at all that he ought not to be disturbed at whim when he was in college. All she knew was her need, paramount and immediate, the need to be gratified on the spot, like a child. Of late she was becoming progressively infantile, as if she was regressing into the child she could not have. The other day, at a dinner in the new chemistry lecturer's house, she had suddenly put down her plate and said, let's go home, I'm tired. She had just stopped short of putting out her arms to be carried. The chemistry lecturer and the students who had been invited had gathered round him, talking about the Tarkovsky film they had just seen at the film club, and had ignored her, their youth and their indifference too perhaps, inuring them to the cardinal rule of social conduct—in pursuing the object of your interest, don't neglect to include the spouse. The instinctive worship that she received in her family circles was absent; no one had paid her attention, no compliments had come forth on her clothes and looks.

He was always careful not to draw her mind to their childlessness, nor to dwell upon it himself. He had told himself so many times that it did not matter, that he had begun to believe it. But it must have affected her for it showed in her behaviour in many ways. There was this business with the cat, for instance. Whenever he suggested that they get the cat spayed, she protested vigorously. So, every few months, when the cat littered in the balcony, they had to go through the nerve-wracking process of protecting the new-born kittens from the tom cat and the crows and, sometimes, from the mother herself. Surprisingly, Lily, who rarely bothered with things that did not affect her directly, was genuinely fond of the cat and quite devoted to it.

There was also her growing absent-mindedness. What was he to make of that? The other day he found a strange pair of trousers in his cupboard. Where did these come from, he asked, walking out in the short, voluminous thing. She stared at him, half-smiled and then frowned: the dhobi must have made a mistake. But you know I don't wear black trousers, he wanted to tell her, in all our years of marriage I haven't owned a single pair of black trousers; I've held forth several times on the demoralizing effect of black, not to mention its lint-gathering qualities. There had been two large bottles of stuffed red pickle—something that neither of them liked—on the sideboard once. Expensive too. And she had no idea how they had got there.

'Lily, why don't you ask Balu to get the medicine for you? I'm going to be late today, I told you in the morning.'

He heard her short intake of breath at the other end. He could picture her eyes widening, her lips pouting; he could hear her think. This was the first time he had suggested it so openly. That Balu do the fetching for her. So far, it had only been tacit; Balu, her cousin was their handyman and Suppi, Balu's sister, her confidant.

'He'd be only too happy to do it . . . your devoted slave . . . your Hanumanta . . .' he laid it on.

'The good hearted duffer' was his other teasing reference to Balu, and 'the big fat hen' his description of Suppi, which had elicited peals of laughter from Lily the first time he used it. Sometimes, he was saddened by the facile devices he used to deal with her, that such charades were the only points of easy contact, of light-heartedness between them. In the early days of their marriage he had made good-natured fun of her affectations—of her hors d' oeuvres and dips, of the cheesy, flaky, insubstantial twirls she baked, but now he had given up. She had stopped her baking and they had nothing to talk about.

Most people—strangers and servants usually—took to Lily immediately after meeting her. There was an air of fragility about her, not just because she was small but in her tentative movements and hesitations, particularly, the way she gestured with her hands about her face, her fingers close together. More effective was the suggestion of mystery in her light, heavy-lidded eyes; the slow sweep of those lids could be mesmerizing, hinting at a great deep secret she carried locked in her heart, despite which she had survived, and which she would soon confide to the other. Only he knew that there was nothing beyond the gaze, nothing in the grey-green vitreous, except a complete obsession with herself.

'Balu?' she demurred unexpectedly. 'I can't ask him. He does too much already. Besides, he's not coming today; he has to go to Coimbatore. How late will you be?'

'We have a meeting scheduled for three in the afternoon. It may go on till late, and after that a few of us may meet up at the club—'

'Oh, the club . . .'

'Yes. Don't wait for me at dinner.'

If every family had a governing principle—some, the rough thumb rule of happiness and unhappiness, others, the dictum of who should be loved and how much—then Lily's family was ruled by a hierarchy of homage and she, undoubtedly, was the reigning queen. Even now her cousins Balu and Suppi spoke of her in the third person in her presence, hushed and fond. It must have been her good looks and her fair skin in a family of remarkably plain looking, dark-skinned people. Although pushing fifty, Lily had kept her looks. She had not put on weight, if anything she had grown thinner, the slightly gaunt look showing off her bones. Her face was still unblemished, the skin taut, its matt texture intact, and her hair, if a little coarse, had just a few strands of grey glinting here and there. When she walked, her waist dimpled, or just—a tantalizing depression, shifting under the thrust of her hips, shown off to advantage by her below-the-navel style sari, a bold thing that had come into fashion when he was in college, which Lily had continued with long after others had stopped wearing the sari that way. Her hands were still plump, unknotted by veins and her nails, ever since the beauty parlour came up below their flat, always painted.

Shrinivas Moorty had inherited Balu and Suppi along with Lily when they were married. She had grown up with them in their large joint family, the kind in which you could not tell which child belonged to whom. In Balu and Suppi's barometer of adoration, the mercury scaled a bursting high when it came to Lily. Every detail of her routine, every small concern, was theirs. Whether they had a life independent of Lily he did not know, nor did he care. Balu, if he recalled, was trading in edible oils; the rare evening when he did not visit them Lily would say he had gone to his godown in Kalasipalya, or on a 'business trip' to a nearby town. He had a grown son in engineering college, whom Shrinivas Moorty had last seen as a small boy, and he had lost his wife a long time ago to complications arising out of typhoid. From what Shrinivas Moorty understood, Balu's life revolved round the crumbling family mansion two streets away from Ammanagudi Street, his 'business', and visiting the many members of his family scattered around the city, particularly his adored cousin Lily on whom he and his sister waited hand and foot. Suppi, fat and buck-toothed, had deserted her post briefly when she married a widower with grown sons—the family agreed that they were lucky to come by him—but had soon arranged her domestic life to the detriment of neither party in order to continue her visits. Every evening, come rain or shine or bundh, they were there, the 'nasty, brutish and short' creatures, sitting in front of the TV in his drawing room, watching for a signal from Lily, waiting to interpret every gesture, one with her in her joys and disappointments. But Lily's needs—shopping and visiting—were their own; the three were in perfect harmony.

The only time Balu and Suppi did not accompany Lily and him was on their honeymoon, and on reflection, he was surprised by that. For the very next day after 'seeing' Lily, when he went to meet her, they were sitting on either side of her in the restaurant. Lily had behaved as if they were not there and he had taken his cue from that. He gave her the red roses and the two books he had chosen, *The Intelligent Woman's Guide to Socialism and Capitalism* and *Jane Eyre*—they were two of Geeta's favourite books—and Lily duly passed them on—the roses after looking them over with the slow maddening sweep of her eyes and the books without looking at them—to her cousins as if they were installed there for the very purpose.

Lily, he had tried telling her, we cannot have those two hanging around all the time. They are my family, she had replied, I love them and I need them. Besides, you keep such long hours. Once, just once, he had decreed that Balu and Suppi would not visit. They had invited Geeta and Jairam over for dinner, just before Jairam left for the US to work on his doctorate. It was a disastrous evening. Everything was perfect, for Lily was a good housewife. Geeta and Jairam had sat on the sofa, as if aloft a mountain, looking uncertain while Lily, her organdie sari standing stiffly about her, whirled in and out with little swirls of this and that, and dainty sips of drink. He had watched Geeta and Jairam view the food with alarm, biting gingerly on the spongy crusts, waiting, as alien flavours and juices flooded their mouths. There was little conversation and just as they settled down to something, Lily would thrust a tray between them, with her latest offering from the cookbooks. They had left early as Geeta, three months pregnant, was tired. Barely had Geeta and Jairam left than Balu and Suppi entered the house, as if they had been waiting all along in the corridor outside the flat, asking after the pudina petites and ignoring him completely.

Geeta and Jairam had invited them back 'for a glass of wine'. They sat in the crowded drawing room with the TV blaring and Jairam's father sitting in front of it, shirtless, his sacred thread hanging over his stomach. After a while, he got up and went inside and Geeta served warm sweet red wine in thick-bottomed glasses smelling of onion.

After that he made no more attempts to make a foursome or to resist Balu and Suppi. Instead, he came to look upon them as allies; they distracted Lily while he got on with his life in peace. Suppi was Lily's shadow of comfort, her maid in waiting, while Balu was the ideal handyman. There was nothing he could not fix, and he had no qualms about plunging his hand into a clogged drain. Both of them were always available and could be counted on. Besides, they were tactful enough to defer to him, and tried to be as unobtrusive as their large frames would allow them.

<h1 style="text-align:center">3</h1>

He remembered the gradient too late. The scooter bucked and spluttered, and a spasm of pain seized him, reminiscent of the morning and he cursed afresh the planners of NR Colony and the makers of Milk of Magnesia. SVK's house was situated on a sharp upward incline, right in the middle of it, just where unwary drivers started fighting with their gears. SVK would never know what that meant for he had never owned a vehicle of any sort—not even a bicycle. The house too was as he remembered it—one of the old fifties Trust Board houses where all the rooms opened out into a central 'hall' and the bottom half of the walls was slicked over in green oil paint.

He had not waited for Jairam, nor had he left word; he had just sneaked away well before 1 o' clock.

SVK's son—Lenin or Stalin, he could never tell which was which—was standing at the gate. The only time in SVK's life when his wife had made trouble was when he had named their sons. SVK had insisted that Lenin and Stalin would be their 'given' names but she declared that she would call them Rama and Krishna. And so, they were, properly, S. Lenin Rama and S. Stalin Krishna in the school registers.

Lenin hurried forward as soon as he saw him and clasped him by the hand, his eyes brimming over.

'How is he?'

'Not well, not well at all. We are afraid—'

'Don't say that.'

'It was Gorbachev—'

For a second his mind boggled. Was there a third son, about whom he did not know?

'My father could not believe how he betrayed the movement . . . the USSR.'

USHA K.R.

Shrinivas Moorty was nonplussed. He could only press Lenin's hand in return.

Then he heard afresh, as if it were only yesterday—'The USSR!'—bell-like, SVK's ringing tones in class summoning up a far away paradise, of scarves and samovars, proud peasants and tireless workers and clean, piston-pumping factories, a paradise they would all reach one day, but which, in reality, SVK Sir had neither seen nor had any hope of visiting.

It was true then, the story making the rounds that SVK had taken the break-up of the USSR personally. Since then, it was said, he had started going downhill. His evening visitors were lectured about the 'counter-revolutionary conspiracy', how it was a 'plot by the CIA' and, uncharacteristically, SVK would not let anyone oppose him; he who had encouraged debate and promoted controversy would not allow anyone to slip in a word edgeways.

The coffee in SVK's house as always was excellent. Unlike Jairam and a host of others, Shrinivas Moorty had not stayed in touch with SVK after the first few years. But everything was exactly as it was when he had been a student and a regular visitor. The metal chairs—the only items of furniture in the room—were as he remembered, as was the photograph of SVK's parents on the wall, the only ornament he did not consider a symbol of bourgeois decadence. SVK Sir's wife, exhibiting her intransigent streak, would not budge when it came to her plastic-bead animals in the show case, assembled just above Deutscher's volumes of Stalin's and Trotsky's biographies. Also eternal were the noises from the kitchen—the clinking of steel vessels and of glass bangles as the unknown sari-clad shoulder scrubbed vigorously at the kitchen sink.

SVK's illness appeared to have united all the rival Marxist factions. At the other end of the room Shrinivas Moorty recognized Bhupaty, quite bald, now DGM of a nationalized bank but, in those days, a Trotskyite. Jairam and he himself had been members of the Circle for the Study of Dialectical Materialism, set up by SVK, while Bhupaty had belonged to the opposing Circle for the Study of Scientific Socialism. He did not know whether the study circles were still active but in its salad days, the CSDM had met every Thursday in the modest premises of the Centre for the Study for Socialism, above hotel Shanbhag in Gandhi Bazaar. There they discussed the classics of Communist literature—from *The Communist Manifesto*, to *Anti-Duhring* and even Gorky's *Mother*—over cups of coffee that SVK paid for. The CSSS, on the other hand, moneyed, decadent, met at Hotel Ginza in the posh Cantonment area. No one quite knew what they did there but there were rumours of Chinese food. In the only public debate between the two factions, he remembered Bhupaty's fervent Trotskyite declaration of 'permanent revolution' and Jairam's own weak, sobre, reasoned response. Bhupaty had trounced them, slipping in a last ringing accusation of 'petty bourgeoise revisionism'; Jairam had been all at sea.

Bhupaty had not noticed him. He was deep in conversation with two others. The faces of the two men seemed very familiar but Shrinivas Moorty could not recall their names. After some searching he recognized one but his name still eluded him. This one had been an adherent of AIDSO, the All India Democratic Students Organization, which owed allegiance to the hard line SUCI, also known as the Zalim Lotion Party for like the mysterious Zalim Lotion, the SUCI existed largely on the white-washed walls of the city, or so the other Marxist parties claimed. The third person's name came to him in a flash and then he realized that SVK must be very ill indeed; perhaps he was on his deathbed.

'It's the nose, I'd recognize it anywhere. Alfie man—' Even as he put out his hand he regretted his uncharacteristic spontaneity for the three men had broken off and were looking at him uncertainly.

'Oh Shrinivas Moorty,' Bhupaty said at last, tepidly. 'So you heard . . . You're here too . . .'

But it was the other man, 'the nose' that Shrinivas Moorty was interested in. Alfie, Alfred Rosario, had been neither CSDM nor CSSS nor AIDSO. He was part of FUG, the Freedom Unlimited Group, which both the CSDM and the CSSS believed was funded by the CIA. Alfie had gone on to study comparative religions at Heidelberg and become a Buddhist. Somewhere in between, for a brief while, Shrinivas Moorty and Alfie had developed an intense friendship, sitting in Cubbon Park and discussing matters of consequence, till the policeman, who regularly weeded out pimps and prostitutes from the park, had shooed them away. He had heard that Alfie had disappeared for some time and then surfaced in a non-traditional, non-conformist boarding school, set in acres of land in the Western Ghats.

'So what are you doing these days, Alfie?'

'Oh! Teaching . . .' Alfie was looking beyond Shrinivas Moorty at something at the other end of the room.

'Most of us have ended up as teachers . . .'

'Chosen, Shrinivas. Not ended up. Bhupaty, they've come out. Will you find out—'

The door to the only bedroom in the house opened and Jairam emerged hurriedly (so, Jairam had arrived before him!), followed by a short stout man whom he recognized as Prabhakar Rao.

It was only when he saw Prabhakar, striding forward with such authority and with finality that he was reminded again how serious the matter was.

'We're shifting him immediately to hospital,' Prabhakar put his arm round Lenin's shoulder. 'I've called for the ambulance.'

Bhupaty caught Jairam's eye. He nodded and came towards them. 'Ridiculous . . . the man can barely breathe and they've shut him up in that cold dark room . . . I told them. Prabhakar has already asked for an ambulance . . . no time to be wasted. He has to get back to his meeting; the chief minister is waiting . . .'

'And we have ours at three—' Shrinivas Moorty said but Jairam had already walked away to talk to Prabhakar.

Principal secretary to the chief minister, Prabhakar Rao was reputed to be truly dynamic, with the risk-taking ability rarely seen in a bureaucrat. He was known in his circles as the Turnaround Man, for he could turn around any department in any degree of shambles within two years. His methods were what he impatiently described as in keeping with the spirit of the law and not the letter. Shrinivas Moorty remembered him in college as president of the Toastmaster's Club. Extempore speeches on any subject had been Prabhakar's forte; he had ready reckoners in politics, philosophy, history, religion and science on his finger tips and was known to read five newspapers a day. On his last outing at the Toastmaster's Club, he made a brilliant speech, extempore, on 'Vedanta and its Impact on International Relations' and won the first prize for it. It was later pointed out that he had read his topic wrong; he was supposed to speak on 'Détente and its Impact on International Relations'. But it was too late; he had been awarded the prize, much to the chagrin of his arch rival from a women's college, a serious-looking girl with a long plait who had gone on to join the UN. He was just as ready, Prabhakar had declared, to come back and speak on Détente, only, they'd have to give him the prize a second time.

There was a stir at the back of the house and a small procession of women came from the backyard into the room, crowding it. Shrinivas Moorty recognized several of them as SVK's former students, some of them his classmates. Mrs SVK came first and Prabhakar and Lenin spoke in low, urgent tones with her, while Jairam, Alfie and Bhupaty waited in a respectful semi-circle. The women formed a second, uncertain ring round the men.

She was the last to come in from the backyard, and at the sight of her his heart did a little flip—of pleasure, of guilt even after all these years and, also, of relief.

'Hi Geeta,' he said as casually as he could. She smiled and his mind was set at rest.

'Come, let's go out. These people are busy. You don't have to hang around do you. I'm dying for a smoke.' She held his elbow with an old familiarity and he slipped again into the role of escort, twenty-five years rolling back in a moment.

They stood under the lone tree in the backyard, in relative privacy. He watched her as she undid the gold clasp of her handbag. Why, he wondered, had Geeta not outgrown her trousers and graduated to something more womanly, like a sari or even a salwar-kameez. For her jeans only seemed to show up the impedimenta of her hips, and her t-shirt the droop of her bosom. He was glad Lily did not wear trousers, though he was sure she would look

USHA K.R.

good in them too. That was one thing about Lily—clothes looked good on her.

'Benson and Hedges?'

'Always.' She leaned back, smiled and blew him a smoke ring and once again, his affection for her surfaced, despite Jairam, despite everything.

She held out the packet to him but he shook his head.

'No? Never? You want two cigarettes perhaps—' she giggled suddenly and he smiled at the memory of the incident.

They had been sitting in her balcony, he, Geeta and another girl whom he did not remember now. Those were the girls' early smoking days and both of them had audaciously struck up in the house, knowing that there were people about. Geeta's parents were known to be liberal and many other girls had sighed over her good fortune, but casual though they were about her friends, even they would frown upon such bad habits as smoking. And sure enough, the girls had just enough time to hand him their cigarettes before Geeta's aunt walked in. She gave him a severe look and, after he left, lectured Geeta on the influence of 'such boys'. Later, much later, when Geeta announced that she was getting married to a classmate, the aunt had said, not to that boy who smokes two cigarettes at a time, I hope, and Geeta had replied in all honesty, no, not to him.

'I've tried to give up,' she said ruefully, flicking at the ash with her long fingernail.

'Hey, watch it—'

'Sorry . . . this is one bad habit that just persists.'

'You seem to have acquired several others. What's with these rings? Even Jairam wears a similar Sai Baba ring. But I remember he wouldn't let your father give him an engagement ring . . . said he didn't hold with men wearing ornaments. And that tilak? Getting religious, is he?'

'Not religious, spiritual . . .' she touched the ring on her middle finger defensively and switched her cigarette to her ringless hand. 'You need to look inwards as you grow older—your intellect can't sustain you forever, you know. The whole man . . . even Marx wouldn't object . . .' she added, recovering her self-possession.

'Have you settled down in your flat yet?'

She looked up quickly, alert for any innuendos, traces of mockery or envy, and satisfied that his remark was innocent, said, 'We've moved in but the workers still come in every morning.'

Ten years ago Jairam had bought shares in a fledgling information technology company. A friend of theirs from college who was one of the partners in the company had made them an offer when it went public. Jairam bought every single share on offer and borrowed money to buy more in the open market. Shrinivas Moorty refused the offer despite Jairam's advice. One was never sure, he said, how these things would turn out. He would rather trust the nationalized banks and their savings certificates, than these instruments of virtual value. He had joked that there was no shark worse than a lapsed Marxist and Jairam retaliated that only a fool would fail to recognize that the wheels of the economy were turning. When the share market boomed a few years later, Jairam sold part of his shares and bought a duplex flat in a quiet upmarket area—away from Ammanagudi Street where he had grown up.

Jairam had had an elaborate grihapravesh ceremony some months earlier. The flat was a grand split-level construction, and after a conducted tour Shrinivas Moorty summed it up as 'US-returned affectation competing with Indian nouveau riche glory'. There were so many people that he found himself pushed from the kitchen—an open kitchen with an 'island' in the middle to house the cooking 'range'—into the pooja room, large enough for Jairam's father to do a sashtanga pranam in front of the deity in comfort. The door of the pooja room was carved intricately into niches, like a beehive, with a bell suspended from each niche. Jairam had not stinted on the black polished granite which was there wherever it could be accommodated and the wash basin, Shrinivas Moorty was perplexed to find, was a large glass bowl in which, if you spat, the membranes in your spittle were refracted in the layers of the thick glass. All the toilets were Western style; not a single squatting-on-your-haunches type Indian one, Jairam's father was heard complaining loudly in the middle of the ceremony.

Some of the furniture—chairs made of pale slats of wood with mattresses for cushions—had already arrived as had the bunk beds in the children's room. The smoke from the homa had filled the rooms and the chanting of the priests boomed through the building from which the scaffolding had still not been removed. Shrinivas Moorty was embarrassed for Jairam, at the vulgarity of the whole affair and was about to remark upon it in an undertone to Lily when he caught the expression on her face. Lily had been silently contemplating the flat all along, noting every detail, her eyes turning cold with what he thought was disdain, but later understood to be envy. They did not stay for lunch for she complained that the homa fumes had given her a headache. When they reached home she immediately locked away the beautiful heavy silver cup that she got as a gift from them, as if she could not bear the sight of it. She refused to go to their house for dinner that night, despite his coaxing, despite his inviting Balu and Suppi as well. Her envy angered him, he thought it cheap. Much later he deduced that her silence and her sulks had been directed at him; if only he had played his cards right, if only he had been a little resourceful, that grand flat could have been theirs, hers.

That evening, the newly consecrated flat was cleared of the remains of the morning's homa and before dinner the guests were subjected to a variety entertainment show by the children in Jairam's extended family. His son and daughter, dressed in satin costumes 'break-danced' in front of an admiring audience. Their dancing grew more frenzied as the tempo of the music increased—the boy's spectacles misted over and he had to stop for a minute to hand them over to his mother, who watched anxiously from the sidelines. That evening, standing on the balcony by himself in their brand new tenth-floor flat, distanced equally from the fun and games going on inside and the panoramic city lights which stretched below, Shrinivas Moorty acknowledged that he had moved away irrevocably from Jairam and Geeta, at one time his closest friends.

'My in-laws will be moving in with us,' Geeta grimaced as she lit a fresh cigarette with the butt of the previous one. 'I've told them not now, let's settle down first.'

He said nothing to that. Don't grudge them their son's success, he wanted to tell her, you were a late entrant. The image he carried of Jairam's father, 'Imperialist' Radhakrishna, was of a short, bald, stocky man, in a banian full of holes and a dhoti turned up at the knees, eternally standing in the sun as he supervised repairs to his compound wall. Like his own house then, Jairam's too had constantly been in need of repairs and there was never enough money to get it all done at once. 'They're old,' he couldn't help saying, 'they'll keep to themselves . . .'

'That's what you think—' Her belligerence, he realized, was a reaction to his support for them. 'His father keeps arguing with him for every little thing. And Jairam has so much on his mind these days—take SVK's illness. It's Jairam who's been doing all the running around—those sons of SVK's are useless. BNS is paying for the treatment of course, but they turn to Jairam for everything.'

B.N. Swamy. His largesse accounted for so much. One of the first among their pre-university batchmates to go abroad after his degree, BNS was among the first wave of successful entrepreneurs to emerge from Silicon Valley—the real one. He was a legend in the business circles, the subject of endless articles in the press—even his stodgy middle-class marriage had been worried to its core on the pages of a gossip magazine for any symptoms of romance. His success was documented in a case study which was essential reading in so many business courses; the young lecturer of business management in National Trust College, the one who dressed in a raincoat, taught the life and achievements of BNS with awe and pride. And BNS had paid his debt to his alma mater in full: the Bennehalli Nagasimha Swamy Trust had decided to gift the college a new building to house the new courses to prepare the students for the new world. All facilities would be state-of-the-art, on par with the best anywhere in the world. 'I barely had enough money to pay the fees and the principal waived them so many times. I owe whatever I am today to National Trust College and my teachers,' he declared when the college had a special ceremony to honour him. He was particularly grateful to SVK, the sun in the teaching firmament. And so it was B.N. Swamy who had under-written all the expenses of SVK's long drawn-out treatment for a failing heart, down to his frequent flights to Madras to consult the specialist there.

It was this, the sharing of the spoils of the BNS Trust, that had opened up the rift in the staff committee, and a decision would be made one way or another in the afternoon's meeting, if Shrinivas Moorty had his say.

'That's another headache. Being administrator of the Trust has been giving him sleepless nights. It doesn't help that the committee is being stubborn and ignoring the writing on the wall. He only wants what's best for the college . . . to abide by BNS's instructions . . .'

He grew alert at that half-wheedling tone, he remembered hearing it before. Surely Geeta was not trying to influence him to change his mind. Had Jairam put her up to it? What did she think? That they were still in college and she could play one off against the other as always?

'I've thought the matter through—' he began rather brusquely and stopped. Jairam, Prabhakar and some of the others had come out onto the porch. A little later they saw SVK being carried out on a stretcher and into the ambulance that was standing outside the gate.

He hurried forward for he had not seen SVK at all but the ambulance doors banged shut just as he reached. Jairam got into the front with Lenin.

'You boys,' Mrs SVK clutched at Jairam and Prabhakar. 'You are truly loyal to him . . . you have saved my mangalya.'

three

~

1

The meeting with the programme director went off better than Balaji expected. And it was shorter too. The PD had said just one thing: Shape up or ship out. But he knew better than to take it seriously. Most of the letters that poured in—through the post, SMS, e-mail or on the phone—were in praise of him and his programmes. He was a natural performer; he had a way with people; he was simply the best. Voices from Heaven could not do without him.

He sifted through the envelopes on his desk quickly—passes for a music show, an invitation to a book release—he had learnt to throw such things directly into the dustbin. The letter from National Trust College, on yellowing paper, complete with the 'coat of arms' and inspirational motto, the date with the printed 19__ struck out and turned into 2000 in an indifferent blue hand—surely it wasn't written on a *typewriter*—but so it was, and one with a worn ribbon too—thanking him effusively for his recent seminar on Radio Rediscovered with the media department. That had been a good afternoon—the college principal patted him avuncularly on the arm with each statement that he made, mistaking him for an ex-student, the students went wild with excitement and their questions came thick and fast. The teachers were stiff in the beginning but he soon had the women giggling—one of them even took his autograph for her daughter and begged him to read out her response to the 'Know Your City' quiz in the next programme. The men were either condescending or grumpy; one of them in a vegetable-dye print bush-shirt that held up his stomach, was persistently sarcastic—he had killed him, though.

His email inbox was full. He recorded the first correct answer to the Know Your City quiz—this had been an easy one. The mandate was to make the questions as easy as possible, getting more people to participate, more e-mails and phone calls and SMSes. There was the usual mail from Nelly—she wrote to him everyday—agonizing over something or the other. Move on Nelly, he replied, as he had told her in the morning, as he had been telling her these last few months, let yourself heal naturally . . . time to forget and forgive. Maybe he would ask her to call in on the Broken Hearts special he was planning the following week—there were so many soulful Hindi film songs on that theme.

As he shut down his computer, he realized that he still had an hour before meeting Chantal. He did not want to go home, though he had his own keys and a separate entrance to his room and could probably catch an hour's sleep without anyone knowing that he was home. But he did not want to chance it. His father might be in, and ever since he got his RJ's job, he kept the peace at home by sleeping in till his father left home for work and returning after his father had gone to bed. His mother, though, waited up for him, however late he was, to give him his dinner, at least a glass of milk or a banana if he had eaten out. The more he came to depend on seeing her first thing in the morning and last thing at night—for he always came home to sleep in his own bed, after tarrying awhile in Chantal's—the less he had to say to her. Moreover, in this latest 'disagreement' she was on his father's side; he could sense her disapproval even though she said nothing to him directly.

In the final year of his five-year engineering course, Balaji Brahmendra had opted out. Not that he was doing badly, but his heart was just not in it. It was then, when his disenchantment was at its peak, that a media mogul visited the campus. Tall, large and white, owner of a successful television and broadcasting company which had begun to proliferate wildly through the world, he spoke about the opportunities provided by the miraculous opening up of the airwaves. Come, he invited them, join the party, get your slice of the cake, your place in the sun. He had spoken of radio as the more imaginative, more romantic medium; with more reach than television, more nuanced and therefore more potent. A voice without a face had so much more freedom: you were not bound by your body or your looks. And because of its reach, radio was more malleable, you could do so much good with it.

A few months later, that same corporation launched an FM radio station, the first in the city and he, Balaji Brahmendra, compere for innumerable talent shows and beauty contests, signed on as a radio jockey with Voices from Heaven. Once the deed was done, however, he was afraid to go home for his parents had no inkling of what he was up to. This was a year ago. He still remembered how he had sidled in through the back door, crisp contract in hand, and told his mother. She said nothing to him all evening but as soon as they heard his father's car at night she ran out and told him all, not waiting for him to park the car and come in. His father had stormed into his room, pushing open the door with such force that the bolt was wrenched off its moorings. He recalled how his father's body had rocked to and fro in anger while his mother stood behind his father, looking very satisfied with herself.

'So, you think nothing of telling us before chucking up your studies! Is this what we deserve . . .'—his father reached for his ears, plucked the earphones off and hurled them along with his portable player against the wall—'. . . for feeding and clothing you all these years!' He followed Balaji into the drawing room. 'Did I sell my land in the village for *this*! For my son to become a radio announcer—' he reached for the panchaloha idol of Lord Vishnu that stood on the TV, keeping the TV cover in place, and Balaji made a dash for his room.

His father followed him furiously, barging in again, looking round the room for something else to throw. And suddenly almost as if defeated he sat down heavily on the bed. Balaji flinched for he hated anyone else sitting on his bed, but he didn't dare say anything to his father, at least not right then. His father looked round the room carefully, as if seeing it for the first time and his eyes grew baffled as they took in the bean bag in the corner, the posters of unwashed men and women on the wall, the boutique chairs and the Chinese lampshade, the computer and the large, dangerous-looking shoes on the floor. Then he got up and left without saying a word.

'The principal said I can defer the final semester; come back after a while if I want,' Balaji offered from behind his door as he locked it securely.

There was no response from the other side and he was able to breathe again. And incongruously, as if it were a sentient being with a black sense of humour, the tape recorder, broken but still working, continued to sing from the floor where his father had thrown it. Freddie Mercury nee Balsara, unabashed, crooning to a forgotten love, '... *Radio gooogooo, Radio gaga ... Radio, someone still loves you ...*' The song had made a come back when Voices from Heaven started operating.

His father started on his mother after that. Balaji heard him in the kitchen, '*You!* You're responsible for what he is ... *spoilt* him ... waiting on him hand and foot. Your *precious* son ...' and decided to stay in his room till his father went to bed. His mother knocked on his door and gave him his dinner once his father was asleep. He did not tell her then that he was moving out of the house that very night.

He did not go home till, three days later, his mother rang up the friend he was staying with and begged him to return. He could have a separate entrance to his room, separate keys; he need never speak to his father. He had always intended to go back; he just wanted to see how long it would take for her to defy her husband.

No, he would not go home and take a nap. Instead he slipped on his headphones and decided to listen to the recording of an old programme. He often did that, listening to the ones that had the highest listener ratings to boost his morale when he had had a bad day. This one had won a listener's poll as the most memorable evening of the year and people had asked for it to be broadcast again; of course, part of the appeal was that superstar Yashwant had appeared on it, but still. He fast forwarded the announcements, the promos, even the cute little spot that Chantal did that was repeated four times a day—a take off on the local slang in the accents of a bumbling rustic—adjusted the headphones, closed his eyes and sat back to listen to the sound of his own voice.

'. . . yes, I remember. Thanks for the number of SMS reminders, Ruhi. Today is the train special—the Rajdhani, the Shatabdi, the Mail, the Passenger, the broad gauge, the metre gauge, the narrow gauge and the steam engine special. Say guys, where would we be without the Indian Railways, how would romance thrive on the screen, how would our film hero impress his heroine without hanging on to the door and leaning out dangerously, and, above all, where would our guest for the evening be—welcome, Yashwant, hero of the mega blockbuster *Chuku-Buku Express*! Guest's privilege—the first song we play today will be of your choice.'

'Thanks Bali Brums. Great being on your show. I love that train song from *Aradhana*, a true classic—'

'Much before *my* time but no doubts on that one . . . our man with the mysterious appeal Rajesh Khanna following *alongside* a train in his car, singing to his sapno ki rani . . . Oh my, wasn't Sharmila Tagore coy . . .'

'Our listeners are waiting to talk to you Yashwant, but before we put them on, the song that's been rocking Bangalore these last few weeks, *your* song from *Chuku-Buku Express*!'

'Hi, this is Sneha . . .'

'Hi Sneha—Friendship—one of my favourite names.'

'I can't believe I'm talking to you, Yashwant Sir!'

'Then pinch yourself Sneha. As host of this show I command you, and you should see Yashwant here, grinning away to glory . . .'

'Sir you say you like my name but you were so mean to me in *Train Hudugi* . . . you wrote my name in the sand on the beach but my friend's name you wrote on paper with your blood . . .'

'What to do Sneha, that was what the story line said. The director ordered me to reach Mridula through Sneha . . .'

'Hi Yashwant, this is Madhu. I loved you in *Mahamastabhishekha*, but can you tell me why you wore a muffler throughout the film?

I mean it looked very nice and you kept changing into different coloured ones, but was it just the wish of the costume designer or did it have a symbolic meaning?'

'What a lovely observation, Madhu! It is my good fortune to have fans like you. You may have noticed that I played a cold character in the film, a man who cannot express his feelings, a man whose words get stuck in his throat, who cannot tell the girl that he loves her . . . so that warm muffler was . . .'

'A muffler that muffled your voice, good show indeed! For you Madhu the train special from *Train Hudugi* . . .'

'Hi, this is Nelly—'

'Hi Nelly!'

'I want to say hi to Bali Brums—'

'Of course, he's as much as a celebrity as I am. You're the talk of the town Bali . . . I saw your photograph on page three at least twice last fortnight . . .'

'Well Nelly, how are you this evening?'

'Not too good.'

'Why, do you have a cold?'

'No, I've been dumped.'

'No, don't say dumped, Nelly. Say you've moved on, to greener pastures . . .'

'This guy . . . playing games with me . . .'

'Never mind Nelly, plenty other fish in the sea. He doesn't know what he's missing . . . casting pearls before swine, I'm sure . . . You sound like a lovely person . . .'

'Thank you Bali. I want to get even with him . . .'

'Ah well, all's fair in love and war. Just see that you heal . . . whatever it takes. You'll find someone better. And here's a song just for you from your other favourite . . . Shah Rukh Khan doing his thing on the train top in *Chaiyaan chaiyaan* . . .'

'Yashwant, Sheela wants to know—'

'Yashwant avare, you are my top star, but my mother who is a great fan of your father says he is the better actor. But Bali Brums, I want to tell you that I love your voice, I recognize it in all the ads also—you sound great even in that cough drops ad.

Your croak sounds real sexy—'

'Now, now Sheela, watch the language! This is a family programme, remember.'

'You mean in a family programme the word—'

'Talk to you later, Sheela. Gadi bula rahi hai, seeti baja rahi hai . . .'

'I must interrupt you Yashwant to put the director general of Bangalore Police on air. Here's what he has to say to all you two–wheeler riders who absolutely refuse to wear helmets . . . we never think it will happen to us . . .'

'Hi Pushpa Rani. How are you doing today, Flower Queen?'

'Fine, couldn't be better . . .'

'Your voice sounds lovely, Miss Pushpa Rani . . . like a bubbling brook . . .'

'What a compliment, and that too coming from you Yashwant avare. Many of our clients too say that when they hear my voice on the phone. I want to convey my father's wishes to you Sir. Unfortunately he is bed-ridden and cannot speak to you right now. He is a great fan of your father's, especially the mythologicals . . .'

'What a privilege, to hear from my father's fans. I seek your father's blessings . . . it is only with the good wishes of elders that I can progress. I want to say to all my fans out there who are listening . . .'

'Thanks Yashwant for being on the show and before we bid you goodbye, the stock index figures—tech shares are booming on the Bombay Stock Exchange . . . Nifty is nifty . . .'

'The results of yesterday's Know Your City quiz. When was the first railway line built in our state and which two places did it connect? I know it's a tough one . . . I'm sorry so few of you got it right. It was built, back in 1864, by the Madras Railway Company, between Bangalore and Madras. Great job Pratibha, you've won a date with Yashwant! Coffee with him at the Taj on Thursday evening. Don't be late . . .'

He slipped off the headphones and eased his back against the chair. That had been good. He had listened to this programme several times before. It was the best antidote to the blues, a sure fire pick-me-up. It never failed to revive his spirits. He had held his own against superstar Yashwant. Every time Yashwant started taking off in his self-important way, he had cut him off, quite abruptly a couple of times. Plus, two of his regular listeners, Nelly and Pushpa Rani had phoned in, making it clear to Yashwant that they had called not to talk to him but to *their* superstar. That was why it was *his* show. No matter how big anyone was, finally, the finger on the trigger was his.

2

'We must hurry. The temple closes at twelve.'

Antonia Larson, the visiting social scientist from Leeds, had long waited to see a temple. Not the ISKON temple, she said clapping her hands over her ears, that was for tourists. In all her years here, she had seen most of the large magnificent temples—Vitthala in Vijaynagar, Belur, Halebid and Somanthpur, Brihadeeshwara in Thanjavur, even the Bull Temple in Basavanagudi; of the erotic sculptures in Khajuraho she had had her fill, but she had yet to see an ordinary, day-to-day temple, visited only by its regular worshippers, where the grime and the vermilion had not been cleaned up for visitors, nor the idol prettified, nor the entrance besieged by ingratiating souvenir sellers. She did not want to venture into one on her own for she was afraid of being turned away because of the colour of her skin and hair, or being thought of as a hippy or even a spy.

I'll take you, Neela had offered kindly. The Mallikarjuna Swamy Temple is very old. It's my father's family temple; they keep making regular donations to it. He has been going there since he was a boy.

I feel equally at home in a church and in a temple, Neela had told her in one of their first meetings and it was this, Neela's ease in church and temple alike, that first caught Dr Larson's finely tuned researcher's antennae. Neela, product of a Kannadiga Smartha Brahmin doctor father and Tamil Catholic nurse mother, signifier of the 'changing patterns of kinship in a dynamic society' was enrolled or, rather, her parents were into Dr Larson's longitudinal study on the subject. She visited Neela's home, spoke to her parents, who assiduously filled out the fat forms that Neela brought home for them from Dr Larson year after year, believing that they were contributing to the expansion of knowledge.

The social scientist was now an old India hand. And of late, after the country had become easier to visit and the people and their institutions more accessible, she had many irons in the fire, many projects with research organisations and NGOs and spent almost half the year in guest accommodation at the Centre for Socio-Economic Studies. She was now thinking of getting a flat in the city which she and her research associate Alka could share.

That morning, the excitement over the snake had delayed them and Neela fretted. We must hurry, she kept saying, the temple will close. The traffic was heavy and the roads bad. There were many diversions and many roads seemed to have been declared 'one-way only' overnight. Neela snapped at the office driver who pleaded ignorance. The last time he had been on this road, it hadn't been a one-way, he said.

'This place has changed so much in such a short time. The traffic was not so bad last year.'

'I don't come to work on my two-wheeler anymore, I take the office bus,' Neela said.

'And the rents, they've gone sky high. You can't get decent accommodation for less than five thousand rupees a month,' Alka said, 'I'm glad I share—'

'It's all those software companies . . . too many outsiders with too much money—' Neela cut her short, realizing too late that Antonia Larson was an 'outsider' too, worse still, a 'foreigner'. 'The good thing is,' she added quickly, 'more jobs . . .'

'Yes, but what kind of jobs,' Alka said, unperturbed. 'That's part of the research we're doing . . .'

Neela would have been happier if she could have had Antonia Larson all to herself. But that was not to be. Alka, her research associate went everywhere with her. But Alka was sitting in front, next to the driver, while Neela sat in the back with Dr Larson. One of the many 'would-not-dream-of-doing' things in Neela's list was not sitting next to the driver in the office car. She never went to the common canteen either, but sent Sukhiya Ram to fetch her food from there and water in a bottle from the cooler.

They *were* late. When they reached, the doors to the garbha griha were closed. A hand-written notice—in Kannada and in English—pasted on the wall informed them that since it was Dhanur masa, in the first two weeks of January, the pooja would be held between 5 and 9.30 in the morning and 6 and 7.30 in the evening. There was nothing else to do so they wandered about, studying the façade and appraising it.

It was a small temple and not really eye catching. The architecture was not remarkable, nor its walls and gopura particularly embellished with sculptures. The rusting blue metal plaque implanted outside declared that the temple was a protected ancient monument. 'Be warned,' Alka read out in a mock threatening voice, 'that under section three of the Karnataka Ancient and Historical Monuments and Archaeological Sites and Remains Act, 1961, whoever destroys, removes, injures, alters, defaces, imperils or misuses this protected monument shall be punishable—'

'Read that out again—injures . . . imperils . . . destroys . . . defaces . . . It sounds like poetry,' Antonia Larson laughed, sitting on the open ledge of the courtyard, her legs swinging slightly.

'. . . whoever destroys, removes, injures, alters, defaces, imperils or misuses this protected monument shall be punishable with imprisonment which may extend to three months or with fine which may extend to two thousand rupees or with both as per section twenty-six . . . by order of the director.'

The sprawling banyan outside the temple and the grimy stone dhwaja stambha in the courtyard gave the temple the appearance of antiquity. They wandered for a bit in the courtyard, then climbed up the four steps that led to a portico, and stepped across a high threshold into a fairly large pillared hall, at the end of which they confronted the closed doors of the sanctum sanctorum. The original ornamentation of the ceiling in the hall had long fallen off and it had made do with a replacement—a re-inverted lotus in stucco—and the joints and beams of yore were held together with bandages of cement wherever they threatened to give way. The doorway to the garbha griha was mounted with an elaborately carved brass panel etched with human and animal figures entwined with a creeper that grew lush between them and curled round the conches and the drums that they held. Right on top of the panel was a linga, guarded on either side by Nandi bulls, signifying that this was a Shiva temple. The humped bulls were watched over by two winged creatures.

'Look!' Alka pointed, 'a panel in the door is open.'

And so it was. If they stood up on the wooden threshold and reached up on their toes, they could peep inside the sanctum sanctorum through a small square opening in the door. Neela went first to check it out. Inside it was pitch dark, with a single lamp placed strategically on the floor to throw its light on the face of the idol, and there shining in the dark was the golden face of Mallikarjuna Swamy, shielded by the hooded serpent, clothed in a new white dhoti and fresh flowers. And then they noticed outside the closed door in a niche in the wall, a small plate with the flowers and the teertha, the vermilion powder and the vibhuthi, and the stray coins left by latecomers like themselves, and they rejoiced in the thoughtfulness of the Lord in accommodating people who were not familiar with His hours.

Antonia Larson was happy. She rang the bell mounted in the arch of the doorway as they came out into the courtyard. She wrapped the flowers, the bilva leaves and the vermilion powder that she had helped herself to in a paper napkin, careful to do them no irreverence, wiping the excess from her fingers, while Alka who had barely touched the vermilion to her brow with her little finger wiped it off surreptitiously, leaving her forehead correctly clueless though her trousers would carry the smear of red till they were washed next, and Neela took out her compact and looked into the mirror to make sure that the temple vermilion had not exceeded the bounds of her stick-on bindi.

They sat on the steps leading down from the portico to the courtyard for a while, looking around them.

USHA K.R.

'There seem to be some houses too, on the premises,' Antonia Larson remarked.

Behind the temple, a little away from it but in the same compound there were two outhouses with tiled roofs. One of them had a scooter parked outside. A child rode on a tricycle close to the house, away from the temple, while a woman washed clothes under a tap. The clothesline against the wall already had a string of dripping clothes.

'That's where the priest lives,' Neela said.

'What are they doing?' Antonia Larson asked Neela, pointing to the women who had gathered at the base of the banyan, its vast girth girded by reels and reels of thread that people had tied round it.

'Making a wish,' Neela said. 'This is a wish-fulfilling banyan. They go around it, tying all that thread . . .'

Just then the temple priest came out of one of the houses. He saw the three of them and came hurrying across the courtyard. Neela got up and introduced herself. 'I am Gopalrao's daughter, Gopalrao doctor of the . . .'

The man was all smiles. 'We did the abhishekha, the archana, in his name this morning. I thought you would come earlier. I've kept your prasada for you.'

She would have to get a plastic bag, Neela thought with annoyance, to carry all those dripping leaf containers, and sometimes a single plastic bag wasn't proof against those liquids. But when the priest brought the prasada, thankfully, all evidence of the morning's ritual ablutions with milk, honey and ghee, had been confined neatly in plastic containers, each labelled according to its content—teertha, khara pongal, sweet pongal, puliyogare, satyanarayana prasada—no mess, no smell, no flies. The boiled gram alone came in leaf donnes. All made right here, the priest explained. Not in the temple of course, he was quick to add, for that would be defiling its sanctity, but in the twin outhouses in the same compound where he and his elder son stayed. His son had set up a catering business, cooking only for religious ceremonies and he also performed home ceremonies—satyanarayana poojas, thread ceremonies, grihapraveshas and a variety of other homas—the demand for poojas had gone up of late. He lamented that the number of visitors to the temple had fallen with people preferring to go to the newer ones—the slick, tiled ones where the gods were decorated fancily in butter or grapes or pomegranate seeds each evening.

'This,' Alka said, pointing to the gram, 'is rich in protein—boiled, you will notice, not fried—with coconut and coriander for garnishing. Even these,' she tapped the plastic containers, 'sprouted moong, are very healthy. The sweet version has jaggery, not sugar, mind, and ghee, and the spicy version has pepper, rice and desiccated coconut—a perfectly balanced meal.'

But Dr Larson would not be induced into tasting any of it. She passed her donne on to Alka, who quickly put them all, leaf cups and plastic containers into her capacious bag—it would save her from cooking that night.

'I thought,' Dr Larson said, 'that the idol would be made of marble or of stone but this seems to be made of brass.'

'No, not brass. This is a panchaloha idol,' Alka said. 'Idols meant for worship in temples are supposed to be made of an alloy of five metals. Pancha is five and loha is metal; in this case an alloy of gold, silver, copper, brass and iron. It is prescribed in the shastras, the Shilpashastras, and details of the proportions too. If I remember correctly, there's a large amount of copper and quite a bit of gold too.'

'And the serpent above the idol's head? The multi-hooded serpent? It looked duller than the idol.'

'Was that so? I didn't notice. I just had a few seconds on that perch. But we have a tradition in metallurgy that goes back in time, even before the birth of Christ. Mohenjo Daro's famous bronze Dancing Girl? Five thousand years old. And the process the craftsmen have used to cast this idol,' she gestured towards the garbha griha, 'is the same lost wax process that the craftsmen of Mohenjo Daro used. In the south, the temple idols are usually made of panchaloha. I took an art-history course one semester,' she smiled at Antonia Larson's questioning look. 'Marble idols are common in the north, where marble is available. It's a question of locally available materials, and perhaps the fetish for fair complexions,' Alka, north Indian and fair complexioned herself, so fair that the acne stood out pink on her cheeks, said. 'But there are some Jain temples where the idols are made of black marble. It's all there in *Indian Iconography*, Shastry's dependable basic tome. Our library has a copy in the reference section.'

Neela sat next to them on the steps and chomped glumly, already feeling excluded for she knew none of these things about balanced diets and protein rich foods, or marble and panchaloha idols and books about them. She was about to get up and walk towards the car, so that they too would be forced to stop talking and follow her when Alka said, 'Look. Over there—'

'Who is that?'

'Isn't that the girl we hired for data entry last year?'

'Oh yes, Pushpa Rani.'

Neela looked up, a sharp contraction stabbing in her chest at the mention of the name.

'Are you sure it's the same girl? She looks very different. No . . . yes . . . it is Pushpa Rani.'

'I'm sure it is her,' Alka said. 'She was on the cover of *Nation Today* some months ago. I remember her from that.'

They saw a tall girl, very young, barely out of her teens perhaps, hair loose and flowing, coming down almost to the low waist of her jeans. It was Pushpa Rani and it wasn't. She broke away from her companion with a quick word in his ear and walked towards them from the banyan tree. Her loping walk was the same, as was her wide smile.

Two years ago, when the rush of projects had grown too heavy, they had hired Pushpa Rani as a daily-wage typist to help with the reports. One of the other executive assistants had pleaded her case—the girl needed a job, she was willing and hard working and not fussy at all, the family was in trouble, the father was an invalid and no longer had a job. So they had hired her. Even after the work load eased, they kept her on. We could do with an extra hand, Neela said when Dr Subramanyam asked her. All right, he said, her wages are not much, just make sure we pay by cash against a voucher each month. Neela had thought that Pushpa Rani would be a willing dogsbody, someone to fetch and carry when Sukhiya and Daisy were not around: run to the canteen will you, could you go to the library and enter these books into the register, rush to the gate and fetch me an auto . . . But she found that she had misjudged Pushpa Rani. First of all, she showed none of the gratitude that was proper in someone who was desperate for a job and was the 'sole bread winner' of the family. Then, she allied herself with Alka Gupta and Antonia Larson whose reports she typed, and soon they were getting along like a house on fire, a sisterhood almost. With Sukhiya Ram and Daisy, she struck up a giggling ease. They all ate together in the same room—high smelling food of clashing dispositions, ground mustard mingling with garlic. Neela made sure she did not step into their room after lunch or the smell would cling to her clothes and her hair. Once, an important circular had gone missing and she discovered that Daisy had used it to cover her computer keyboard while eating lunch at her work station—she had given the three of them a good tongue lashing after that.

However, for Neela, their greatest transgression lay in their insistence on behaving in *human* terms, their utter disregard for the niceties of what was due to whom, and their refusal to understand and respect their appointed place; their behaviour reeked of insubordination. It was dangerous too for they challenged her authority in a way so subtle that she could not name it and hence could not take appropriate retaliatory measures. She had to resort, as always, to equally subtle, non-official means to get even with them. She dared Pushpa Rani, by her manner, to address her with the familiarity that she did Alka, by her first name, and daunted, Pushpa Rani addressed her with nothing at all, allowing her sentences to hang without suffix or prefix. Neela got back at her in various ways—by keeping her back late, knowing that she had to travel halfway across the city and then to a distant suburb to reach home and her bus left at six. The Alka Gupta–Pushpa Rani camp would find, suddenly, on the morning of their presentation to Dr Subramanyam that the computer would not respond to their command or that the keys of the filing cabinet were misplaced, or that a crucial document they had searched for all week was on their desk all along. There were other ways of marking territory, to Neela's mind, than lifting your hind leg like a dog.

Then, after working with them for two years, without warning, when the workload was at its heaviest, Pushpa Rani upped and left to join a call centre. Neela was intrigued when Alka explained the concept to her—people in India who answered queries about the local weather in the US, or the status of some one's credit card or a routine returns request from a departmental store, messages that travelled through satellites in the sky and cables on the ocean floor so far from where they originated or mattered. That something she had always imagined to have belonged in the realm of telepathic communication should be made so literal filled her with disbelief, even disappointment. How diminished were the sky, the stars and the clouds, home only to artefacts as accomplished as the aeroplane and as aesthetic as the paper kite, or the oceans, in which fish and sea horses and anemones and submarines frolicked, if they housed such matter-of-fact queries.

'Hello madam. Hi Alka.'

Neela, Pushpa Rani ignored or perhaps she did not see her standing behind the other two. There was a round of warm hugs in which Neela pointedly did not participate.

'How *wonderful* to see you, my dear. How *are* you?'

'Very well, Dr Larson, couldn't be better. How are *you*?'

'Oh Pushpa, how is your father now?'

'Much better, thank you. He is more steady now, under control. Is that project complete—the one on gender and health commissioned by the government department?'

'How *clever* of you to remember! That was so long ago. But you were always sharp—yes, the report was completed well on time and submitted to the ministry.'

'And you Alka? Did you find a new flat? If not, I can give you some leads; I know a lot of people.'

It struck them all immediately, the new muscle in Pushpa Rani's voice, a tonal imperative that demanded parity.

There were some more exclamations of surprise and pleasure, after which Pushpa Rani fell in step with them, while Neela straggled behind.

'This is a beautiful temple, isn't it?' Pushpa Rani continued, conversationally. 'I've come here after a long time. I come whenever my shift timings permit. Yesterday, I was put on a new shift, so I came this morning. But the temple is closed . . .'

But the temple is closed—the words hung in the air, their forlorn appeal such a contrast to the sunny chimes of a moment ago.

'I love this temple,' she said, recovering herself. 'It gives me peace of mind. Besides, I like the face of the deity here: it has such a sweet expression. And Mallikarjuna is my chosen god.'

They gathered round her solemnly, contemplating her—low waist blue jeans, purple lipstick and a silver faux-leather handbag. Gone was the synthetic salwar-kameez and the single plait taut with hair oil. Her eyes too were unfettered from their thick glasses. Even Neela could not but be impressed by her; to strike such a note of confident intimacy with god, to talk about the sweetness of His face, of *her* preferences, as if He was just one among many to be picked. All she could boast of was a proprietary interest in the temple and its priests whereas this girl claimed friendship with god Himself, on first name terms.

'How is your job?' she asked tartly. 'I believe you have to get up to all kinds of monkey tricks—change your name and your accent.'

'No big deal. It's actually pretty cool. It's just to make the caller feel comfortable. You're not expected to fake an accent. Just speak more clearly, which is a good thing even for you.'

'What a terrible thing to be cooped up for hours on end, as if in a cage—'

'No different from any other desk job—' Alka said quickly and Neela threw her a searing look. 'The offices look really swanky in the photos—fully air conditioned, international standards—'

'I was more cooped up at the Centre,' Pushpa Rani said with an easy smile, as if she was confident that it was a thing of the past, '. . . not even a desk of my own!'

'But you have to keep talking for eight hours at a stretch!' Neela laughed and turned to the other two.

'Not for long. If you're good and learn fast you get promoted to a non-voice job. Like me! I've just been made Team Leader.'

'Congratulations!'

'Thank you. I worked very hard for it.'

'We know you're a hard worker, Pushpa, and a quick learner too.'

'Thank you, madam.'

'I believe the callers can get abusive?' Neela persisted.

'It's not as if other offices aren't abusive. There are subtler ways to inflict damage.'

Neela blushed, and said nothing, ambushed by her many past unkindnesses, the delayed payments and the meannesses.

'I saw your photograph on the *Nation Today* cover,' Alka stepped into the silence, 'the Business Process Outsourcing special and I told Dr Larson, "Isn't this our Pushpa Rani?"'

'Oh that!' Pushpa Rani shrugged and glowed with happiness.

'How is your health?' Neela tried, one last time. 'You have to work through the night I believe, to suit their timings in the other half of the world.'

'I'm quite comfortable working at night; my body is pretty used to it now. I've started practising Yoga. Actually, the office insists—they have a centre and a Yoga teacher right on the premises. My stamina has improved since I started Yoga. The office provides transport—I get picked up and dropped at my door in an air conditioned taxi, so no more riding in public buses.'

And then Alka and Dr Larson bore Pushpa Rani away, eager to speak to her and Neela hurried after them, determined to listen. Bits of their conversation floated over to her. Pushpa Rani had taken a loan for her father's heart surgery, he was to be fitted with a pacemaker. She was earning fifteen thousand rupees a month. Fifteen thousand rupees! Neela could not believe her ears. That was much more than even what she earned. Alka too, for that matter. And Pushpa Rani was a PUC fail! She had got a compartment in science and had had to carry it over. Her only skills were typing and shorthand, and the ability to talk endlessly and with great certainty in her bad English. Soon, I will get to be supervisor, Pushpa Rani was saying, and my salary will increase.

On the way back to office, all three of them were crammed into the back seat, for Alka slid in quickly after Dr Larson. Neela had seen the joint light of excitement in their eyes, and sure enough they began discussing a possible short-term research project. Here was a transformation they could see before their very eyes. The New Economy and the New Woman—Alka said she could sew up the research in a few weeks' time.

'I got her mobile number, and she said she'd be happy to be part of it. There's a whole community out there that we could involve—'

They praised Pushpa Rani, her ambition, her resourcefulness and her courage, and said how happy they were for her for having improved her prospects. Neela thought Dr Larson's interest in the lower orders, in 'people and their stories' as she called it, regrettable. First Sukhiya Ram and now Pushpa Rani. The two of them had roped Sukhiya Ram too into one of their projects, and she had to grant Sukhiya time off from work legitimately to sit in a chair opposite Alka in her office and speak into a tape recorder about his travails, his migration from the village to the city, as part of their new fangled ethnographic study on the subject.

And then, when Neela Gopalrao had been lulled into her usual state of mild resentment, came the question that she had been expecting these many weeks but which she was most unprepared to answer.

'What happened to that young man who did our reports last year? I thought Dr Subramanyam had hand-picked him to report on the activities of the Centre, you know, as a kind of central conduit of information. If I remember, there was some talk of making him the face of the Centre—'

'Prithvi Kumar. He left.'

'Pity. He was quite bright. The place needed a person like him.'

Neela cleared her throat to relieve it of his name. 'I don't think his contract was renewed,' she managed as her throat closed up on itself again.

'Do you think we can have lunch at MTR?' Antonia Larson said, changing the subject and Neela was glad.

Alka and Dr Larson were soon immersed in the details of the project and Neela was left to herself to mull on the issue she thought she had safely pushed to the fringes of her mind—Prithvi Kumar, the unsent letter that sat in her drawer along with Alka's cheque, and the elusive nature of love.

four

~

1

As she walked in the sun, the noon-day winter sun, feeling it sharply on her back, warming her bones, Pushpa Rani felt better, much less anxious. It was true, what she had said to Bali Brums in the morning, the sight of the rising sun *was* the most glorious in the world. Perhaps the next best thing was feeling it on your skin, feeling your blood leap and your pores tingle and your spine uncurl as you stepped into the sunlight after a long hibernation. It hurt the eyes in the beginning, glorious as it was, till you got used to it. For a whole month she had left home after dark, at six in the evening and come back at five in the morning, before it became light, and was fast asleep by the time the sun rose, waking up only after it had set. To be honest, she preferred those hours. She had not lied to Neela—she *was* comfortable with the dark, she had no problem with irregular hours. For as long as she could remember the household had woken up—all except her father—in the very early hours of the morning, much before the sky even began to lighten, to receive the baskets of flowers that would arrive. Her mother was a professional garland maker. Two small rooms—that was all they had—one in which her father slept on a wooden bed and in the other, she, her mother, her sister and her brother spread out their mattresses at night. It was in this room that the baskets were unloaded and the flowers strung together and they had to roll up their mattresses to make room. The four of them, her brother included, would sit amidst the sweet-smelling jasmine in summer or the milder sevanthi or even the odourless kanakambra to string the flowers. The garlands had to be ready before dawn when the agent, who supplied the flowers, would return for them and they would then be distributed to households and temples and markets all over the city, in time for the morning's pooja.

She felt a special kinship with the small hours of the morning, mingled as they were with the scent of jasmine. Even now when she rode alone in the office taxi at night, alone most of the way—'Princess' the others called her—through the sometimes dark, sometimes lit-up streets, she felt that the streets had emptied themselves of the maniacal crowds and the traffic of the daytime for her alone, and that only she was privy to their true secret self, and this kindred feeling was such a slight thing, a suggestion, a whisper really, and would be gone by morning. And yet she was also the child of the sun, for her shift permitting, she would work through part of the night, watch the sky lightening through the glass-fronted windows that stretched from floor to ceiling, and see the sun come up. And the prospective customer to whom she was trying to sell insurance or the irate man who was calling to retrieve some piece of information half-way across the world in America, was truly blessed, for the waves that carried her voice across ocean or sky carried also the magic of sunrise. One such morning when she was new in her job she had admitted to pleasant-sounding Mr Joe Chuffnel of Phoenix, Arizona—call me Joe—that she was actually from Bangalore, that her name was not Pam and that she had just seen the sun rise right in front of her eyes. It was an omen of tremendous luck for him, she had added at the spur of the moment, departing completely and unprofessionally from her script. Joe Chuffnel had bought the insurance she was trying to sell him. They still exchanged occasional emails; she had given him a recipe for curry and had learnt from him what a 'high five' was.

Pushpa Rani had much to thank Neela Gopalrao for. If it not had been for her bullying, she might still be stuck at the Centre, typing reports for fifty rupees a day, less than what a contract sweeper was paid. Besides, the work was also uncertain: she did not know when she would be sent home. Come back after a month, we don't need you now, the report will be ready only next week, Neela Gopalrao would say with relish. Or she would spring a fat two-hundred-page document on her at four in the evening, even though she had had it with her all day long, and she, Pushpa Rani, would be the only one left in the building, with the menacing security man at the door, typing away into the night. There was no point, she told herself whenever she dwelt on the past, on her now inconsequential days in the Centre, thinking about Neela Gopalrao's bitchiness, of making herself unhappy again, when it did not matter anymore. If her new job had taught her anything, it was to shed the baggage of the past, and as Bali Brums the RJ from Voices from Heaven put it, to think positive and prepare for a better future.

It was in one such miserable lull, when she was sent home without work, that she spotted the full page advertisement: Do you want to be a call-centre professional? Do you have the confidence for a global encounter? All it asked was for you to be young, ambitious, resourceful and English-speaking. It was the girl in the advertisement who caught Pushpa Rani's attention. She was dressed in black trousers and a black T-shirt and her hair was cut short in a fringe across her forehead. She wore no jewellery except for a watch with a very large dial and a thick black strap and her black polished square-toed shoes gleamed from the floor. Her hands were crossed across her chest and she smiled up at the camera—sharp, cocky and warm. Just what Pushpa Rani would like to be, and how she would like to be seen.

She spoke to no one about it, consulted nobody. One day, at the Centre, when she got a few private moments at the common computer, she looked up 'call centre' on Google and tried, in round about ways, to question Alka Gupta, the research scholar whose reports she sometimes typed. The only thing that bothered her as she prepared for the interview was that she did not have a pair of jeans and a t-shirt. But making bold, she walked into the best of the two rows of shops in Sundarapalya where she lived, and bought her first pair of trousers and the blue t-shirt that flapped in the wind, on display outside the shop. Good choice, the shopgirl told her, came just this morning from Bombay; you will look very smart in it. Knowing her mother could not bear it if her daughters could not wear the flowers she strung, Pushpa Rani did not cut her hair. At the interview, one among a sea of young, smartly dressed boys and girls who flooded the lobby of the three-star hotel, she felt not a moment of doubt or anxiety.

'We need youngsters who are strong and can handle pressure. Can you keep a cool head in a difficult situation?' one of the men on the interview panel asked her.

'I am strong. I can lift my father off the bed and sit him up all by myself, without my brother's help,' she said. 'As for difficult situations, I face one every evening when I come home . . .'

The men received this in silence.

'You will be required to listen a lot, to people with different accents, to interpret their speech patterns correctly.'

'I have a flair for languages. I know three south Indian languages which I picked up just by listening to people speak. As for interpreting people's accents, if you can make sense of what a person in pain mumbles, you can make sense of anything.'

'Where did you learn your English?' the man who asked her the first question said, with what she thought was a hint of a smile.

'At St Michael's Convent School, Sundarapalya,' she replied confidently. 'Whatever happened my father made sure we got an education.'

'Would you be willing to work the night shift?'

'Yes. Any shift, any time of the night or day—'

'You haven't completed your pre-university. Our ad clearly says you have to have a ten-plus-two.'

'I can complete it in six months as an external candidate.'

'By the way,' the friendly man asked when she was about to leave, 'are you really eighteen years old?'

'I turned eighteen last week.'

The early days had been such fun. The training sessions of the first few weeks were a revelation, a departure from all that she knew and had been taught. The voice training classes were difficult—it was tough to get her tongue around and between her teeth or climb the back of her palate and produce all those funny sounds—and it also made no sense to unlearn her correct English and catch an approximate version of it. But the films they were shown on the states and festivals of America were as exciting as watching the latest Kannada films, and listening to the tapes on the frequent mistakes made by people while receiving and answering calls were really funny. She marvelled at how much she learnt about the world in those first few weeks. She had intimate glimpses into the lives of people, entered their glossy homes and their open kitchens, mowed their lawns and travelled in their cars, learnt what they liked to eat and drink and play and how they kept their money, all in a part of the world that had never crossed her mind. She was also surprised to find out that it was not her knowledge of English but her high score on 'potential to be trained' that had helped her get in, and here she more than fulfilled their expectations. It was no exaggeration to say that she was the trainer's favourite—willing, eager and capable, she proved to be better than the graduates and even the engineers training to be technical support. Straight away after the training they had put her on the night shift and she took to the work immediately. People usually complained about doing the late shift but for her the most difficult task was waking up the taxi driver and every evening there was a huge tamasha on the street in Sundarapalya. The pick-up taxi, a luxurious Qualis, would park in front of her house in the evening since she was the first to be picked up. When she came down at eight, well in time for the ten o' clock shift, she would find a crowd of people admiring the brand-new car and the driver fast asleep inside. No amount of knocking on the window or even shaking the car would wake him up. She would call him on his mobile phone, see the screen light up and hear it ringing on the dashboard and still he would not stir. Finally, just as the boys of Sundarapalya were helpfully offering to smash the windscreen open with a cricket bat, the driver would wake up, shake himself alert and they would drive off. Sundarapalya was truly far flung, so she rode alone for most of the journey and she made it her job to watch out for the driver and make sure he did not keel over the wheel on the long empty stretches of road. The six of them in the taxi often bet on the number of times his eyes would close and on particularly dangerous days, they pulled over at a dhaba and had tea.

And then came the *Nation Today* cover. After a country-wide poll, the leading magazine chose her as the face of the country's burgeoning Business Process Outsourcing industry. She hardly recognized herself in the photograph: her skin an even matt, her eyebrows perfect arches, her eyes almond-ed with kohl, and her smile—oh, her smile, that was the best feature—pink lips with a silvery sheen parted to reveal a dazzling row of white. She looked better than even the girl in black who had featured in the advertisement that had first attracted her. For weeks after that strangers had stopped her on the road and spoken to her, gazing at her with admiration. Her father was so proud. Even her mother said, Imagine, my daughter on the cover of an English magazine! *Nation Today* sent a photographer to their house and though it was one of his bad days her father made an effort and she sat at his feet to be photographed. It was the only photograph she had with her father, only she wished he looked a little less scruffy and his bed not so crumpled. She told the reporter everything about herself and the article carried a few lines about her father and her background. They had quoted her saying, 'My inspiration? My father. Though he is ill he keeps smiling. Life has treated him harshly but he never forgets to feed the sparrows on our balcony each morning. From him I have learnt what courage and determination mean.'

That cover face had been lucky for her. It brought her a promotion and, just last week, the bank loan for her father's operation was sanctioned. It also won her a new friend. Till a few weeks ago, Ranjit was the tall boy in technical support she used to see in the cafeteria and wonder about, the one whose shift ended just as hers began, but then one day he came over and spoke to her. Your face is your fortune, he joked, and she had the wit to retort, Not my face but my talent, my ability. My face is just a mirror.

The cover had also caused much heart-burn on the floor. Many of her colleagues were convinced that her out-of-turn promotion and other perks had come because of it. She had been angry at their insinuations for the truth was that she was so much better than them. The customers were happy with her service, as the customer satisfaction surveys consistently showed—she finished her calls in less than average time, and there was no hanky-panky with her, like disappearing into the loo every now and then or sneaking her mobile in to make personal calls. The girl who had made the most fuss was the one who fell asleep on the job and had to be shaken awake by the team leader at least once every day; the same one who kept her earphones off her ears, more on her cheeks, and so missing half the things the caller said. Apparently there was a buzzing in her head if she positioned her phones exactly over her ears; of course she had been shunted off. Then there was the boy in the cubicle next to hers—the one with the thick accent which no amount of training could erase—who kicked the walls of the partition when she took calls because she had complained about him and the girl whose head buzzed disappearing into the loo together. Well, he got his comeuppance. He was caught trying to divert an unfavourable customer response to a false e-mail id. He was caught almost immediately; they were very good at finding such people out. Of course, it was a monotonous job; the counsellor had said as much. But there were ways of handling it like an adult, which they all were. She herself had taken to Yoga—it had done wonders for her back. She, Philomena, who worked on another floor, and Ranjit were taking the western dance classes that were held in the basement once a week. They were gong to perform in the Employee's Day celebrations soon.

Pushpa Rani knew now that the others saw her as a shining star—brilliant, perfect but distant. They all aspired to be like her but they knew that they could not, so they were jealous of her. They could not come to terms with their own imperfections, so they blamed somebody else for them. It was the same with the abusive callers. It was all a question of seeing things in the right perspective.

Remember, you are there to help the other person, to solve his or her problem, her trainer had told them, and you will see yourself as a giver. The skills we teach you are primarily to make you a better person, to add value to you as a human being, and not only as a professional. We build your inner strength so that you can be flexible when required. So, when a caller was short with her or even called her a 'stupid Indian bitch' or enquired whether she wore anything other than a loin cloth, she knew he was frustrated over his lack of information, or perhaps he was cold and lonely or had lost his job. Such people were angry, afraid of things they could not control, so they took it out on someone who could not retaliate, who could not say anything other than, 'I'm sorry for your trouble, sir, but I'll do whatever I can . . . I'm sorry we had to keep you on hold for so long . . . could you tell me what the problem is . . . you haven't been issued a receipt? Could you confirm your date of birth, Mrs Sarah? And your address please? Could you please look at the bottom right hand corner of that blue slip of paper you are holding and read out the sixteen digit number . . .' She had successfully handled a variety of dissatisfied customers—from men whose accounts were overdrawn to those who confessed that the only human voice they had heard in days was the one at the end of a toll free number. There was one caller, a woman, who wanted to sue the credit card company because she had ripped her finger open when she had tried to open the letter the company had sent her announcing she had won a holiday for two. The staple-pin holding the two sheets of the offer letter together had cut her and she was afraid of third world infections. She would not believe that the letter had been posted from a local American office. Then there was the man who insisted that she call him Daddy Darling because that was his nickname and all his friends called him that. Those two were the only calls she had forwarded to the supervisor so far. You were born to customer care, her supervisor once told her. You have a great future in this line, but you must take care to become a total professional. It is a demanding environment out there and you must be ready to push the limits of your performance.

Which was why she was annoyed with herself for having risen to the bait so easily with Neela Gopalrao at the temple that afternoon.

To think that she had actually taken that woman seriously and allowed her to affect her temper. She had no patience for that kind of pettiness, for the likes of Neela Gopalrao, with her ridiculous airs and enormous spite, who, she now understood, was insecure, threatened, and—she searched for the phrase from the training manual that she was so fond of—'lacking in self-esteem, in positive, feel-good emotions'. In fact, Neela would make the ideal abusive caller. She could be profiled for the training manual and her own responses to Neela could be recorded and played to trainees to illustrate what not to do, how not to handle an irate caller.

She had walked for more than a kilometre from the temple, when the sun began to burn her back.

'Ammanagudi Street,' she said to the auto driver, sure that he would not refuse.

2

Pushpa Rani had always believed in omens and symbols, in coincidences and accidental signs to show her the way, and of late she had become particularly mindful of them. However, what saved her from becoming fatalistic or even contemplative for too long was that she was first a creature of instinct, wilful and confident in equal measure. So every lizard that chirruped on the wall only confirmed her train of thought, the weekly horoscope told her what she already knew for she was always ready for the unexpected, and when she left the house she always arranged the slippers neatly so she would not find one of a pair inverted against the other for that could mean only one thing—the final journey. Because Pushpa Rani, believer in omens and symbols, also believed that she had been reborn in this very lifetime.

As a child she had been sickly, prone to bouts of fever that left her weak and dizzy most of the time. She was so thin that she could almost see the bones beneath her watery, insubstantial flesh and the shifting muscles and tendons of her bare legs and thighs frightened her into sitting still and not moving. And her father, she was convinced, had exchanged his health for hers. Like the emperor Babur who when asked to give up what was most precious to him to save his son Humayun who was gravely ill, had not produced the Kohinoor diamond, but had simply gone round his son's bed thrice, after which he had taken to his bed and his son restored to health. Some such pact, Pushpa Rani was sure, her father had made with god. He returned from a pilgrimage of the seven holy rivers and gave her a locket, a circular thing the size of a twenty-five paise coin, with a red stone in the centre, a stone of many facets, with a pleasing angularity. The locket was made of gold and had been expensive. Her mother had scolded him for buying gold without her mediation but the locket never left Pushpa Rani's neck from that day. Her father had asked her to keep it on even when she bathed, for the holy man who had blessed it had said that as the 'gold water' washed over her, she would be cured. But no such cure had worked for her father.

To see her father now it would be impossible to believe that he had been perfectly healthy once, that it was she who had been sickly and practically confined to her bed. Her mother, in her usual brisk way, had revealed that there were times when she thought her eldest daughter would not recover from her latest bout of fever. That same briskness of approach had helped her mother, head bent over her patch of vegetables or her pile of flowers, go about as if *that* was the business of her life and all else—children, husband, illness and death—were distractions. But her father was not like that. The many evenings when she lay listless and peevish, her mother clicking her tongue impatiently every time she tossed or turned or asked for water, it was he who, immediately on coming home, even before undoing the bicycle clips from his trousers, sat next to her and told her about the fat man in his office with the pig tail or amused her with the painted mud toys that he had picked up from the weekly market. It was he who would cajole her into drinking her bitter medicine, lacing it with honey or bananas, while her mother watched, snorting that he was spoiling a grown girl.

They had lived in a village then, far away from the city but close enough to the highway. It was one of the many villages which formed the market garden fringe of the city and supplied its daily quota of vegetables and fruits. Pushpa Rani remembered her father setting off before dawn every day, cycling for miles through the fields surrounding their house to deliver the vegetables to the van that stood waiting on the closest tar-road. He would return, bathe, and set off again on his cycle, park it in a shop by the bus stand and catch the first of two buses to Majestic in Bangalore where he was head clerk in a small firm and also the proprietor's right hand man. It seemed a cruel joke that those indefatigable legs, which had pedalled almost to Bangalore and back every day, should have failed him.

They had had little to complain of in the beginning. Though they had a small plot of land and could only grow vegetables on it, and flowers when the season was right, the division of family lands had been amicable. There were no ugly fights as with the other families in the village, and they did not have to live in constant fear of their lives, wondering which uncle or cousin would attack them the next time they ventured into the fields alone. Her mother managed the vegetable garden by herself, with the help of her children and hired hands when required. And then, in the first of a series of ill-advised moves, her father sold their piece of land and invested the money in 'business'. Within months both the money and the business were gone, and they had shifted to a one-roomed house in Sundarapalya, closer to the city, its last outpost, refuge of those who could no longer afford to stay in the city but did not want to leave it.

The village in which Pushpa Rani was born and raised for the first twelve years of her life had been a sedate hum, a cluster of modest houses, with the biggest house belonging to the biggest landlord, which in time added another floor and came to be distinguished by its curlicued balconies and the colour pink, and a dish antenna on the roof. Everyone knew who was who and what was what and, except for the minor government officials who were transferred periodically, there had been no new settlers in the village as far as they could remember. Sundarapalya, barely twenty kilometres from Pushpa Rani's village, turned out to be a true and permanent half-way house, caught unawares as it were in the afterglow of a city that had suddenly been thrust into the limelight itself; Sundarapalya was just outside the lime-yellow arc, in the penumbra of greyness, destined always to be just out of reach.

Two rows of shops housed in indifferently built buildings, their bare cement blocks now blackened, with iron rods still sticking out unevenly from the beams, made up the main 'square' of Sundarapalya. Away from the square, new buildings were coming up haphazardly, dwarfing the older shabby houses, even hutments sometimes of the original inhabitants, all of them separated by mud tracks; there were no pukka roads in Sundarapalya except for the main road. The only mud tracks that were maintained in some state of repair were the ones leading to the 'farm houses' that the new rich of Bangalore were constructing, and laden trucks made their way on these tracks off and on, followed sometimes by bright cars with their black windows rolled up. Sprouting in the middle of fields filled with parthenium—that deadly weed, harbinger of respiratory disorders and skin allergies—Sundarapalya had little charm, seeming more a random settlement than a planned colony. But there was no denying its energy. It had the knowingness, the half-knowledge and the erratic growth of an adolescent whose voice has begun to break, whose face has broken out in a rash of acne and whose body has become equally a site of embarrassment and excitement. Sundarapalya might receive only the backwash of Bangalore, but the lights winked in the distance, the promise of adulthood lay just round the corner.

Pushpa Rani had not cared much for the bank or the school or the commission agents and depots that came up on the fringes of Sundarapalya, nor did the increasing traffic of lorries register. She knew only the bakery and the clothes shops in the square, and the cinema theatre further down the highway. What she, her brother and her sister associated most strongly with Sundarapalya and lusted after in vain were the foreign-made, highly-coloured packets of potato chips, lined with silver foil on the inside, which each shop had strung up at the entrance. These packets, plump with promise, had come to replace the local red-spotted chips in the greasy, transparent, cheap plastic packets, which split open even before you reached home, and whose price you could never tell from the speckled bits of paper with the hand-written details that were inserted into them. The newcomers, puffed up to capacity like balloons and claiming that the contents were untouched by human hand, quite literally turned out to be full of hot air for the fat packets never contained enough and the chips sounded like seeds in a rattle when you shook them, and Pushpa Rani and her brother and sister were always accusing each other of having taken more than their fair share. The empty packets proved indestructible too, turning up in every field and furrow, their silver innards shining in the moonlight, as they made their way to distant mountains and streams. Now, of course, when she didn't want them, Pushpa Rani could have any number of these packets free in her cafeteria. There was also a surfeit of pizza and biryani, which the office ordered regularly, so regularly that she no longer remembered a time when they had been treats just to dream of. But Sundarapalya, lop-sided as it was, was to serve them well for it had an English-medium 'convent' school and it was here that their mother was inducted into the flower-stringing business. Since there was little to do but hang around in the square, Pushpa Rani threw herself into her studies, going for tuitions in maths and English after school. Spurred by the competition she encountered from the girls who came from the newly built houses, better off than she was but less alert, less aware of their disadvantages or the opportunities that may pass their way, Pushpa Rani set out to excel.

In Sundarapalya too her bouts of fever disappeared, as easily as if she had shrugged off a heavy cumbersome garment, but the first signs of ill health began in her father. It had begun innocuously—he would rub his left eye off and on, claiming he could not see very well out of it and sometimes, when he was holding his tumbler of coffee, his hand would go numb and he would not feel the weight of the tumbler. They noticed that he walked rather stiffly at times and though he never admitted to being in pain, his face would be black and drawn. He also seemed to find more and more excuses not to get on to his bicycle. They tried to think of a number of explanations for it. They had moved to Sundarapalya at the wrong time, a cousin said. His grahachara is not right, has never been, her mother said. Another relative, after consulting an astrologer, said the vastu of the house was faulty, so they moved to another house a street away, paying a higher rent for a smaller place, for nothing else was available and the rents had gone up since they first came there. They also decided to consult a doctor. The series of tests and probes yielded no name and the symptoms refused to conform to a pattern, but the treatment began to chisel away at their savings. When he started to make mistakes with the accounts, adding the same numbers twice and entering them in the wrong columns, his firm quietly pensioned him off—by then the proprietor had retired and his young son was in charge. Her father settled for a lumpsum payment, which dwindled considerably over the next two years, going towards his frequent, short, fruitless stays in the local hospital, from which he emerged worse than before. After many years and several doctors, the elusive symptoms were pinned down and the disease was diagnosed, still tentatively, as multiple sclerosis of the galloping variety and it was little comfort to them that this was more commonly a white man's disease, rare to the tropics.

At that stage, Pushpa Rani took matters into her hands. She made up her mind one evening, after the landlord forced his way into the house and told her father off in a particularly insulting way for being behind with the rent. She quit her pre-university course in St Michael's Junior College, and made her brother give up school to take up a job packing glassware for a crockery distributor who had just opened a depot in Sundarapalya. She refused an offer of marriage from her mother's brother, and another offer from a well-off cousin to go to Bombay to mind his house and his children while he and his wife went out to work. Instead, she set her face resolutely towards Bangalore, whose lights were fast approaching Sundarapalya. She struck a deal with a relative who was a tout of sorts and set herself up on the pavement outside the high court with the only asset she possessed—her father's typewriter—to type out petitions for the stream of people who went in and out of the red bricked building, till she got a break at the Centre for Socio-Economic Studies as a daily-wage typist. It was a long haul: travelling a minimum of four hours each day on a series of buses, six days a week, eight hours a day, at the beck and call of a temperamental mistress. But it was a clean office and the canteen had subsidized food.

Pushpa Rani was not given to reflection—it slid invariably into self-pity—and that helped her live through those two years. When she left early in the morning, her father would seem all right, even insisting on making her a cup of tea but when she returned late in the evening she would find him in bed, knocked out in pain or exhibiting yet another symptom. Her mother, watching one of the lurid serials on television, would tell her composedly, your father couldn't swallow his food today or the doctor has recommended a new series of tests, you had better draw some more money from the bank, or he has started wetting his bed now . . . She had remonstrated with her mother once, and her mother had replied: I do my duty by him, by all of you . . . You cannot shed tears over a person who dies every day.

A little bit of money and mentoring could change your life completely, Pushpa Rani learnt. As voice-help in the customer care department in Trix Marketing Solutions, in one stroke, she was earning ten times as much as she had as a casual typist at the Centre. Within six months of being confirmed in her job Pushpa Rani shifted her family out of Sundarapalya—after extracting a hefty sum from their landlord for evacuating the house—and into Ammanagudi Street on the recommendation of a new colleague. She made her brother give up his job in the packaging warehouse and put him through a call-centre training course after which he joined a sister concern of Trix Solutions. Her sister, chafing to get out of school and start working, was rapped on the knuckles and enrolled in private tuitions to help improve her marks and keep her from hanging around the square with unsuitable friends. Pushpa Rani's decision to shift to Ammanagudi Street, again, had been against the advice of her uncles. The rent was too high, they pointed out, and what was the point of moving into the crowded heart of the city when seasoned city-dwellers themselves were moving to the outskirts? Her brother and she, Pushpa Rani told them, would manage the rent—it was a small outhouse after all—and their mother's earnings would be enough to run the house. Moreover, she pointed out, it had become impossible to continue in Sundarapalya, so far from hospitals and bus stops, in a second-floor house, when her father was bed-ridden. They were lucky to get an outhouse on the ground-floor in an area as central as Ammanagudi Street. Besides, Sundarapalya, cheap though it was, was so far off that no auto would even wait for her to finish saying 'Sundarapalya', before driving off in an exhaust-blast of disdain. (Not that she could afford to travel by auto in those days; it was always the mofussil public bus, unless it was to take her father to the doctor.) Pushpa Rani had never felt particularly intimidated by her relatives, nor the need to defer to them as her brother and mother did. And now she was ready to take anyone on. Now, when she put on her headphones, smiled into the mouthpiece as she had been taught ('when you smile it reflects in your voice and in your heart') and said, 'Thank you for calling. How may I help you?' in an accent free of the influence of her mother tongue, she knew that she was straddling the world, reaching across oceans and continents to another person in a place she recognized only as a pink splotch on a map, to help him, to make a difference in his life.

Yet, despite her natural confidence and optimism, Pushpa Rani was foremost a believer in symbols. Was it so easy then to turn the tide, to cheat destiny, to get the better of fate? The thought made her so fearful that she clung more fiercely, with deeper desperation and faith, to her symbols and omens, afraid that her luck would turn. And the fear that lurked in her heart all the time, which insinuated itself in her every movement, and stole upon her thoughts unawares, was that she would lose her father, that suddenly one day he would be gone, and after that things would just fall apart. For Pushpa Rani also knew that her mother could not manage the feral creature their household was growing into—her brother who raged at having to work by day and study by night and sometimes did not come home for days, her sister, not yet thirteen, but who already had the sinuous sulkiness of girls who were ready to come out, her mother, unmoved by anything, attaching herself only to the task on hand, and she herself who felt too much the burden and often wished, much to her shame, that it would all end and she could be free.

Her mobile phone rang when she was in the auto, half way to Ammanagudi Street. It was her mother. She braced herself . . . Will you go to the homeopath and get his medicines, her mother asked, and while you're at it tell the doctor about your back as well. Your father is fine, she added, Mani Nurse is with us.

At that, Pushpa Rani relaxed against the plastic-covered seat of the autorickshaw and gave thanks to the angelic Mani Nurse. God did move in mysterious ways. Mani Nurse was proof of that. Between them, Mallikarjuna and Mani Nurse would see things through. On moving to Ammanagudi Street, the one convenience that had been beyond Pushpa Rani's reach was a male nurse to come and attend to her father for her mother could not manage him alone anymore. But then her mother had run into Mani Nurse who stayed close to their house, just behind Ammanagudi Street. She came regularly to give her father his injections and between them, her mother and Mani Nurse managed to help him bathe and took him for short walks, but more than anything else, Mani Nurse's visits cheered him up considerably. And she charged so little, sometimes nothing at all. Her mother too seemed to have found a friend in Ammanagudi Street at last; it was always Mani Nurse this and Mani Nurse that. Pushpa Rani had seen her only once and that too through a haze of sleep for Mani Nurse came in the late afternoons, when she was between shifts. Mani Nurse had flashed her a smile and Pushpa Rani had mumbled a greeting from the sofa where she slept, and even in her half-asleep state she had noted that Mani Nurse looked very familiar; she bore a strong resemblance to someone Pushpa Rani knew but could not recall.

Part III
~

five

~

Whenever Mani Nurse caught sight of Gopalrao Doctor, her heart stopped for a moment before coming back to life, like the self-lighting candles on children's birthday cakes. She watched him approach the window where she was on duty and go past it, and the expression on his face, in repose, was what she could only describe as 'goodness', that open-eyed look of wonder at the world and affection for it. His eyes, the best feature in his already impeccable face, were large and appeared naturally to be lined with kohl. He visited Modern Nursing Home twice a week for the ultrasonography scan—he was a radiologist—to sound out the bellies of expectant mothers and tell them that their babies were fine. Theirs was a small, private nursing home and the number of patients was not enough to warrant a daily visit. One thing intrigued her though: she never understood why he carried his own case of equipment while his assistant walked ahead of him, empty-handed. Immediately, she put this down to his innate goodness that recognized no difference between high and low.

She contrived to have herself posted on afternoon duty, despite having done the night shift, so that she could greet him with an 'Afternoon doctor!' two times a week. That was easy for she was the one who assigned all the nurses their shifts and helped the matron make up the duty roster. After three weeks of 'Afternoon doctor!' and 'Had coffee? Why don't you try our canteen sometime . . .' and a bit of bold banter, Dr Gopalrao decided he liked what he saw—bright eyes that beamed their adoration of him and a white smile in a luminous dark face. He took up her invitation for coffee and soon one thing led to another.

Six months later, the day after she told him she was pregnant, he stopped coming to the nursing home. It was then that she learnt other things. He was not a radiologist; he was not even a qualified doctor. He was simply the man who carried his radiologist brother's bag for him—the non-descript man who had always walked ahead of him, who was eclipsed by the radiance of his brother's looks. True, he came from a famous family of doctors. His father and his three brothers and two sisters were all doctors, each specializing in different parts of the human body; he was the proverbial black sheep. His family had got him a seat in a medical college and he got through the first year. But after having failed his second year four times, he dropped out. The family then created an administrative slot for him, with a suitably important-sounding designation, in one of the nursing homes they owned. It was purely by chance that he had come to Modern Nursing Home where Mani worked—the radiologist brother had injured his shoulder and needed help with his heavy bag, and Gopal had been pressed into service.

God had willed that they should meet, Mani said. But when she walked up and down the footpath outside the fortress in which he lived—guarded by a watchman and several large dogs of daunting pedigree—and his 'secretary' returned all her calls with 'Gopal Sir is in a meeting at present', the enormity of the situation hit her. How could she, a girl who lived away from home in a crowded hostel for nurses, with no one to call her own in the city except an old aunt, and no money other than the small amount her brothers sent her, have dared to hope for more? So she did what she had promised herself she would never do: she ran home to her brothers in Nagapattinam, from where she had run away to Bangalore in the first place.

A few days later Gopalrao was told by the servant that he had visitors. He walked into the drawing room, unarmed and defenceless, to see two hirsute thickset men, their two pairs of thighs easily occupying a sofa meant for three, staring fixedly at the open front door. It was a particularly inconvenient day for them to have come. His father and eldest brother were leaving for a conference of surgeons in Geneva late that night. The travel agent, the foreign currency supplier, the shop man who delivered winter clothes to their home, and sundry others were going in and out. The household flowed past the two men, uncaring, completely ignoring them; there could be no one sitting on the sofa as far as they were concerned. Even the servants knew that Gopal's visitors did not matter. When he discovered that the two men spoke no language other than Tamil, Gopalrao still thought he could get out of it, but a helpful servant stood by to translate. We run a transport service in Nagapattinam, the two men said, mainly taking pilgrims to the shrine at Velankanni. Everybody knows us there; we are a respectable family.

Let us go out and have coffee, Gopalrao suggested, wanting to get them out of the house as quickly as possible, wondering how much these two would want and how and when he would ask his father for the money. They walked through the garden grimly, lost to the lawn, the beds of flowers and the ornamental fountain, even the watchman who looked at them curiously.

And there, outside the gate stood Mani, in a bright yellow sari, her stomach already showing.

'I hope . . .' she said, swallowing so hard that her throat heaved, her anxious eyes darting about his face, 'I was so afraid that they would hurt you . . .'

And at that there was just one thing Gopalrao could do. He reached out for her hands and took them into his own.

And so they were thrown together—Gopalrao and Mani Anthony— to build a life together from scratch. Mani never got to step inside the family mansion, the one she had anxiously waited outside for days, for the couple was banished to a small flat far away from the family home, on a side road off Ammanagudi Street and Gopalrao was assigned a pharmacy to run in one of the family nursing homes. After that the family washed their hands of them, except for Gopal's sister, the only one who was not a doctor and who lived abroad. Her own family, Mani voluntarily banished; her mother was old and could not travel and as for her brothers, while she was grateful to them for having intervened, she could not forgive them for humiliating her Gopal. She would never forget the look on his face when they had marched him out of his own house—round-eyed with fright and shame, all trace of his habitual benign majesty gone. And so, when she developed complications in the seventh month of her pregnancy, it was not one of the super-speciality hospitals in which her husband's family had stakes that she went to, but the modest Modern Nursing Home where she was still nurse, and through all her complications it was Jessy, her friend and fellow-nurse who attended to her. Pray that it's a girl, Jessy said, only a girl will survive. And a girl it was. A one-and-a-half kilogram weakling who shilly shallied for a few weeks in an incubator before coming home to a house bare of all furnishings—even the kitchen was perfunctory—but ablaze with buntings and flowers and a coloured thermacol sticker on the wall that said, 'Welcome home, Neela Mary'.

Less than six months after her daughter was born, Mani was back at work for she had learnt enough of her husband to know that, as usual, she had only herself to rely on. Herself and the medallion of Mary of Velankanni that she wore on a gold chain round her neck. She accepted her husband's irregular contributions to the household money and his regular extravagant gifts with equal composure. And he, in return, loved her. It was a novel experience for Gopalrao to be, so obviously, the centre of someone else's life, and he quickly grew used to it, especially since so little was demanded of him. There were things he noticed, stray domestic details that marked his changed life. Waking up in the morning and seeing the woman of the house going about her work with a vast, bare, vermilion-less forehead, seeing the vessels in which food was cooked and those in which it was eaten heaped together so promiscuously in the kitchen sink—these departures from the familiar sent such a thrill through him that he grew to savour these differences. But the food in his home would always taste strange; he never quite got used to Mani's cooking.

When Neela was a year old, Mani sent tentative feelers to her family. Not to her brothers but her older sister Miri who was a nurse in the Middle East. The next time she came to India, Miri visited them and it became a yearly feature. In many ways Miri was a first—the first person in the family to work abroad, the first to leave off the sari and take to skirts, to cut off her long hair and wear it short. Her mother and brothers did not say anything to her for her cheques had cleared the loan on the tempo traveller and paid for the renovation of the house, and every year when she came down for Christmas, she came laden with gifts for her brothers' wives and children.

The first crease in the smoothly stretched fabric of Mani and Gopalrao's marriage was caused by Miri. During the ten days she spent with her sister, Gopalrao gave Miri a wide berth but even when he watched TV in his drawing room, he was only too aware of her, sitting in the balcony with his wife, her legs propped up on a stool, uncaring of her skirt riding high, smoking cigarette after cigarette, casually flicking the ash off the balcony railing. She made no effort to conceal her contempt for him, to make clear that she thought it was her sister who was the worse off for the bargain. If pressed he would say she was a vulgar termagant, but he held his tongue. It took him two weeks at least after each visit to undo the damage she had done and bring his wife back to her own meek, loving self. Above all, it was the knowledge of a liberating world outside, that rasping edge of unpredictability, the suggestion that anything was possible that Miri brought with her and infected his wife and growing daughter with, that made Gopalrao uneasy.

For one, she effected a change in Mani's church-going habits. To please her sister, Mani gave up her local church, where she went unobtrusively every Sunday with Jessy, where the priest preached in Tamil and on whose steps Neela played with the other children, chasing the geese that the watchman kept, munching, as a matter of course, on the round white pressed wafer that her mother put in her mouth. Instead, Miri dragged her sister and niece off to her grand red-and-gold church at the other end of the city, to a congregation of well-dressed strangers who listened to the young priest of unclear extraction preach in quaintly accented English. This was the church Miri was bidden to by her Dubai friends. It had recently been resurrected by a group of youthful evangelists from Spain and the exchange group of young Spanish priests was given time at the pulpit, which they made the most of.

Some things, if understated and done quietly, can last a lifetime. In the early days of their marriage, Gopalrao's sister Lakshmi had staked an equally ostentatious claim on the territory. Before they had moved into the flat off Ammanagudi Street, when they were still shifting their things, she had come in a hurry one morning, placed a portable gas stove on the kitchen counter, snipped open a quarter litre sachet of Nandini milk, made it boil over in a perfunctory house warming ritual and installed a large patha of Venkataramana Swamy in a prominent place. When they moved in, on a shelf next to Lord Venkataramana, to show no undue favour to either, Mani arranged her own icons to which she lit a candle each day. But there was something that Mani had done when Neela was born—rather Jessy had done and Mani had weakly concurred with. Neela had been so gravely ill that Jessy was scared: if the child was destined to go how could they send her off just like that? She hastily conferred with the priest of her church and in one brief interval, when the baby was brought out of the incubator, her crown was moistened with a drop of holy water carried in an empty Pepsi bottle, her forehead anointed with oil and a feint of salt placed at the corner of her mouth. The child was in effect baptized and Jessy, by default, became her godmother. Coming as he did from a community awash with rituals Gopalrao assented to it because he thought it was yet another ritual, one among many that did not matter, and also because he had not expected his daughter—weak and sickly as she was—to survive. But survive she did and grew large and strong, with a certain aggression of temperament that he saw in his sister-in-law.

True enough, as a child Neela waited eagerly for Miri aunty's Christmas visits, for the many presents she brought wrapped in shiny scented paper, for the smart skirts and high-heeled shoes she wore, for the air of festivity, of vigour and purpose she brought with her, that touched her placid mother as well. Till she grew old enough and saw the same skirts and shoes as tacky and felt a little ashamed of being seen with Miri aunty in public. There were other certainties too that yielded to doubt as she grew older. To the simple question, 'What does your father do?' her reply, 'My father is a doctor', became more tentative, but 'My mother is a nurse' never changed; it was cast in stone. As a child she learnt to sense disturbances in the air, the shifting masses of cold air that periodically marred the sunny climes of her house. They arrived in the form of her relatives: her Miri aunty and her Lakshmi aunty—her father's sister—who, like Miri, came once a year and looked her over with suspicious concern for signs of damage, as if she were a precious object that had been left to the care of servants for a brief while.

Neela saw her father's people for the first time when she was five years old. Gopalrao's eldest brother, the distinguished surgeon, came home one day. Their father had suffered a sudden stroke—perhaps it was the shock of their mother's unexpected death a year ago, and they were known to be very attached to each other—and needed round-the-clock trained medical care. The family had decided that he should stay with Gopal and Mani since Mani was a trained nurse after all; they could have kept him at home but there was no one to supervise the nurses. Not for nothing had he been given the flat and the job, Gopalrao now understood; he had to make good. His brothers' wives would not look after the old man nor could he be left entirely to the care of servants. His father, an accomplished surgeon with his much written-about 'hands of a dancer' till the other day, a man who moved from one operation theatre to the other effortlessly, with no sign of tiredness, had become a lump of flesh overnight. Of course, Gopalrao's brothers added, Mani must be made aware of the sensitivities . . . their father was so particular. Perhaps they had better get a Brahmin woman to cook for him . . . keep his things separate . . .

Mani gave up her job at Modern Nursing Home and began tending to her father-in-law, who refused to look her in the eye or call her by name; the more his limbs atrophied, the more acid his tongue became. She bore it with the good cheer of a nurse dealing with a difficult patient and made sure her daughter came nowhere near the old man.

One afternoon, when Neela came home from school, she found her mother agitated, her grandfather's bed empty and workmen hammering away at the bathroom window. In the last few months Gopalrao's father had made an almost-miraculous recovery and insisted on using the regular toilet instead of the bed pan. That day, despite his daughter-in-law's entreaties, he did not ask for her help and he also locked the bathroom door from within. When there was no reply from him even after several calls, Mani climbed on a stool and peeped through the window. She saw him fallen on the floor, bleeding profusely from a cut on his forehead. When the window was finally hammered through—the door would not budge—she climbed in through the hole and even before she knelt by the supine figure she knew that she would find no sign of life in it.

Right through the eleven days of funeral rites, the bit of the wall that had been hammered out along with the window grills and shutters stood on the drawing room floor, witness to all the obsequies, overseeing the old soul's journey to Vaikunth. After the thirteenth-day ceremony, the brothers pronounced their verdict: their trust in Gopal had been misplaced. He had neglected their father; the accident in the bathroom should never have happened.

Perhaps it was this that drove Gopalrao to reckless abandon. He handed his daughter over to Miri's ministrations, and they no longer needed to be subtle. Miri read the unwritten postscript correctly. And so, at the age of twelve, five years later than it should have been, as Miri grumbled, Neela was confirmed in the grand red-and-gold church, in a ceremony that her father did not attend. Even now, the white dress she had worn and her lacy veil smelling faintly of balsam oil, and the sari that Miri aunty had worn, the only time anyone remembered her wearing one, lay at the back of her mother's cupboard. After that, there was always a flurry of church activities, especially around the time of Miri's visits. Neela attended a summer camp where in the recognize-the-hymn competition she won her first annotated Bible. For several weeks after that, she, along with some older girls, did the flowers and cleaned the green glass candle stands on the pulpit and arranged the hymn books in the pews. The high point of her involvement was the week in which she was chosen to hand the chamois cloth to the presiding priest, in full view of the congregation, and wait while he wiped the silver chalice that would soon bear the host. Under Miri aunty's tutelage she prepared short sermons on topics like 'The Strength of the Family' and 'The Significance of Hymn 47' which she read out falteringly into a microphone on the dais. What she liked best though was the singing in the end. The visiting Spanish priests, declaring that a mass without a rousing hymn was like a prayer without soul, had put together a special set of hymns striking high and plaintive notes, and Neela especially liked hymn thirty-two from the 'To Our Lady' series—*Maiden Mother, Meek and Mild*—though meek and mild was not what she'd be when she grew up. But she did not have much of a voice and much to her aunt's disappointment, did not shine in the singing.

As soon as Miri left, however, Mani would go back to her own church, the one around the corner where the preacher preached in Tamil and summer camp meant working in slums. Neela did not know Tamil and she discovered that she did not like working among the poor either, despite her aunt's exhortations—she found them ungrateful and dishonest, especially after her purse was stolen in a slum that she had gone to uplift. By the time she reached adulthood her church-going dwindled to attending the annual Christmas eve mass with her aunt, and the few occasions when her mother or Jessy sponsored high mass in the Tamil church. It was the pendant of the Arokya Mata of Velankanni, Mary, Giver of Health—after whom her desperate mother had named her when she lay still and unmoving in the incubator—that she clasped and prayed to each night on her knees, before she went to bed. Thankfully, her other aunt's visits did not clash with Miri's; Miri aunty came in winter and Lakshmi aunty in summer. She too demanded a share in her brother's life, a slice of her niece and she put Neela through the paces of her choosing—a naming ceremony and an annaprasan, where at six months Neela wrote the Kannada alphabet in a plate of uncooked rice with her father's gold ring, her right hand guided by her father and her aunt (it was another matter that she turned out to be left handed) and was then fed her first rice meal. When Lakshmi aunty visited, among the trips to relatives was the mandatory look-in on the family temple. Neela went through the motions mechanically, for as far as she knew a flame, whether it burns in a green candleholder or an oil wick in a brass lamp, is the same and consecrated water feels the same on the tongue or the top of one's head despite its different infusions, that the ash of incense smells the same and gathers in small grey heaps, and flowers are flowers everywhere.

When Neela finished school and entered college both her aunts tried to nudge her in the direction of eligible young men of their choosing; her Miri aunty more half-heartedly as she had chosen to remain unmarried herself and had advised her niece in a moment of weakness to never trust 'them' and to hang on to her money. Neela immediately saw that as a reflection on her father. Nevertheless, Neela did not rise to the bait offered by either of her aunts for each had instilled in her, while assuring her of their love, a distrust of the other. Miri had made it clear that her father's family was perfidious while Lakshmi aunty had hinted that her mother's family was not in the same league. Neela did try to give the boys her aunts had chosen for her a fair chance, but the boy who sang in the church choir, who could strum a mean guitar and wore an Elvis puff on his forehead, preferred Jessy's daughter Molly to her. She had tried to win him by watching him avidly out of the corner of her eye and then crushing him when he tried to speak to her, by which time, Molly, open and unambiguous, caught his attention and soon he was teaching her to sing and play the guitar. When she was a little older Lakshmi aunty, after mysterious references to him for months, introduced her to a 'brilliant engineer with great prospects', only he turned out to have a withered arm. Neela rejected him, turning on her aunt angrily. But given your 'contaminated' background that is the best you can hope for if you want to marry within the community, and why should his arm matter so much, her aunt said. I do not want a man who will hold me with just one arm, she wanted to tell Lakshmi aunty, but held her tongue. Her aunts, on their part, had not stopped trying; their efforts were unflagging as ever. When Miri aunty came, there was at least one dinner with 'an excellent family'—a congregation of men and women, children and adults, where the 'boy' was usually an NRI who stood out because of his accent and the ease with which he sat in his suit. Not to be outdone, Lakshmi aunty had registered Neela's name in a matrimonial bureau run by the local temple, where things were run like a government office, complete with forms and photographs in triplicate, and which even had computerized horoscope matching. But nothing had come of all their efforts and things were getting more difficult as Neela was fast approaching the age when she could no longer be presented as an enticing prospect. They also found that their niece had become less pliable and now that she was thirty-two years old, they could not barter away her Sundays without her consent, which she frequently withheld.

Her one weekly day off from work—Sunday—Neela now spent largely on attending to her person; the mornings on her hair, her hands and feet, for the magazines had told her that those are the first things a boy notices about a girl, and she also looked to her legs, just in case, and the afternoons were spent at the movies with Molly, who had trained to be a nurse like her mother, or eating chaat in the new snack bar in Ammanagudi Street and catching up with the magazines. Molly was the only friend she had, the one she went shopping and to the movies with, but she was not wholly satisfactory. She was completely biddable, which suited Neela, but too good-natured, which irritated her, and simple too in many ways. But she always came in handy; that much she could say for Molly. Some Sunday afternoons, Molly and she would pore over the magazines—she loved the names, *Elle*, *Cosmopolitan*, *Vanity Fair*, *Marie Claire*—that they found at a second-hand bookstall that sold old copies of foreign magazines at reduced rates, along with the Indian editions that were much easier on the pocket. While Molly giggled over the pink perfect faces (they were too bland), the red mouths (they belonged rightly to vampires), the blonde tousled hair (uncombed!), and the clothes (they looked either dull or like underclothes), Neela looked at them

all with fierce concentration. Most of what she had learnt about
the secret recesses of her mind, her pulse of the world, her cues
to behaviour (when she was not caught unawares) was gleaned
from the glossies. Till now, she had taken every test for singles
in the magazines—If you and your partner go to a party and you
see another man you fancy/he starts flirting with another attractive
woman . . .; How far would you go on a first date? 1) just coffee
2) holding hands 3) kissing and canoodling . . .—with her ideal
invisible man. Each such test confirmed her as confident, friendly,
outgoing, fun loving, full of attitude and self-esteem, and yet the
chances of her imaginary ideal man becoming flesh and blood
receded. I want to make friends, she confessed to Bali Brums of
Voices from Heaven, the only one she felt she could trust of late.
Try the Internet, he suggested, a chat group of your choice, there's
a whole new world out there.

And in the face of it all was the spectacle of her parents' love
for each other, the indecent intimacy that they projected just by
being in the same room together, which Miri's battering ram had
failed to breach. It showed on the glow in her mother's face, in
the samplers that she embroidered carefully with brightly coloured
thread and hung on all the nails in the house—The Lord is my
shepherd. He dwells in this house and is our Light.—and the
plaque that her father had hammered outside the door—I am the
master of this house and I have my wife's permission to say so.
This love of theirs fed Neela's vague longing for a house of her
own where she could arrange fruits in a wooden bowl and not eat
them, where she could stand a single arum lily in a long-stemmed
glass vase, where the wooden boards of the kitchen would gleam
in the evening light, where her imaginary man and she would be
snuggled up on the duvet that was advertised in *Cosmopolitan*,
till it grew into a succulent but still amorphous need. The plaque
outside the door angered Miri every time she saw it but Mani only
laughed. Miri tried to explain to her sister the mindlessness of a
man gifting his wife a set of marble angels inlaid with semi-precious
stones when he would not pay the electricity bill, but Mani did
not care. Despite everything she would not hear a word against

USHA K.R.´

her Gopal, even if it confirmed her suspicions about him and she in turn, would always be his 'Kanmani'. 'As my Mani says . . .' was a standard preface to his statements.

Some evenings, in his more tender moments, Neela's father would stand her mother against the mantelpiece and like a film hero of yore, a Shivaji Ganeshan or a Raj Kumar, he would sing an old Kannada song, extolling the virtues of the peerless wife, his Penmani . . . his Kanmani . . . who rose at the crack of dawn, finished her household chores and begged her elders for more opportunities to serve them; then off to school (for she was a child, merely) to learn good things, to be serene and peaceable; who never praised her mother's house in her husband's, nor spoke lowly of her in-laws, who won her husband over with sage and timely counsel; a girl who could draw a beautiful rangoli, sing tunefully and meet fame and adversity with equal animity. And Mani would listen to him, beaming, believing every word and rejoicing in it. 'See you my Kanmani . . . my Penmani . . .' his eyes would linger fondly on her face as he set off in the mornings; his Mani would not ask him where he was going and when he would be back for she was sure he would be back, wherever he went, and she firmly believed that a man must have his space.

six

1

On his first day at college, it was not the girls—massed six to a bench, sitting across the aisle at arms' length—Shrinivas Moorty had noticed, but Jairam. And of course, SVK. The general English class of more than eighty students was literally a sea of faces. Left to himself he wouldn't have looked twice at the wiry, undersized boy, wearing a shirt so well-washed and so tight that it strained between the buttons and at the armpits like a woman's blouse; he much preferred the flamboyant Cantonment types in Levis. And had SVK not been standing on the podium, forcibly demanding their attention, he would not have looked at the self-effacing man in khadi either. An English teacher in a dhoti! Surely, he had not come to college for this.

SVK had taken an elaborate roll call on the first day, telling them that it would be the last time—they could attend his classes if they wanted to, but he was not answerable to irate parents. He paused at each name, giving its bearer a quick sharp look, as if to imprint the face in his mind, and moved on. At Jairam's name he paused a little longer and, betraying revisionist and sectarian tendencies perhaps the only time in his life, said, 'You are Sir H.K. Shastry's grandson, aren't you?' his voice softening.

Jairam, one could tell, had been waiting for this moment, perhaps even gratified that it had come so soon. He stood with bowed head for a few moments till the whole class had fixed its attention on him. 'I must confess,' he said in a mock lugubrious tone, the voice surprisingly strong in one of almost puny build, 'my grandfather was indeed a bootlicker of the British . . .'

The class tittered; SVK looked at Jairam with a smile of delight and Shrinivas Moorty knew instantly that Jairam would be his friend and that he too would be complicit in the bond that had just formed.

SVK began his first class with a poem from their poetry text, a poem that Shrinivas Moorty had done in school—'The Palanquin Bearers'. More a song than a poem, his school teacher who loved it had said, written by a woman who wore many hats—socialite, hostess, friend of Gandhi, first Indian woman to be president of the Indian National Congress, to be the Governor of a state, and poet in English.

As the class waited, SVK read the twelve lines of the musical and rhythmic poem without any expression and Shrinivas Moorty felt the first stirrings of doubt. He had heard so much about SVK as a teacher. Was this all there was to him? For a moment, a chasm of boredom yawned before him and he wondered how he would last three years in college. What good was this dhoti-clad man if he was felled by a poem as easy as this one?

Then SVK read it again, recited it rather, with emphasis, leading them along, making no comment but showing them what to make of it.

'*Lightly*, o *lightly* we bear her along . . . *Softly*, o *softly* . . . She *sways* like a flower in the *wind* of our song—unfortunate word that, wind, I would have suggested "breeze" to Ms Naidu—She *skims* like a bird on the *foam* of a stream . . .'

Midway, he stopped, looked over the class, his eyebrows dancing, and said, 'Would you like to choose your *fanciful* favourites?'

Shrinivas Moorty got in first: 'Line four, She *floats* like a laugh from the *lips* of a dream . . .'

Jairam was right behind: 'Line eight is better, She *hangs* like a star in the *dew* of our song . . .'

SVK smiled at them and rubbed his hands together, a gesture they were to get well-acquainted with over time.

'It is a beautiful poem—' a truculent voice sounded from the front benches.

The class went quiet.

'Ah! Miss Geeta, isn't it—' SVK said as a tall, dark-complexioned girl with large eyes and full moist lips stood up on the extreme right.

'Convent school . . . English type . . .' someone sniggered and the boys in the back benches began to boo softly.

'Yes Miss Geeta, carry on,' SVK said encouragingly.

'The poem is rhythmic and musical, you can dance to it—' Geeta stopped, closed her eyes and took a deep breath, as if she were internalizing her sense of affront. 'The images are so delicate, so precise, and the poet is celebrated as the Nightingale of India—'

SVK bowed deep, acknowledging her courage. 'Tell me Miss Geeta, have you ever seen a nightingale?'

Geeta looked at him uncertainly and said nothing.

'Has anyone seen a nightingale? Even a picture of one?' SVK stepped off the podium and started walking up the aisle. '*What* is a nightingale? Supposedly an English songbird. *Ode to a Nightingale. The Nightingale and the Rose.* It is a notion foisted on us, and we parrot it blindly—The Parrot of India would be a more suitable title. Stop for a moment, madam—' He stood next to Geeta and regarded her gravely, his chin resting on his steepled fingers. 'The poem purports to be a song sung by palanquin bearers who are carrying a woman, perhaps a bride. Think. Visualize the image. Four grown men carrying a woman, transporting her like a precious package, an inanimate thing, somebody's prized possession. What is it that the poet you admire so much does here? Gives back to us images of ourselves tempered in their steel, made the way they want to see us, in *their* language. Thankfully she spares us the physical images of muscular brown bodies. And why would the men want to celebrate their burden?'

'But sir, don't we have our boatman songs, rousing songs that labourers sing as they work to the natural rhythm—'

'Is this the same thing?' SVK strode back to the podium.

The fire quickly spread. It was not the same thing someone said. It was one thing to be a labourer composing his own song to keep his spirits up while battling the elements, and quite another for a woman, who had probably never lifted anything heavier than a pencil in her life, to celebrate men carrying a woman in a box.

USHA K.R.

'The poet was jailed during the freedom struggle,' one of the girls countered. Perhaps Jairam should remember that before pouring scorn on her.

'And the right way to pronounce the word is pala-keen, not pa-lan-quin,' Geeta said, trying to have the last word.

'Why palanquin? Why not palki, the Hindi word, or palakki as in Kannada?'

'What does it matter, palanquin or palakeen, the poem remains the same.'

SVK sat back and smiled, stepping in only when the voices grew too loud or one person persisted in speaking all the time.

In the next class, which nobody slunk out of, with a small smile of triumph on his face, SVK thanked the students for thanking him for a stimulating class and making known afresh a poem that they had all done in school—'Many of you came to see me later. That's very well, but please don't crowd the entrance to the staff room, remember it is meant for the lecturers . . .'

At the end of the first week SVK went up to the blackboard and wrote on it the words 'res publica'. The public cause.

'In the conversations we have had so far, you think you expressed your individual opinions, conclusions you had arrived at by dint of your own mental efforts, words that sharpened and cut through the clutter of images in your head. Now, let us see to what extent we are conditioned by our circumstances.' SVK put down the piece of chalk, dusted his hands and rubbed them together. When he spoke again his manner was deliberate. 'So Mr Jairam, you like Huxley's *Brave New World*, and you, Miss Geeta, would prefer *Jane Eyre*. Miss Saraswati wears a langa-davani while you, Mr Alfred Rosario, wear American jeans. Why do you wear them?'

'Because I like them—'

'Because he likes to show off, sir, that he has relatives in the US who send him clothes. They pay for them in dollars—'

There were a few uneasy titters at that. It was rare for them to take such liberties in class in front of their teachers, but SVK, by suggestion, encouraged them to speak their minds, to go beyond in fact, and perform.

Alfred Rosario did not deign to reply to that dig, but it was true; a pair of Levis was the ultimate status symbol. It didn't matter if you wore the same pair every day; the more faded, the more attractive they were. What they signalled was that you were well-connected, that you had access to the West, 'contacts' who sent you clothes that were not available in the shops and could not be imported into the country.

'But why do you like them, Mr Rosario? How did you come to like them? And why are they not sold here? Why does the finance minister think that a pair of coarse, indigo-dyed trousers—impossible to wash and dry I am told—can threaten the economy of the country?'

And they understood that all English classes would be as this one: the prescribed text finished off in the first ten minutes, or so interwoven with digression that no one would remember whether it was a prose text they were doing or Shakespeare, and the rest of the class devoted to 'res publica', to politics, economics, history, sociology, and English literature possibly, reflected in the world around them. The morning's newspaper became their textbook and catalyst of the many grand debates that the classroom witnessed over the next three years. Capitalism vs Communism, the USSR vs the USA, Indira Gandhi vs the Opposition, Men vs Women. SVK usually kindled the discussion by making a provocative statement or reading out a news item from the newspaper and then, as people began to take sides, he would stand aside, smiling slightly, his chin resting on his hands joined together, making an innocuous statement here, throwing in a word there, pretending to be a neutral referee but steering the proceedings, till, just before the bell went off, he would clinch the discussion with his argument. And the cycle began again the next day. Geeta usually spoke for the majority of the class, carrying the flag for Capitalism, the USA, Women and also Indira Gandhi, triumphantly and newly re-elected as prime minister of the country, while Jairam and Shrinivas Moorty formed the less popular but more vocal opposition.

Sometimes, the discussions took on the shades of a carnival. One day SVK came to class with the morning's newspaper,

R.K. Laxman's cartoon displayed prominently on the front page. Laxman's hapless 'common man', the anxious-looking Mr Everyman, clad in a dhoti and checked coat with an umbrella rolled under his arm, who suffered the daily grind stoically and commented on it through his creator's column, had just mis-read Mrs Gandhi's famous slogan 'Garibi hatao' as 'Garib hatao'. A discussion on Mrs Gandhi's policies and governing style followed, Geeta defending her as 'a friend of the poor' and Shrinivas Moorty and Jairam branding her as 'populist' and 'vote grabbing'. Others recounted more of Laxman's cartoons and Jairam, revealing shades of his 'organizing' self immediately launched on a project to have an inter-college cartoon contest and perhaps invite the cartoonist himself to give away the prizes at the next annual day celebrations, a project the class enthusiastically backed.

It often seemed that they chose to be on opposite ends of an argument—Geeta on one side and Shrinivas Moorty and Jairam on the other—out of a spirit of lively competition, encouraged by SVK. Their exchanges were always brisk and sometimes long drawn out, with SVK guiding them from the banks of ideology to the currents of international events and relations. Sometimes the discussions grew acrimonious: one particularly quarrelsome week when much rhetoric was traded was when the American policy of food aid was discussed. What would the right-thinking world do without America's help, Geeta wanted to know. The very notion of America invoked the ideas of freedom, frontier spirit and democracy. Which other nation had the courage to script in the pursuit of happiness as a fundamental right? And they helped spread their notion of the good world very concretely, with their money and their men and their military might, as they were doing currently in Vietnam. Closer home, what would India do without American wheat, feeding us through our droughts and shortages? The very rotis and bread (and biscuits, Jairam added with a wink to Shrinivas Moorty for Geeta's father was the general manager of a multi-national company that manufactured biscuits) they ate at home may be made with wheat they got through the public distribution system that relied on the American Food for Peace programme. SVK would allow Geeta and the others to have their say and then turn to Jairam and Shrinivas Moorty, knowing he could rely on his shishyas. What Jairam and Shrinivas Moorty's side lacked in numbers, it made up for in vociferous and clear-cut arguments. You had to be very naïve, Jairam countered, if you thought that the food aid that the US sent out under its Public Law 480 was a benign, good-hearted thing that came with no strings attached. It was a clear ploy, a tool to contain Communism. But India's newly signed treaty with the Soviet Union would put an end to American scheming. And then, invariably, the heat would shift to the Machiavellian Mrs Gandhi, for whom even SVK had a sneaking admiration. For once he had been on Geeta's side in praising Indira Gandhi's diplomacy and negotiating skills.

Towards the end of term, on a Friday—the day of the week when attendance was thin for it was also the day when new films were released in the cinema theatres and most students rushed to see the 'first day first show'—SVK asked them all to go and see a film that was running in town. It was the first time that a teacher had suggested that films could be more than mere entertainment or 'a waste of time' as films were considered in their homes, and it was with considerable triumph that Shrinivas Moorty announced to his parents that he was going to see a film at the express instructions of his teacher to buttress the portions on Imperialism. Lateral ways of thinking and gathering information were equally important, SVK said. On a rainy Sunday morning the class turned out in full force to see *Queimada*, though many of the students were as sceptical as their parents that a habit-forming leisure activity could actually educate. The film was about a revolution in a Portuguese colony in the Caribbean, incited by a British agent provocateur in the name of freedom but actually to serve British interests in the sugar plantations on the island. Most of the students were just happy to be out of the house on a Sunday morning with a legitimate excuse and did not understand completely nor care for the twists and turns of the story, but *Queimada* met Shrinivas Moorty with the potency of first love. He saw it again, all by himself, and then a third time. For days after, he could think and speak of nothing else. He discussed the film incessantly with Jairam, dwelling on the details of the narrative and marvelling at the sequence of its plot, the haunting organ music that alternated with silence, the panoramic sweep of the camera and the lush colours of the natural scenery, the contrasting presence of a consummate actor like Marlon Brando and the unknown black hero, the way the whole was used to convey the machinations of colonial power. (There was also a three-second shot of a woman's breasts—completely uncovered, which had somehow escaped the notice of the censors.)

Shrinivas Moorty made enquiries and found out that there was a fledgling film club specializing in 'foreign art films' run by an NGO in an unused garage somewhere in the suburbs. He sought it out and, lying about his age—he was yet to turn eighteen, became a member. But, he found out, one needed to be a real enthusiast to persist. The screenings were erratic, the prints would not arrive on time from the archives in Poona or they would be damaged, or they would receive a letter from the Higher Authorities with the dreaded stock response 'permission not granted', or the electricity would fail mid-way. Once they were summarily asked to pack up and leave by the owner of the garage. But Shrinivas Moorty's Saturday afternoons were now spoken for and he persisted, cycling all the way, often alone for Jairam and Geeta had signed up with an amateur theatre group. There was so much to choose from, so much to do after college. Other than films and theatre, there was a literary club, a humour club, and the study circles—SVK's Circle for the Study of Dialectical Materialism or the opposing Circle for the Study of Scientific Socialism, or the Freedom Unlimited Group, which the non-conformists, the apolitical and the girls preferred.

2

On Sunday mornings, Jairam went through the firewood–and–castor-oil bath drill. Almost at the crack of dawn—before he had read the newspaper at any rate—he would head for the firewood yard to order and collect the week's supply of firewood that would heat the household's bath water. It was a tricky job for the man always tried to sell him short or pass off raw sticks of wood. After the logs had been chopped, the man would cart them to Jairam's house. Sometimes, when there was no one else in the shop, he asked Jairam to mind the yard while he delivered the wood and came back.

The shop was on Ammanagudi Street—Shrinivas Moorty and Jairam cycled to college and back with each other, Jairam living a little off the main street—and while Jairam waited at the depot he would fetch Shrinivas Moorty to wait with him. When Shrinivas Moorty saw his friend—curly hair flattened with the thick oil, his forehead glistening and his eyelids gummy, haggling with the depot man, who was rude and a cheat, too, he was glad of his AEH, his all-electrical home, and his enlightened father, for Jairam's father 'Imperialist' Radhakrishna insisted, even in the year 1971, that there was nothing like bathing in water from the wood-fired hande, fragrant with wood smoke and heated just right, to induce a good nap on a soporific Sunday afternoon. Water from the electric boiler just did not compare.

There were other embarrassments that Imperialist Radhakrishna subjected his son to. Those white accretions on Jairam's forehead, for instance. Shrinivas Moorty had thought them to be patches of dandruff sitting low on his forehead, or the overnight accumulation of geej from his eyes, not quite washed off. But he was startled to discover one Sunday morning, after Jairam had washed the oil off and neatly slicked back his wet hair, that the white marks on either side of Jairam's eyes were mudres, distinctive caste marks in sandalwood paste, stamped with a mould, and he marvelled afresh at his friend. Of course, Imperialist Radhakrishna was a dyed in the wool conservative and he would insist that his son wear those marks. Sometimes, in the mornings, it was difficult to conduct a decent conversation in Jairam's house in his alcove because of the noise his father made in the pooja room. His own father, Shrinivas Moorty was happy to say, would never dream of letting his sacred thread outline itself under his banian.

'What does your father do?' Geeta had asked Jairam in the early days when they were getting to know each other.

'He's an imperialist,' Jairam's lip had curled in disdain. (They were fresh from their political theory classes and from SVK's influence.) 'He expropriates the labour of the workers in other countries and sells it in ours, pocketing part of the profits while the main fills the coffers of his capitalist masters.'

It turned out that Imperialist Radhakrishna had a small-scale industry that manufactured castings for sugarcane crushers and furnaces that cured tobacco. Most of the pig iron for the castings was imported. But under the draconian quotas of the Mineral and Metal Trading Corporation of India, the margins were slim and Imperialist Radhakrishna was perpetually struggling with the restrictive laws. There was an interesting story about him making the rounds; it might have been apochryphal but it gave evidence of the resourcefulness that he was said to lack. When a particular batch of castings meant for the tobacco curing furnace was proving to be too brittle, cracking under the heat repeatedly, and no one knew what the alloy lacked, Imperialist Radhakrishna had added jaggery to it—and produced perfect castings! To Shrinivas Moorty's mind, Imperialist Radhakrishna was more petty bourgeois than imperialist, but trust Jairam to want the best in everything.

His own home and circumstances, Shrinivas Moorty thought, were modest, till he saw Jairam's. A shelf on the wall and a table and chair below it were all Jairam had unlike Shrinivas Moorty who had quarter of a room to himself. On his first visit to Jairam's 'alcove' as he referred to it, Shrinivas Moorty had scanned the shelf quickly, relieved to find a mix much like his own. He ran his hand along the spines of a row of battered Alistair MacLeans to more recent acquisitions of James Hadley Chase—MacLean's clean-cut, straight, fair-playing, honourable hero, the stuff of adolescence, making way for the gritty fringe-world of Hadley Chase where the truth was clouded, the men hard-boiled and tough and the women no angels. Shrinivas Moorty had read his first James Hadley Chase just a few months ago and the shock of enlightenment about the seamy world that lurked beneath his own had been so severe that he had wandered for days in a daze—the streets suddenly had more hard-bitten shifty-eyed men and he mentally separated the women he saw into those who would look good in skirts and have long legs and those who wouldn't. The books on Jairam's shelf were so well-thumbed that the pages were curled and greasy to the touch; no doubt acquired by Jairam, as were his own, when the local circulating library held its annual sale of discarded books.

'This one I haven't read,' Shrinivas Moorty's hand rested on the spine of *No Orchids for Miss Blandish*.

'Take it. Keep it if you like,' Jairam offered.

In the row behind, stacked together were much-thumbed copies of N. Narasimaiah's *Purushottamana Sahasagalu*, adventures of the legendary detective Purushottama, the finest among men. Rubbing shoulders with Purushottama were back issues of *JS—Junior Statesman*, the clever magazine from Calcutta, another favourite.

'Do you still have these? I have this one too, I just couldn't give it away . . .' Smiling, he looked at the cover of a large, illustrated book of poems by Pushkin, from the ever-dependable Soviet Books, heavily subsidized, without whom he doubted he would have owned a single book in his childhood. Most of the 'good' books then, the illustrated fairy tales and the Enid Blytons, were printed abroad and priced in dollars and pounds which were beyond the ken of the rupee. His knowledge of the Russian classics, and later, the works of Karl Marx and Lenin he would owe to the life-saving duo of Raduga and Progress Publishers.

In the days that followed, through college, many of the books on their shelves were relegated to the back row to make place for new enthusiasms, newly found allegiances. All that SVK recommended for instance—Brecht, *Aid as Imperialism*, *The Communist Manifesto*, Edgar Snow's *Red Star over China*, Gorky's *Mother*, Frantz Fanon's *The Wretched of the Earth*. Just as Alistair MacLean had made way for James Hadley Chase, *The Four Just Men* did likewise for *The Godfather* and the fluffy adventures of Purushottama for the iron-in-the-soul poetry of Siddalingaiah. Nevertheless, the Sunday morning castor-oil-and-firewood drill remained a constant and for many weeks as the man chopped and slipped in as many raw sticks as he could, Jairam paced the depot and read out choice bits from the latest book he was reading, always in a state of excitement, to Shrinivas Moorty.

'Do you know that the great Sir Cecil Rhodes . . . yes, the man who instituted the scholarship that we all clamour for year after year to go abroad and study . . . when he found that the whole world, all the markets were taken, it so shook his imperialist heart that he fantasized about colonizing other planets. He actually gave it serious thought!' Or it would be some revealing statistics on industrial practice or the state of society: 'Beggars swarmed Europe in the Middle Ages. The ones who harass us at traffic junctions or the tourists at the Taj Mahal are nothing . . . In the seventeenth century, one fourth of the population of Paris consisted of beggars and in Switzerland the rich had hunting parties to cull them . . .'

In retrospect, one could say the firewood depot on Ammanagudi Street was their consecrated ground and Sunday mornings their propitious time. A small yard, fenced off from the street by barbed wire, damp in the rains and smelling of moss, the ground bald but for a few patches of unhealthy-looking grass, where one of them sat on the stump of a tree while the other stood, would perhaps not count among the ideal spaces for inspiration. But it was here that their best ideas struck them and they spun their schemes, some which even proved workable. Their new enthusiasms inspired their first competitive project: a poster designing competition organized by the local branch of the Communist Party for an all-India Youth Summit. Their subject was the depredations of the mill owners in Manchester in newly industrializing England. While Shrinivas Moorty paraphrased Leo Huberman for the text, Jairam inked illustrations of the conditions under which the spinners worked, his hand shaking equally from nervousness—this was their first project after all—as from his anger against the mill owners, who had driven their workers to work eighteen hours a day without water, and fined them for such transgressions as opening a window to let in air, washing themselves, or even whistling. England in the early nineteenth century had shortages similar to ours now in the nineteen seventies, Jairam remarked morosely as he tried to swipe the castor oil smears off the poster. The Manchester spinner, it turned out, was fined the heaviest if caught repairing his drum with his gas light burning and spinning with the gaslight on for too long in the morning, a reflection perhaps on Jairam's own electricity- and cooking gas-less house that still depended on firewood. Their posters won them a set of Lenin's works, hardbound in red cloth with the sickle and hammer embossed on it, which Shrinivas Moorty allowed Jairam to keep.

It was here too, in the firewood depot that they conceived of their magazine, *Anger*, with its mascot Adulter-Ant, who like Laxman's common man, bemoaned the lot of the masses. Early industrializing England was all very well, but they had to look to their own late-democratizing backyard. We must be subtly political, yet satirical, Shrinivas Moorty maintained as he supplied the ideas which Jairam illustrated. Corruption in public life and the shortage of essentials were the most popular targets of cartoonists and newspaper editorials and Adulter-Ant was perpetually pitted against Thrifty Housewife. So there was Adulter-Ant, sad-eyed and whiskered, pushing along a large white boulder, only to realize that he had been tricked; the white grain left behind on the dining table by Thrifty Housewife in a careless moment was actually salt, not sugar. In the next issue of the magazine, Adulter-Ant was weak and gasping for breath for Thrifty Housewife, true to her name, did not spare a single grain of rice for him, giving everything to her own hungry family. In the final issue of the short-lived *Anger*, Adulter-Ant breasted the tape marked 'Life', exultant; he had just escaped death because the insecticide issued by Corrupt Official to Thrifty Housewife was adulterated.

Once Jairam had had his castor oil-hande water bath, they would cycle over to the second-hand bookshops in Majestic or M.G. Road to try their luck. Shrinivas Moorty, not quite as single-minded as Jairam in his loyalties, was happy to find copies of Orwell's *Animal Farm* and *Nineteen Eighty Four*, and the new American classics, *Of Mice and Men* and *Old Man and the Sea*. They also scoured the second-hand record stalls on the pavement, hunting for the elusive Alice Cooper or Led Zeppelin long playing record. It was Jairam who weaned Shrinivas Moorty from Radio Ceylon, from

Gentleman Jim and Dawn. But the separation was not without a pang. For right through his high-school and pre-university college days, every morning was a battle with the transistor, turning it this way and that on the window sill, waiting for the crackling to reduce, for that vital connection across the narrow Palk Strait—so narrow on the map that you could probably walk across and shake the Radio Ceylon announcer's hand—to come through. Shrinivas Moorty could well say that it was the voice of Vernon Corea that had seen him through puberty. At a time when Indian radio stations did not play any 'English' music, Radio Ceylon was a lifeline. It was true that the callers were neverending and the songs few and far in between: with unflagging enthusiasm Vernon (and Vernon it was for they knew him so well) would list all the uncles, aunts, cousins and nephews who were greeting Shanti Solomon of Belgaum either on her birthday, her exams or Christmas, and at the end of five minutes, play 'But You Love me Daddy'. He himself had sent a request, for Dawn's 'Knock Three Times' and Abba's 'Fernando', but Vernon had not played either.

In return Shrinivas Moorty, with his instinctive frugality, showed Jairam how to make a rupee last as long as possible. That was their pocket money: a rupee a day, thirty rupees a month, which Jairam with his mindless extravagance finished off in the first two weeks, but which Shrinivas Moorty could stretch well into the next month. He lent Jairam money readily, sometimes foregoing a rupee here and there. He made Jairam see the stupidity of watching films from the upper stalls in the cinema, at one rupee fifty-five paise, when the middle stalls cost only sixty paise and, better still, a place on the matting in the tent cinema that came at fifty paise. Besides, if Jairam could convince his mother to pack him sandwiches or even a bun for lunch every day, like Shrinivas Moorty's did—they couldn't squelch through curd rice from a steel dabba in college as they had done in school!—it would save him the thirty-five paise he paid for the masala dosa in the college canteen. In which case Jairam would be flush with funds for all his books and records on Sunday mornings, and even the occasional book or record they bought for Geeta when they visited her. But however flush with funds they were, Jairam would not eat out on Sundays; he insisted on going home for lunch. For on Sundays his mother made kootu with sandige for lunch, and nothing, according to Jairam, could equal his mother's pumpkin and peanut kootu.

3

If one considered SVK objectively, it would be difficult to say why he had such an influence on generations of students. His appearance was not attractive—he was always dressed in a white dhoti and a khadi kurta of no particular colour, his eyes were blurry behind thick, black-framed spectacles—and his English was so thickly accented that one, especially an impressionable eighteen year old, tended to dismiss the mind and thoughts of the speaker along with the agglutinate twang of the words. Perhaps it was the sense of freedom that they experienced for the first time in their eighteenth year, no longer treated as children who spoke out of turn, a nuisance really, but as 'people', accredited members of an adult society, who could think and whose opinions and ideas mattered. SVK seemed to truly believe that his students were assets and that he was an instrument in opening their minds and in doing so, he seemed to be enjoying himself. For the first time too, his students experienced that 'studies' could be a joy, that 'knowledge' was not a rock to be hefted for three years and then put down, that there were pleasurable, day-to-day avenues to it. And SVK played no games with them, there were not the usual tussles of ego with him, the eyeball to eyeball confrontations, or, the 'I will see you in the examination' sort that they had with the other teachers; they could speak their minds with him and he, the generous fount, gave openly to them. How much they drank depended on how thirsty they were; each of his students remembered a favourite class or discussion, had in his cupboard a 'rare' book that SVK had lent him and he had forgotten to return, could recall an SVK-ism with delight and spoke of the number of cups of coffee he owed SVK, which SVK had promised to collect when he got his first job. It was only much later that they understood how much they had been shaped by him, without their knowing it, and they were grateful that he had made men and women out of them.

Before the end of the first term Shrinivas Moorty and Jairam signed up as members of the Circle for the Study of Dialectical Materialism—the CSDM—a study circle run by SVK. Geeta refused to join but was persuaded to visit as an observer; the boys knew she could not resist an argument of any sort. She had a sound mind but all the wrong ideas, SVK said; nothing a little education could not repair. With equal generosity Geeta admitted that SVK was 'not bad for a Communist'.

As the sharpest members of the CSDM, Shrinivas Moorty and Jairam were picked by SVK to attend their first political event—a mammoth four-hour meeting addressed by the chairman and veteran leader of the Communist Party of India, a small, spare, articulate man who had till then been only a black-and-white photograph in the newspaper bearing the legend S.A. Dange. He turned out to be a more dramatic and rhetorical version of SVK, and seemed to animate the concepts and theories that SVK discussed in the classroom and the CSDM meetings. That evening when Dange spoke, even the phlegmatic pillars of the town hall, in their conventional majesty, seemed to reverberate with his call for change. They came away from that meeting, their minds achurn, transformed, and almost immediately they volunteered for their first taste of res publica—an anti-Vietnam War demonstration.

The Vietnam War was a subject that ended all other discussions, that caused the most studious student in class to close her textbook and pay attention, and which engaged tempers so violently that teachers from neighbouring rooms often sent the peon to bang on the closed doors of their classroom. Geeta, as usual, argued that Vietnam was the crucial crucible; if the Vietcong geurrillas with their Soviet backers won, all was lost to freedom and democracy. A photograph in the newspaper of a young Vietnamese girl running on the street naked, her clothes just burned off her back, after the Americans had dropped a napalm bomb on her village had silenced Geeta momentarily. (But it had rankled with her, for many years later she had brought it up when the three of them were together, pointing out that the girl in the photograph had eventually sought asylum in a Western country, and become one among the 'capitalist roaders'.) The photograph had goaded Jairam into organizing their own anti-Vietnam War demonstration.

'We want to stand up to be counted,' Jairam told SVK, 'We want our voices to be heard. Our class discussions and our study circle meetings have not been fruitless . . . We want to plan it all by ourselves, Sir, but we want you to lead the march.'

For Shrinivas Moorty, the spur had been Satyajit Ray's *Pratidwandi*. In an unforgettable scene, Ray's out-of-luck, quiet, brooding, charismatic hero, played by Shrinivas Moorty's current favourite, Dhritiman Chatterjee, had replied fatefully and to his detriment at a job interview that the courage of the Vietnamese people under attack was more important and inspiring and significant than man's landing on the moon. Shrinivas Moorty immediately identified with the hero's sense of alienation, his being completely out of step with the world in which he lived, but bruised by its nihilism all the same.

Since it was Jairam who first suggested the anti-war demonstration, he canvassed support for it in the college canteen. Together, they visited other colleges, inviting students from all over the city to participate in the protest meeting. 'We have successfully created a groundswell, Sir,' Jairam reported to SVK. 'If the college authorities don't ban it, we should have hundreds, perhaps even a thousand students in the procession.' For days before the event, the canteen was covered with banners and placards in various stages of preparation, and copies of the pamphlet they had put together with the money they collected from the students. With SVK's help they drafted a formal petition on behalf of the 'concerned student population of Bangalore's colleges' condemning the 'barbaric carpet bombing of Vietnam'. There were a few moments of uncertainty when they contemplated whom to hand over the petition to—the United States Information Service office in the city had shut down the previous year as a cost-cutting measure, a loss they were still recovering from since it had closed the world of American literature to book lovers. The Soviets had been cleverer, everyone said, for they recognized the best way to a people's heart and mind is through literature, and Raduga and Progress, thank god, were still hard at work, bringing out Russian classics at throwaway prices. Someone then found out that though the United States Information Service office was no longer operational, there still was in Langford town, where the office had been, a minor functionary who represented the American government.

On the day of the event it was not the expected one thousand students who gathered but twenty, mostly from their own college, three of them girls. Geeta was not among them; surprisingly, a couple of quiet girls from science had shown up. It had been decided that everyone would meet at the base of Queen Victoria's statue at the head of Mahatma Gandhi Road, and Jairam who had been looking forward to his crowd spilling over on to the road or into neighbouring Cubbon Park, chafed. He had got permission from the police and arranged for the press to follow the procession, but there was not a policeman or a press reporter in sight. They had been assigned the two o' clock slot, and as the hour crept on to three, the handful who had gathered started getting restless.

'Jairam expects a full police bandobast and a battery of reporters . . .' said the economics lecturer who was to lead the demonstration with SVK, and like him, was a veteran of protest marches.

'We must be happy that there are twenty who are committed,' SVK said, 'and not regret the hundreds who are not. Come, let us begin.'

'Placard holders at the back and the middle and, remember, we will give the sign for slogans from the front . . .' the economics lecturer cast one last, professional eye over the group.

Before they began, SVK made a formal speech. 'This is a historic occasion, mark it well. We are commencing this demonstration against Western Imperialism and Capitalist hegemony from its very fountainhead, or its symbol so to say,' he paused and bowed his head to the statue of Queen Victoria, 'and our route lies along Residency Road, Hayes Road, Richmond Road and finally into Langford Town. We are marching along the signposts of our colonial past, in the hope of destroying a monstrous colonial serpent that has a sister country in its coils.'

It was an early summer afternoon, too salubrious to lend itself to a task of such energy and exertion, too far removed from the killing fields of Vietnam. The gulmohurs and the African tulips threw up a profusion of red; a flowering jacaranda shed a purple flower or two on them as they walked slowly down St Mark's Road. The stragglers on the footpaths and a few passers by gave them curious looks, especially when they raised slogans, the traffic made way for them quite readily and their progress was smooth. The group marched slowly, their sense of importance and momentous purpose, of being part of the 'wash of history' as SVK said, mingled with the immediate and slightly disorienting sensation of being differently related to familiar landmarks. The stone building that housed HMV House they took in their stride, but they had to avert their faces from Koshy's and KC Das with their homely suggestion of food and conversation; the next hundred yards helped them steel themselves and they marched on the well-known pavements without a pang, for there was only India Garage on the left and a Sulabh Shauchalaya on the right. They stopped a while at the circle opposite the State Bank of India, and there they felt the group warming up.

'Dhikkara! Dhikkara!' Jairam shouted, hoarse, full-throated, as if to make up for the missing one thousand.

'America! Down Down!' Shrinivas Moorty replied, feeling a very real surge of anger.

'Lal Salam! Laaaaal Salaaaam!'

'We shall overcome . . .' someone began singing in the front.

'. . . deep in our hearts . . .'

'. . . we do believe . . .'

'We shall overcome some day . . .' the chorus of twenty took up.

Shrinivas Moorty and the serious-looking girl from physics stepped out and handed pamphlets to the autorickshaw drivers and chauffeurs waiting to pick up the students of Bishop Cotton's, for it was time for school to give over for the day, and when they passed Cash Pharmacy, they went in and left a pile of pamphlets at the counter: 'a prescription for the mental health of your patients', they told the cashier.

The march was over in an hour; they walked past a watchful uniformed guard (who had been forewarned) into the United States Information Service office, housed in a beautiful old British style bungalow with monkey-tops on the windows, and handed their letter addressed to the President of the United States over to the courteous receptionist as the minor official was not in.

On the way back, before the group dispersed, SVK said, 'We have registered our protest. We have shouted in their ear. Every voice matters. Well done!'

As they walked towards the bus stop Jairam, Shrinivas Moorty, SVK, and the two other lecturers, stopped for tea at a roadside shop. There, as they sat on the rough wooden bench, Jairam with 'Hang Nixon' resting on his lap and Shrinivas Moorty with 'Down with American Imperialism' standing up against his shoulder, SVK said what they had been waiting to hear for weeks, that would make them the envy of the others in class: 'Why don't you drop in for a cup of coffee? A few of us meet in the evenings at my place, you might enjoy the discussions.' And so they won their spurs, the three of them—Shrinivas Moorty, Jairam and Geeta (by default)—to the inner circle, the gathering of poets and film directors and writers, and (they had heard) men on the run, and everyone knew that invitations to SVK's house sessions were handed out sparingly to students. It was a fitting end to the day, a quiet underscoring of their sense of elation, that they had set a current in motion, just a ripple perhaps, but one that would gather strength, that their concern for the world outside had not gone unnoticed by it.

4

One afternoon in the canteen, a crowd was gathered around Alfred Rosario. There was nothing unusual about that for he was quite a magnet, but this time it was not the usual gang of girls but an assortment of boys, some of whom Shrinivas Moorty and Jairam did not recognize immediately. From where they stood, on the other side of the canteen, it looked as if Alfred Rosario was handling some sort of instrument which the others were examining—and it was not a guitar. As they watched, they saw Alfred Rosario's face tense and then his neck and shoulders seemed to quiver while his eyes bulged and his face started turning red.

'It's the Bullworker! Remember, he said he'd bring it to show it to us,' Jairam said, almost running across the canteen.

'Let's see Alfie, let's see it,' Jairam said.

But Alfie was putting it away, back into its cardboard case. Shrinivas Moorty managed to catch a glimpse of shining metal handles attached to a central chamber and white elastic cord before it slid into its box.

'What is it made of? Silver?'

The boys laughed.

'Not for skinny rice-eating boys . . .' Alfie said as he moved off. 'Better stick to the debating society . . .'

'Better still, have the sand kicked into your face . . .'

'I say—' Jairam began hotly but Alfred Rosario and the others did not wait.

For a minute they turned glum; Alfie and the others were just jealous. But both Jairam and Shrinavas Moorty had longed, secretly, to possess the Bullworker, the wonder machine that would build their muscles and shoulders and put some meat on their frames. The comic strip that advertised the Bullworker was responsible—it managed to shame them and reassure them of their manhood simultaneously; it suggested that they were thin and weak and unattractive but that the situation was not beyond repair. At the end of each Phantom and Mandrake comic, on the last page was the story of the Bullworker, in five neat frames. Skinny boy and his girl are sitting on the beach. Well-built, muscled creep kicks sand in their faces. Skinny boy can only fume, hands on hips. Worse still, his girl tells him not to let it bother him. Six weeks later skinny boy and his girl are back on the beach; only this time skinny boy has turned into muscle man, thanks to exercising with the Bullworker. When the creep appears again, skinny boy makes short work of him and his girl looks at him adoringly.

In their minds they were muscle man, though they might look like skinny boy, but it was difficult to convince the world of that. Jairam had half-heartedly toyed with the idea of ordering the Bullworker by VPP post—delivered in fifteen days, at a price of two hundred and twelve rupees—and suggested that they could share the cost. The thought itself had given them muscle and confidence. And now Alfred Rosario had actually gone and done it. Knowing him, he would not be content to just have it, he would use it. The thought was unpalatable, offensive even, but it made them glum.

Alfred Rosario may be a thorn in their side but he taught them many things. They may consider it adventurous to wear white t-shirts with 'Workers of the World Unite' and 'Russia has a Plan—Gosplan' painted on them, but the true mark of consequence was having a pair of Levis. They may master a Bullworker just by internalizing all that it had to offer, but it was material to actually possess one; and finally there came a lesson from Alfred Rosario in the most unexpected quarter—they learnt from him the importance of having a sister. Not the kind they had, but the right kind, the kind who wore Levis herself and roared off on a moped, her step-cut hair blowing in the wind. Alfred Rosario was living proof of how much the sibling glamour quotient was tied up with one's own.

Some mornings at the Ammanagudi firewood depot they were more contemplative than usual, their mystified silences—rare for the two of them—always brought on by the thought of the girls in their class. There were fewer girls than boys and they thought of them in the abstract, as distant, unfathomable creatures (Geeta, of course, did not count), desirable but unattainable. Girls, they understood, moved together through the corridors of college from classroom to classroom like shoals of fish through a sluggish sea; they giggled when one spoke to them, their eyes darting here and there, and even a casual encounter with them caused a high degree of disorientation and embarrassment. Their hearts beat for the divinely plump Malini, Mango Malini, so coy, so unapproachable, so virtuous. She had sworn not to let any boy sit next to her on the bus the day of the college picnic, but once they reached she had plunged into the Kaveri at Talakkad and after that had gone berserk. And on the way back home, with her hair streaming down her back, she had sung at the top of her voice and allowed Alfred Rosario to rest his head in her lap! The softener, they learnt later, had not been Alfie's jeans or his prowess on the guitar or even his muscles, but his sister, the one on the moped with her unoiled hair blowing in the wind, whom Mango Malini wanted to be introduced to.

'I have a plan!' Jairam announced a few days after the picnic. 'A plan to woo Mango Malini.'

The boys were right. Their other activities were too heavy, he said, it was time for them to lighten up. It was not as if they were entirely resourceless; they had sisters too, who were learning Carnatic music and Jairam's sister was fairly accomplished, having sung on All India Radio. They would organize an evening of variety entertainment, under the aegis of the newly formed Youth Club, where Jairam's sister would render a classical raga or two and Shrinivas Moorty's would sing some light music. Mango Malini, who played the violin, would be invited to perform, as would Bhupaty who sang old Hindi film songs. But no Alfie, it was decided, they had to keep Alfred Rosario out.

It so happened that the variety entertainment evening got rained out but the Youth Club flourished. There were plans for other outings, promises about other meetings. Mango Malini said she would join the Youth Club and she came, escorted by her cousin. Shrinivas Moorty missed the first event—an antakshari competition held in the garage of Bhupaty's house—and the second—a meeting in Jairam's compound to plan a surprise treat for Malini on her birthday, where, he was told, Imperialist Radhakrishna watched the proceedings from the terrace with a baleful eye and was passed off as 'my servant' by Jairam. The 'carrom evening' turned out to be a dull affair as none of the girls turned up but when the group met to read poetry together, there was a full house.

There too it was quite apparent that Jairam had not made much headway with Mango Malini and that her cousin, a captain in the army, suave and self-possessed, had taken over the reins of the Youth Club. That evening he recited from Tagore in a quavering, high-pitched voice, and more robustly from Adiga, which had the girls swooning. Jairam's asides from P.G. Wodehouse about the stupidity of men who recited poetry were met coldly. His sister was so moved by the captain's recitation that she sang her favourite song for him, a composition in praise of Lord Krishna in the raga Sindhu Bhairavi.

The next time they met, this time in Mango Malini's cousin's house, Shrinivas Moorty found that despite Jairam's edginess, a convivial spirit had set into the group and they were all playing 'coffee pot' together. Antakshari and dumb charades they knew, but they had never heard of this game before; once they were introduced to it by Mango Malini's cousin, it turned out to be great fun. The group would think of an activity, it could be something as innocuous as reading or as momentous as fighting a duel, which was what Mango Malini's cousin, the resourceful captain, came up with. One person, chosen by draw, would go out of the room while the group 'warmed' the coffee pot, and on being called back into the room had to guess what the activity was, with prompts from the others.

'Great, rollicking game . . . can kick up quite a riot if you let it,' the self-possessed captain said.

The opening rounds were tame. Shrinivas Moorty was the first 'den' and he guessed what the others had in mind much before his allotted twenty questions—a game of chess. Jairam's sister went out next, and with many a teasing prompt from the dapper captain, came up correctly with 'a blind beggar singing outside the temple'. When they interrupted the game for tea, all the girls clustered together in one corner of the room while the boys made forays at the ramparts. Shrinivas Moorty noticed that Jairam's attempts at conversation with Mango Malini, who was making reluctant, low-voiced responses, were being thwarted by the dashing cousin, who by virtue of being older and a man of the world, had managed to engage both his cousin and Jairam's sister simultaneously.

'Next,' the cousin said loudly and in an attempt to be charming, 'our young blade—Jairam—could go out . . .'

The group conferred in loud whispers; finally it was Malini who decided to warm the coffee pot.

'Come in, Jairam. You can come in now. The pot is piping hot.' Malini sang out with an air of great mystery. She would not tell the others what she had thought of.

But Jairam was lounging outside by the gate and took his own time coming back into the room.

'You must be quick sir . . . remember, the spirit of the game,' the cousin said, flashing a keen glance at Malini and Jairam's sister.

'Do you like to coffee pot?' Jairam said to Malini.

Her eyes widened a little at his suggestive tone and she sought to catch his eye but Jairam was not looking at her.

'Yes,' she replied, blushing slightly.

'When do you coffee pot?'

Malini looked around for help but nothing was forthcoming, so she said, with dignity, 'Whenever I can.'

'Where do you coffee pot?'

'Wherever I can.'

'Do you coffee pot everyday?' Shrinivas Moorty asked, moving across the room to stand next to Jairam.

'If I can.'

'Which time do you prefer? Morning, noon or night?'

'Evenings are best for me.' With each reply, Mango Malini's voice rose a notch higher.

'Do you coffee pot alone?'

'Yes, but sometimes my friends join me . . .'

'Is it a mixed group?'

This time she caught his eye. 'Perhaps . . .'

'Do you coffee pot for pleasure?'

'Yes, for pleasure.'

'Do you use any tools to coffee pot? Any special equipment?'

'Yes, a sharp instrument.' Mango Malini's voice shook and colour flooded her fair cheeks.

'Murder. Do you have murder in mind by any chance . . .'

'Wrong answer—' the captain said swiftly. 'You've lost, my friend. Your questions are up.'

'The answer is "embroidery",' Mango Malini said triumphantly and everybody clapped. The party broke up soon after.

Mango Malini appeared to have scored over Jairam in some way, as well as over Shrinivas Moorty, and she swaggered in the corridors of college for the next few weeks—'like a fat goldfish leading her shoal', Jairam sniggered.

After their coffee potting session, Shrinivas Moorty's and Jairam's enthusiasm for the Youth Club dwindled and they initiated no more meetings. The Youth Club had an unexpected fallout though; in a few months' time, Mango Malini's cousin, the suave captain, and Jairam's sister got married. At first Jairam held that it was shameful and that he had been betrayed, but as he was swept into the wedding arrangements, he declared that it was a good thing after all and that the captain was 'quite a decent fellow'.

Their Sunday routine, which had been disrupted in pursuit of Mango Malini, was restored. Such pursuits, they decided, were best left to the likes of Alfred Rosario. They bemoaned briefly the fickleness of women, their lack of taste, and their inability to tell dross from gold, but they had no time for regret, not when a whole Sunday waited and they could go out into the world.

It was Jairam's constant Geeta-baiting that brought Shrinivas Moorty and Geeta closer.

How can we take seriously a girl who comes to college in a chauffeur-driven car, Jairam wanted to know. Geeta just smiled good-humouredly as she did most of the times that Jairam tried to needle her. She was a generous girl at heart; her arguments and differences with people were limited to the classroom or the platform of debate, she did not carry them after they were over and, as she told herself, she had won them. Her contrary views—her support for the United States of America, the bastion of Capitalism, and her admiration for Mrs Gandhi, who was completely pro-USSR—were a source of much banter. When Geeta's serious arguments about Mrs Gandhi's anti-poverty policies, her Garibi-hatao campaign in particular or her courage in taking on West Pakistan in defence of East Pakistan cut no ice with them, she ended the argument by saying that she liked Mrs Gandhi's hair style and dress sense. Geeta's confidence possibly came from being rich, or at least so obviously better off than the others around her. She was one of the few people in class whose father had a private-sector job. He was a high-ranking official in a multinational that made bread and biscuits. 'If they can't have bread, let them eat biscuit' was Jairam's favourite quip; when Geeta had repeated it to her father, he had not found it funny.

The anxieties that beset other girls seemed to steer clear of Geeta. She never discussed clothes and seemed to have an endless and satisfactory supply of them, and shoes and whatever else she wanted. From their very first day in college she had not ducked and giggled when she spoke to the boys; she looked Shrinivas Moorty and Jairam straight in the eye, sometimes even making them feel inadequate. After all she was one of SVK's hand-picked few, despite having the 'wrong' views.

They were welcome to her house on Sunday mornings, and they went once in a while. She had a room with a balcony to herself, where a servant brought them potato chips and Fanta. As he ate the chips and drank the Fanta, Jairam sceptically eyed the servants who walked round the house, performing their chores. 'Does he eat the fruit that he waters—' Jairam would muse as Geeta's mali walked past them with the hose or the servant set a bowl of chikoos fresh off the trees in the garden on the table for them. Or, as he watched the maid carefully lift the books off Geeta's table and wipe the surface, he would say, 'Dust thou art . . .'

'Shut up, Jairam,' Geeta would giggle, winking at Shrinivas Moorty conspiratorially, 'they get paid by the company, more than the fathers of many of our classmates—' At which Jairam would turn sober and just munch on the chips.

But Shrinivas Moorty could tell that they were essaying for a fight. (There was also the matter of the picnic and Jairam's attentions to Mango Malini. Geeta had refused to join the Youth Club, even predicted that it wouldn't last long.) It happened ostensibly over *Midnight Cowboy*. The film was released with a 'Strictly for Adults' certificate and glory be, they were well over eighteen. For the next few weeks it became their touchstone. The mean streets of New York and the squalor of its tenements (in a Capitalist haven!) were a revelation, as was the fragile nature of lives—people who upped and left to become anything, even male hustlers; they were shocked and thrilled by the film's explicitness, by the undeniable frisson of sex and vulnerability which came through, but they skirted the subject and eyed it warily, too encumbered by their inexperience. They called each other 'Ratso' and said 'Hey . . .' in a whining Dustin Hoffman way, Jairam even affecting a limp when he was in the mood. They hummed the title song from the film all day under their breath, and swore to join guitar classes, lulled by Harry Nillson's trills. They spoke of the lighting, the camera work, the excellent gloom and the cleverness of the director in casting a tall man and a short man and making them walk down the streets together and silhouetting them on a bridge in long shot.

A few days later they were in India Coffee House on Mahatma Gandhi Road discussing their favourite scenes from the film, and for once the exaggerated turbans of the waiters did not divert them.

'Ultimately, it is story of true friendship,' Jairam said, summing up, 'of true deep bonding between men . . .'

'So, I gather you have been at the British Library, reading up the *Guardian* and the *Spectator*—' Geeta, who had said little about the film all along, said with a knowing smile.

Jairam flushed, but said nothing. It was true. He had been following everything about the film in the Indian newspapers and magazines as well as those in the British Library.

'It makes too much of it, if you ask me, all that male bonding—' Geeta said shortly.

'It cuts women out, makes them irrelevant, which they are at a certain level . . . that's what bugs you isn't it?'

'We have only the director's word for it. If someone were to make a film about female bonding, the sisterhood, it would be equally strong and touching . . .'

'Name one—'

'I can't think of any right away but—'

'Impossible! It just doesn't exist between women. Don't we see it—bitching and back-biting all the time—'

'Don't be idiotic! There's plenty of that between men too—'

'Don't talk about things you don't understand, just to listen to the sound of your own voice. Every time you open your mouth you surpass your own stupidity—' Jairam snapped, unexpectedly. 'I don't know why SVK invites you to his evening sessions. If you had any sense you'd stay away. Look at you! Look at the way you live and the lines you spout in SVK's house—hypocrite!—complaining all the time about his metal chairs; bet you want tubby sofas like your own to sit on and discuss the poor. All you can do is admire Indira Gandhi. Do you have the guts to do what Ajitha did?'

'Now, now, Jairam,' Shrinivas Moorty said, startled by his outburst, 'what does Ajitha have to do with it?'

Ajitha, a Naxalite from Kerala, was one of the few female heroes that they would permit, for she, a girl in her teens, had stormed a police station in Pulpalli, killed the policemen inside, inked her hand in their blood and left a dripping imprint on the wall of the station, before disappearing into the forests of Wyanad.

'Don't support her!' Jairam turned on Shrinivas Moorty. 'She's nothing but a *kulak*!'

'You're such a B—' Geeta began and then stopped because she had started to cry.

Their conversation came to a standstill and they had to make a hasty exit from the coffee house before they grew too conspicuous. The next day Jairam apologized and gave Geeta his precious copy of Gorky's *Mother* to make amends, but it was Shrinivas Moorty who had given her his handkerchief to wipe her face outside India Coffee House and seen her into an auto. So the next morning, while Geeta accepted Jairam's peace-making gift sombrely, Shrinivas Moorty received a warm smile and a squeeze on his upper arm. Perhaps his shining armour had grown into his skin or it was just the timing of the whole thing. For immediately after the fight, Shrinivas Moorty and Geeta found themselves frequently thrown in each other's company, Jairam having gone off as a student volunteer to Mysore for a trade union meeting. While Shrinivas Moorty had set his heart on the film club, Jairam, after winning the poster competition, had joined the All India Students' Federation, affiliated to the Communist Party, so dear to SVK and had also enrolled as a member of their theatre group. One of his first tasks when he was being put through his paces was to participate in the All India Trade Union Congress organized by the party in Mysore, where he had to man the book-stall and sell copies of Lenin's works that had been translated into Kannada. When he returned, he was full of the meeting, the party pamphlets and the translations he had managed to sell, the street theatre groups that had gathered, their impromptu performances and the rousing songs they had sung. If he noticed an unusual closeness between his two friends, he showed no sign of recognizing it for it was his boast that he steered clear of such relationships of one-to-one domination. His own heart, he claimed, now belonged to Miss Rajni Nimboopani, the buxom film heroine of Mario Miranda's cartoon strip that appeared in the *Illustrated Weekly*—no one in the flesh could combine her carnality with her total wide-eyed vacuity.

At the year-end college play, all three of them took part in the series of historical tableaus that the dramatics department put up. Shrinivas Moorty was Julius Caesar to Geeta's Cleopatra while Jairam was Mark Antony. In imitation of the famous scene in the film where Cleopatra first meets Caesar, with Elizabeth Taylor and Rex Harrison playing the legendary lovers, at Jairam's suggestion, Geeta was rolled out of a carpet on to the stage. The scene was quite sensational and was a great hit with the audience. It also scandalized the college authorities who demanded an explanation from the lecturer in charge of the dramatics department—a newly recruited young woman who had just completed her masters. Since she was a 'temporary appointee' the ripples in the staff room and the principal's chamber died down soon. But Shrinivas Moorty and Geeta came to be called Cleo and Julius after the success of the play, and there was no denying that they were 'going steady'. She was such a good sport, Shrinivas Moorty said to Jairam, and admitted to himself that she had a certain glamour, which he had not noticed till she rolled out of that carpet at his feet on the stage.

Much of their conversation in those days, when Shrinivas Moorty and Geeta walked in Cubbon Park or sat in Airlines Hotel on Saturdays, was about Jairam. He had acquired a reputation with the girls, even a kind of notoriety, not by being polished, like Alfred Rosario, but quite the opposite, by a certain shortness of manner, of rudeness almost, which seemed to appeal to the girls; they thought it more natural. It was rumoured that he had got Mango Malini to buy him masala dosa and badam milk simply by threatening to take off his socks in her presence, warning her that he had been wearing the same pair for three consecutive days. They were his friends and they decided it was their duty to save him from himself and his uncontrolled impulses, for underneath all that he had a heart of gold. His own instincts too, Shrinivas Moorty felt, and his heart, were in the right place but unlike Jairam he did not act upon his convictions in such literal ways. In certain other respects too Jairam grew more casual, even careless. It was Shrinivas Moorty who had lent him his AISF membership fee of twenty-five paise and the twelve rupees train fare to go to Mysore to attend the trade union meet, and he knew that he would not see that money again.

In that the final year of college, Jairam tried them sorely, getting into needless confrontations with students of rival Marxist student groups or, in the absence of opposition, acting upon the principle of equal opportunity whenever he could—'simply causing mischief', as the Principal said. On a class picnic to an old temple on a nearby hillside, while the rest of the class played antakshari under the shade of a tree, Jairam struck up a conversation with the men working in the temple garden and the fields nearby. On learning that they were barred from entering the temple, he insisted that they join him and the others in going right up to the sanctum sanctorum, ringing the bell that hung over the doorway, and demanding the teertha that the priest distributed. His classmates, replete after their lunch and resting under the tree, lauded his efforts but refused to participate. (Shrinivas Moorty was fast asleep; Geeta was not there.) The men themselves did not take him seriously. But the temple management complained to the college about his 'unruly behaviour', more so considering that all the students had been fed at the temple, and Jairam was suspended for a week as punishment for indiscipline.

He became a hero then, and in an act of further defiance he came to college despite the suspension and the teachers noted that attendance was unusually thin on all those days. That week Jairam was to be found in the canteen, in the centre of a group of students, holding what he called 'alternative discourses' on a gamut of events and issues intended to raise them out of their stupor. One afternoon it was the 1968 Student Revolution in Paris and another morning it was Lenin's famous secret ride back to Russia in 1917, on a sealed train, to spark off the Russian Revolution or Subhash Bose's escape from Calcutta to Kabul in 1941 to get help from Hitler to free India from the British. But Shrinivas Moorty's perception of his friend's heroism was dented around that time. To soften the blow of the suspension and do something that they normally would not, they decided to see a 'really third rate' film. Since Shrinivas Moorty had to make a very personal gesture and he could not match Jairam's selflessness and commitment to ideology, he bunked SVK's class for a matinee show and since he had to pay for both of them, they decided on the 'matting' class of the tent cinema. Nothing could fit the bill better than *Rani Mera Naam*. It was supposed to have a scene in which a dog confronted the villain with a pistol. They came out of the film in a suitably lightened frame of mind, and Shrinivas Moorty gave Jairam a scene by scene breakdown almost—the story about the dog and the pistol had not been a canard after all—of how much the film owed to the 'original' that had inspired it: Lee Van Cleef's *Death Rides a Horse*. Instead of cringing at the shameless imitation, we should be proud of the film's élan, Shrinivas Moorty said. It is a good way of thumbing our nose at the West, at 'decolonizing our mindspaces' as SVK would say. And in a truly original feminist twist, it was a woman who was avenging the death of her parents here, not a man. Even Geeta would approve.

The next thing Shrinivas Moorty knew, someone in the canteen was passing round Jairam's prize-winning review in the *Illustrated Weekly*. The feature—a review of a popular film by a lay cinemagoer—which the magazine ran, was a great hit, and not just because of the prize money—the princely sum of fifty rupees. If the article went on to win 'review of the year', a trip to Bombay and a tour of a film studio to see a film being shot were promised. Many a student had taken a shot at it, and failed. As it turned out, Jairam's review of *Rani Mera Naam* was, almost word for word, everything that Shrinivas Moorty had said about the film. Shrinivas Moorty read the piece—written in Jairam's usual flamboyant style—with incredulity and anger. He also realized that it caused Jairam no embarrassment for when he went looking for him, Jairam was sitting in the canteen, surrounded by his admirers, taking all the ribbing and the congratulations as his due, laughing uproariously at the lark while putting away masala dosas, which someone or the other kept ordering for him.

'That was mine, you know it. You stole it from me!' Shrinivas Moorty burst into the crowd around Jairam, and knew immediately that it was a mistake. He stood awkwardly on the outside of the group, the legs of the bench blocking access, his view of Jairam cut off by the heads and shoulders of those who had heaped themselves on the bench to talk to Jairam.

'What is it Shrinivas?' Jairam said easily, kindly, as if speaking to a child who is throwing a tantrum.

'Your review is based on the discussion we had after the film—'

They all turned to stare at him and Jairam peered through a gap in the mass of elbows and heads.

'Of course we discussed the film, Shrinivas, but I don't make a habit of recording what I say casually. Anyway, how can you claim ownership of a discussion? How can you say this idea was mine and not yours? Besides, how can you remember so clearly?'

'It could well be that your views were influenced by his—'

'. . . and you could well have stolen his review—'

'Anyway, you should have written it first if you had thought of it—'

'Cool down, Shrinivas. Here, sit with us and have a dosa.'

And that was what he did: sit down and share Jairam's dosa. The more he thought about it, the more petty his own behaviour seemed, and he was glad it died out with the morning's argument. I'm sure the idea must have been yours, Geeta said to him loyally but her assurance was no consolation. Instead, it reminded him of all the other times when the ideas had been his but Jairam had got the most mileage out of them. The prize money made no difference to Jairam's finances either; Shrinivas Moorty did not get back any of the money he had lent Jairam.

seven

~

1

When they were in the university, doing their post graduation, their three years in college done, res publica, the public cause, came knocking on their door quite unexpectedly. It was 1975—the year Prime Minister Indira Gandhi declared a National Emergency. For the next two years their world of daily reckoning seemed to become more efficient, as if a society had pulled up its collar and bent over painfully, negotiating its protruding stomach to tie up its shoelaces and give its much neglected shoes a shine. The trains and buses ran on time, the clerks in all the government offices and banks were in their seats, and the day-to-day struggle, the queues and the rudeness of public servants seemed a thing of the past. But there were stories one heard: of two men, both stout citizens, who had been complaining loudly against the prime minister being dragged off a bus by plainclothesmen pretending to be passengers . . . of young men on the outskirts of Delhi being forced to have vasectomies to meet the quotas of the family planning drive . . . It was a good thing, all said and done, people said. There was always a price to be paid for efficiency. So what if the entire Opposition (except for the Communists), was behind bars; they were just impotent meddlers. Now, the only 'man' in the government could get on with her job of putting the country in order. So the police made a few indiscreet arrests, but if law and order was to be maintained they had to be given discretionary powers . . . Besides, what was parliamentary democracy if not a handout of the British; we had always had strong unifying rulers, right from Ashoka's time—he was the first man to meld the country into one, and that was three hundred years before Christ.

Moreover, the country had suffered much. They had just defeated their neighbour, Pakistan, in a war and helped divide that country and create another—Bangladesh—at great cost to themselves. Agreed, there were problems. Prices, especially of petrol, were spiralling and families had to think twice before setting off even on their scooters. As for things like rice and wheat and dal, even with the subsidized public distribution system, people with large families were finding it difficult to make ends meet. And even as Mrs Gandhi was setting right these problems, the High Court in Allahabad declared her 1971 election invalid on some flimsy grounds. Instead of resigning she declared an Emergency and just put everyone who opposed her behind bars.

In Shrinivas Moorty's house, the see saw of public opinion was reflected in his father's moods. Vasudev Moorty was much exercised about the Emergency but every morning he would change his mind about it. One day he would be gleeful that all the slackers in his office were forced to work, that the working hours of the bank had been extended to his advantage, that public amenities in general had improved. The next, however, his democratic, politically unaffiliated self—the part that made him don a coat and tie once a month and attend lectures on 'Whither Good Citizenship?' or 'What Does Democracy Mean Today?' at the Gokhale Institute of Public Affairs—made him lecture his wife and grown-up children sternly at the dining table on what the suspension of civil liberties meant in a country with a democratic tradition like India. Some days even the newspaper induced a change in tune. One morning, on reading the headlines he harrumphed, 'Some Congress party fool has actually made a public statement that India is Indira and Indira is India,' and he rolled up the newspaper in disgust and struck the dining table with it. 'And we, a country led by Gandhi and Nehru have to put up with it . . .' Yet another day, the middle section of the editorial page was blank to everyone's initial bewilderment, which was followed by hectic speculation on the office bus as to what the editorial could have said that day, for it to have been taken off so hastily, without a replacement, or was it, perhaps, a unique form of protest from the hamstrung editor. All the letters that Vasudev Moorty received those days made him frown for before he proceeded to read the letters or even see who they were from, he would look pensively at the message stamped across each post card and inland letter—'Emergency: An era of discipline' or 'Work more Talk less'. It was mandatory for all postal stationery to carry such exhortations and reminders. 'As if we are a nation of illiterate beasts of burden,' Vasudev Moorty said, visualizing a salaried clerk sitting at the counter stamping a mountain of cards and letters, fretting over the number of man hours spent on such 'unproductive activity' and the money spent—'taken from the taxes we pay'—on the moulds and the purple-inked stamping pads. But 'Emergency: An era of discipline' exercised him more than the other slogans because it was a statement made by none other than Acharya Vinoba Bhave, a man whom he admired for he considered him to be the last of the true Gandhians. When Vasudev Moorty had been a student, just after Independence, Vinoba Bhave had organized the Bhoodan Movement, urging landlords to donate their land voluntarily, which would then be redistributed among the landless peasants. At that time, such idealism had seemed practicable. Now, such an endorsement—calling the Emergency the 'anushasan parva' or the chapter of discipline, a reference to the Bhagvad Gita, the ultimate manual of action in Vasudev Moorty's eyes—from a man he regarded so highly, seemed a betrayal and he expressed himself so strongly whenever he received something in the post, flapping the errant postcard between his fingers in contempt, that his wife was forced to beg him to lower his voice.

Once they were out of college, Shrinivas Moorty and Jairam met infrequently during the week for they were in different departments in the university, but their Sunday ritual—the visit to the firewood depot—remained. For Jairam, there was no escaping the castor-oil bath drill with water boiling nicely in a firewood-lit hande. So their Sunday morning meeting was as cast-in-stone as Jairam's bathing routine. And the yard of the firewood depot—with its scanty grass dying in the debris of wood chips, the stump of wood that served as an axe anvil and a stool, more lacerated, the depot man more grey but still as distempered and deceitful—remained their hallowed space.

One Sunday morning, Jairam brought a friend along with him to the firewood depot. Shrinivas Moorty remembered him from college as Rajan, a brooding kind who had been in science, and was now in one of the IITs. Shrinivas Moorty did not know him very well, though Jairam spent time with him occasionally. Rajan said nothing at all that morning, and making himself comfortable on a stack of logs, pulled out a crushed but carefully preserved twist of paper from his pocket, and proceeded to mix the small grey-green lumps of dried leaf matter that it contained with strands of tobacco, rolling the mixture into squares of paper, licking the ends together expertly to make a small, stubby cigarette. He held out two stubs on the palm of his hand casually, as if he were handing out sweets. Jairam almost snatched one off Rajan's palm while Shrinivas Moorty hesitated before picking up his. Ever since he read Huxley's *Doors of Perception* he had been wanting to try it but hadn't the courage.

Rajan never came on Sunday mornings after that, but sometimes Jairam would produce the familiar crushed packet, and their mornings would stretch into the early afternoon. Jairam took to it more easily; one joint and he would be off.

'Grass . . . at last . . .' he sang, as he tried to roll another cigarette slickly, in imitation of Rajan's sleight of hand, 'ganjika . . . my premika . . . goodbye Mango Malini, welcome Mary Jane . . .'

'Don't be shy,' he exhorted Shrinivas Moorty, 'Lord Shiva himself would approve . . .'

And so he would, Shrinivas Moorty thought, the ash-smeared, snake toting god, his eyes sunk in canna bliss.

'We are in a state of Emergency, remember, we must resort to desperate measures, register a uniquely personal protest,' Jairam said skittishly, trying to pre-empt Shrinivas Moorty's disapproval.

They hid behind the logs of wood and smoked the joints. At first Shrinivas Moorty was racked by coughs that almost felled him to the ground, but then he learnt to draw his breath in slowly and relax, and over the weeks he got it right. The cloyingly sweet smell that one associated with it was deceptive, he realized, when he came to recognize the peppery taste in his throat and palate—a taste almost disappointingly domestic, too close to his mother's kitchen—but he was lulled into a stupor all the same. After a bit, his head would hum pleasantly, his face turned upwards to the brilliantly blue sky, his eyes closing gradually as if his eyelids were oiled, while Jairam paced the yard and talked feverishly, his eyes glittering, and the depot man went off on his rounds with a knowing smile, assured that the minders of his yard would not leave in a hurry and that he would be paid handsomely too in the bargain.

The weed brought out the poet in Jairam. It was not love or nature that inspired him but politics and he could turn quite violently maudlin about his country and his people.

'I am a capitalist,' he shouted, brandishing the depot man's axe in the air, 'save me from strikes—

'I am a worshipper of tradition—save me from revolution

'I am a scientist—save me from the truth

'I have murdered democracy—save me from the people . . .'

And with that last line, he brought the axe crashing down on the blackened stump that was its resting place.

One such morning at the firewood depot, Jairam said, 'SVK Sir may be in trouble. I believe the principal had a talk with him.'

It had been a while since Shrinivas Moorty had visited SVK and he did not know that Jairam was still in touch with him. After leaving college Shrinivas Moorty had continued to attend SVK's weekend sessions regularly for some time, alone for Jairam had slacked off (one of his reasons being that SVK served nothing stronger than coffee), and yet it was Jairam who knew that SVK was in trouble.

'Trouble?'

'That talk of his at the Civil Liberties Centre . . . I believe the college is taking serious note of it.'

'That hasn't bothered the college before. SVK has always given talks at the Civil Liberties Centre. Besides, he has influential friends in the Communist Party—'

'Perhaps. But he isn't truly one of them . . . not a party member. They wouldn't stick their necks out for him. Not now . . .'

USHA K.R.

They also heard then that the two lecturers of National Trust College who had suddenly gone on leave—the physics and Sanskrit teachers, known to be members of the overtly Hindu organization, the Rashtriya Swayamsevak Sangh—had actually been arrested. That was the time, when standing at the bus stop, any thickset man in a jacket and a moustache riding past slowly on a motorcycle made them stiffen. Any day, Shrinivas Moorty and Jairam declared, give them an inefficient world and the freedom to curse it . . . a democracy as they knew it.

At that time the man who was central to their conversation, but about whom they always took care to speak in low voices, whispers even, was the charismatic, tousle-haired leader of the Socialist Party, George Fernandes. 'He comes from Mangalore, same town as mine,' Jairam swaggered. Fernandes had been a fiery trade-union leader and it was then, when his photograph was splayed across the front pages of newspapers for days as he led the striking port- and dock-workers in Bombay, that he caught their attention, especially Jairam's, who was always on the alert for men of action. George Fernandes had gone on to better himself subsequently; as president of the Railwaymen's Federation he organized a nationwide railway strike and brought the trains all over the country to a halt. At his behest, like bees flocking to a hive, hundreds of railway workers had gone to jail and the railways had been paralysed. That is what we look for in a leader; like Gandhi he is able to command thousands with a word, a whim even, Jairam said, sighing over a newspaper photograph in which George Fernandes, pumping his manacled fist high in the air, teeth bared and eyes gleaming with manic determination behind his glasses, was being led away in a police van. But Shrinivas Moorty was more circumspect in granting George Fernandes heroic status for he had borne the brunt of the strike. His mother and he, travelling back from Delhi to Bangalore after attending a wedding, had got caught in the strike and were stranded at Madras railway station, bathing and eating off the platform for two days, waiting for the Grand Trunk express to reassemble and have a connecting bogie assigned to it to proceed to Bangalore. Shrinivas

Moorty had waited long for this trip and till he reached Madras, the thrill of travelling on the grandest train in the country had made him a child again—he had dashed down at every station to fill water, looked forward to the meals served on the heated aluminium trays, gathered with the other men at the door when the train started its famous backward run, waited for the tunnels in the night and watched the reflection of the window grill with his head silhouetted against it on the smooth innards of the hill that had been carved up to make space for the train to pass, and held his breath through the dreaded Chambal Valley in Madhya Pradesh where dacoits were known to attack. But the pleasure of the journey soured when they arrived at Madras, three-fourths of the way, and George Fernandes struck. After two days spent on the platform, they came back in a crowded train, their bookings to no avail as everyone scrambled for seats and, handicapped by his slow mother, Shrinivas Moorty had to give her the only seat he could manage and make do with standing space in the corridor through the night.

However, George Fernandes had gone underground once the Emergency began, to evade arrest, and from time to time Jairam brought thrilling reports of his activities. And then the rumours started that SVK was involved in circulating a letter from George Fernandes urging students to wreck public property—anything that stood for the authority of the government, and commit other acts of sabotage. SVK it was said was getting his students to distribute copies of the letter, and they were dropping the letters in the very post boxes that they urged their recipients to destroy. Jairam claimed that he himself had hand delivered a batch of those letters to a few people, only he had been ignorant of the contents. What had saved SVK, according to Jairam, and the students too, was that the letters, when opened, turned out to be blank for he had done what Lenin had done in jail—written in milk using stubs of bread as pens—but Shrinivas Moorty had not believed that story. That was an old trick. Even the Five Find-outers were writing letters in 'invisible ink' and every school child who read Enid Blyton would guess.

But, the most bizarre story of those times was about the flower seller in Ammanagudi Street, a rather simple-minded youth who suddenly disappeared one day. A fan of Indira Gandhi's or perhaps one who was familiar with the slogans associated with her and who used them to effect, he had a very amusing way of advertising his flowers and every house and shop on Ammanagudi Street bought flowers regularly from him. 'Woman, come out of your kitchen,' he would shout loudly in English, 'buy Indira Gandhi kanakambra . . . madam malliges . . . PM pushpas . . . rashtriya rojas . . . come out Amma . . . the nation is on the move . . . look at this kanakambra and mallige combination—we two our two . . .' He was a familiar figure on the street and people who gathered in tea shops often used him as a conversation piece. Then one day, Indira Gandhi Kanakambra did not appear and people said he had been arrested for having used her name once too often, and in a brazen way at that. He was back on Ammanagudi Street several months later, selling flowers, and was absolutely mum about where he had been all the time. Visiting my village, he would say sometimes, or gone to another locality, you can't expect me to hang around Ammanagudi Street all the time, his manner much less cheerful now and Indira Gandhi's name wiped off his lips.

According to Jairam, two men from the CBI, identifying themselves as Venkatachalam and Venkatachalapathy—looking exactly like Thomson and Thompson, the detectives in the *Tintin* comics, had visited SVK's house, and questioned his wife while he was at college. After that, SVK's well wishers, the regulars at his evening addas decided that anything 'incriminating' should be shifted from SVK's house. Eventually it was Shrinivas Moorty and Jairam who went to SVK's house one afternoon to search his attic, but they found no trace of his correspondence with the Centre for Civil Liberties or with any of the Communist Party functionaries; no trace either of the letter from the tousle-haired opposition leader, now in jail. However, they removed the unsold copies of *Frontier*, his wife's copy of the Bhagvad Gita and the collected works of Karl Marx and even his class notes, to safety. Jairam said he would have kept them, but there was no space in his house. So, Shrinivas Moorty, who had quarter of a room to himself, shoved all the copies of the radical weekly from Calcutta into a trunk in his attic. SVK often read out articles from *Frontier* to them, particularly news reports on the Naxals. Completely sympathetic with their disaffection, SVK would read out in an impassioned way about the 'massacre' of the Naxalites in West Bengal by the police in 'encounter killings'. In those days in their dark, crowded BA classroom, under SVK's tutelage they had each felt an answering rush of sympathy, of anger, and thought that they had just to stretch their hands out to clasp that of a Naxal from Baranagar or Cossipore, or even a brave Vietcong guerrilla.

After college, once removed from SVK's immediate and overpowering influence, for Shrinivas Moorty more than Jairam, the sympathetic urge steadied and took direction, a more concrete form than mere youthful enthusiasm—it influenced their choice of subject in their post-graduation. Shrinivas Moorty decided on history and Jairam on economics. And they declared that they would not take the competitive exams for the administrative and police services as Prabhakar and scores of their classmates were doing; they could not become part of the establishment they reviled or one among the 'pigs' they despised. Shrinivas Moorty's mother's mild comment that preparing for the entrance exams to the Indian Administrative Service required eight hours of dedicated study every day, they brushed aside. They did not want to be reminded that neither of them had done very well in their BA—Shrinivas Moorty had barely got a first class while Jairam had fallen into second class. Geeta had won the gold medal and she joined the university with them to study English.

The Emergency passed, Indira Gandhi's government fell and was reinstated, George Fernandes went on to become a union cabinet minister with different portfolios under successive governments, veering from Left to Right, Shrinivas Moorty and Jairam smoked grass no longer, SVK continued at National Trust College till he retired and the unsold and unread copies of *Frontier* lay undisturbed in Shrinivas Moorty's attic till the house was demolished to make way for flats. When Imperialist Radhakrishna finally bought an electric geyser to heat his bath water—prompted in no small measure by the closing down of the firewood depot in Ammanagudi Street—their Sunday meetings became more and more irregular. Their weekends were taken up with other things. Shrinivas Moorty became an office bearer of the film society, and being one of the few student members, was asked to do most of the running around. Jairam, in turn, was part of the core of a left-oriented theatre group and absented himself from classes for days at a time when the troupe toured the districts. They invited each other for shows and performances. Jairam came for the first screening of Satyajit Ray's *Pather Panchali*, a triumph for the film society. Shrinivas Moorty had worn himself to the bone with all the arrangements and the official permissions, the film reels did not arrive till the morning of the show and he had to pay a hefty sum out of his pocket to have it redeemed from the parcel office; unfortunately he was not able to get Ray himself for the panel discussion that followed the screening. When it came to organization, Jairam had the upper hand; he got on better with people. When his theatre group collaborated with the National Theatre of East Germany, he became their press representative. The arts pages of the newspapers were full of it—Bertolt Brecht's *Caucasian Chalk Circle* to be performed in Kannada with a mixed German and local cast. On opening night, it was Jairam, still dressed in the much-washed, straining shirt, who introduced Fritz Bennewitz, the director of the Weimar National Theatre to the packed house and was given the task of escorting him wherever he wanted to go. And in three brief days, when Bennewitz was free of his 'official' duties and appearances, Jairam was seen everywhere with him—the record shops on Avenue Road, so crowded that they could barely walk on the footpath, buying a fat marigold garland from the flower sellers in City Market, the 'pet shops' in Russel Market, dosas and coffee on the wooden tables of Vidyarthi Bhavan and the second hand book stalls on M.G. Road. At the end of the year, Jairam had two invitations. One, to no one's surprise, from the National Theatre of East Germany to visit Berlin, and the other, to every one's surprise, from the British Council to attend a Young Writer's

Workshop in London. The second invitation came at the behest of a little-known British poet who had visited the city. Jairam had publicly professed contempt for his work, called it hopelessly right wing, but courted the poet nonetheless, which Shrinivas Moorty was not able to understand, till the invitation to the workshop came—Jairam had been singled out by name by the poet. That Jairam was unable to accept either invitation—Imperialist Radhakrishna said he didn't have the money to cover the balance for the fare—was of some comfort to Shrinivas Moorty.

With Geeta, Shrinivas Moorty's relationship remained frictionless and chaste. Complicity over Jairam had drawn them together, and he still formed a large part of their conversation—their 'analysis' of Jairam, his motives, his behaviour and his temperament could keep them occupied for hours. They could not do without Jairam for they had come to know each other in his shadow. Their timid overtures and tentative explorations, how the other walked and talked and ate and sat, the ink-stained fingers, the chipped tooth, the scars of acne and the pits that chicken pox had left behind—all was reflected off a third person and in the absence of the one, the vital one, they grew awkward and perplexed, like the tongue that falls into lisping when a crucially positioned tooth goes missing from the mouth. At the university they sought each other out of habit though they were no longer classmates. They had lapsed into the comfort of companionship, already behaving like a married couple—she asked after his health and commented on his weight and looks with maternal concern, while he took it all as his due, expressing no reciprocal concern over her health and her looks. Their discussions on films and books had grown tame as they were almost completely agreed on them. It seemed as if they had grown to know each other too quickly, had learnt to anticipate each other too soon. But though they might have lacked burning passion, they depended on their familiarity with each other. He loved her, yes, most definitely, and they would get married one day—a time at a comfortable distance in the future. Their future pointed in a common direction and Shrinivas Moorty saw no need to disturb the status quo, not realizing that inaction had its consequences, as strong and as definite as overt action, a tendency that was part of his nature.

2

Television had come late to the city, much after Delhi and Bombay, perhaps even Calcutta and Madras, and later still to Shrinivas Moorty's house. He would not have guessed then, in 1982, that in ten years' time they would be invaded by so much choice, colour and voice, so many enticing representations of the world, that it would become a virtual presence, the third occupant of his flat, his wife's constant companion. Their first television set was a small black-and-white one, the cheapest in the market, bought reluctantly by his father at his mother's insistence. The first programme they saw was Satyajit Ray's short film *Sadgati*. But 1982 was not just the year of television, it was also the year of the taming of Jairam, who was forced to give up his wayward ways and start earning an honest living, as his mother put it. To Shrinivas Moorty, the coming of television would always be linked with Jairam's capitulation.

Shrinivas Moorty's mother's friends had gathered in the drawing room for they had decided to see the film together, as if they were watching it in a cinema hall. Jairam's mother was there too, which was rare for she hardly went out. The occasion demanded a celebration—song and dance, even classical music; the women were dressed for an evening out. What they got instead was a film about a bonded labourer being worked to death by his landlord, which they watched glumly, in their silks and jasmine. Shrinivas Moorty and his father were the only ones that evening who were absorbed by the film.

The film had almost ended when Jairam's maid came running in from the gate. Would Amma come home immediately? Jairam's father had been taken ill. Later that evening, after Imperialist Radhakrishna had been admitted to Modern Nursing Home, the hunt for Jairam began. 'He's never home . . . rehearsing for some play or the other . . . leaves straight from his tacky college—'

Jairam's mother started crying and all the women clicked their tongues in sympathy. 'I keep telling him it is high time he took over the responsibilities of the house. His father is overworked . . .'

Shrinivas Moorty had been teaching in National Trust College, his alma mater, for five years by then, and had just been confirmed as junior lecturer on a salary of five hundred rupees a month. Jairam, after doing another MA, this time in public administration, so that his quest for knowledge and love of theatre could be accommodated, was teaching at Ramgopal College of Secretarial Practice, and was being paid a pittance. But both jobs had been hard to come by and Shrinivas Moorty knew he was lucky to have been slotted into a convenient vacancy. Jairam's application to National Trust College was still pending, despite their avowed preference for their alumni.

That evening, Shrinivas Moorty reluctantly roused himself from his father's armchair to start looking for Jairam. He was somewhere in town, rehearsing with his troupe for the massive cultural meet planned by the Left parties. Jairam was directing *Belchi*, a play based on a real-life incident—the lynching of eleven landless labourers by the landowners they worked for in Belchi, Bihar. It had been all over the papers a few years back and from what Shrinivas Moorty understood the play was very moving and lyrical; it used poetry to reinforce its pathos. There was talk too of an elephant being brought on stage, for Indira Gandhi had visited Belchi on an elephant, unable to access it by road, and Jairam was planning to use some sensational stage effects, things that would make the city sit up and take notice. But Jairam was not in any of his regular haunts that evening. Finally, Geeta remembered the place in Malleshwaram, a hall that the troupe sometimes used for rehearsals.

By the time they reached the place, Shrinivas Moorty had grown impatient and tired and if it had not been for Geeta he would have given up and gone home. The place was so dark and uninviting that they almost overlooked it. But once they ventured in they discovered that though the courtyard and the corridor that led to the hall were ill-lit, the hall itself was blazing with lights. The festive spirit was overwhelming, a little frenzied even, in anticipation of the big event. Knots of people were gathered here and there, talking. A tea boy was going around, pouring from a kettle. On one side of the hall the banners were being readied. 'Welcome to Janotsava, the spirit of the people' one read. 'Janotsava—32nd Conference of the All India Trade Union Congress' was being fixed on to bamboo supports. At the far end was a makeshift stage on which a group—the only one with women in evidence—was singing. They would sing a line or two together and stop, not getting either the words or the tune right. Jairam was nowhere to be seen.

'He's right there, sitting behind the stage with the harmonium player, working out the tune,' an older man, with grey in his beard and hair, a senior in college and now associated with the AITUC, said. 'We are setting Siddalingaiah's poems to music.'

They still could not see Jairam though they could hear the harmonium.

'You know madam,' the AITUC official said, in English, out of deference for Geeta's jeans, 'Siddalingaiah, our Dalit poet, our most important contemporary voice, the burning anger of the oppressed...' he proffered a copy of Siddalingaiah's collection, *Hole Maadigara Haadu.*

'I know—' Geeta cut him short. 'I have this volume of poems.'

The group on the stage was now singing.

'*Nenne dina, namma jana—*'

'Stop! Not like that!' Jairam's voice cut in and he emerged, seemingly from the floorboards. 'Lengthen the "aa"... dinaaa... janaaa... give it some feeling...'

'*Nenne dinaaa... namma janaaa...*' the group sang.

'Jairam. JAIRAM!'

He turned and looked at them vaguely, not recognizing them immediately.

'Oh it's you. What are you doing here?'

'We've come to talk to you. To tell you something—'

'*Kappu mukha, belli gadda, uriyatiruva kannugalu—*'

'Your father, Jairam. He's in hospital.'

'He's had a heart attack.'

'*Dhikkara, dhikkara, shrimantara sokkige*—'

'Stop it, stop. I can't hear these people.'

'I said your father has been admitted to the hospital. You're wanted at home.'

'We've come to fetch you.'

He looked at them, shades of annoyance and uncertainty crossing his face, as if it were somehow their fault.

'You've got to shape up Jairam,' Shrinivas said angrily, repeating Jairam's mother's words, 'You can't go off every day from work to sing and dance—'

'It is high time you took over the responsibilities of the house. Your father is over worked—'

Without a word, Jairam allowed himself to be led out by them, past the surprised official of the AITUC, and all the other functionaries.

On the stage, the group continued to sing, their voices strong on the 'aas' even as the sound receded.

Yesterday
My people
Came like a hill
Black face   Silver Beard   Burning eyes
Everywhere my people stood like water
A thousand streams flowing into the ocean of revolution . . .

PART IV

eight

~

1

January is a cruel month, a cold deceptive month, a month of false allusions for the sky is bright and the sun benign but the cold cuts and your skin can be lacquered into a crust, and everywhere dry leaves heap up in desolation.

January was the month Neela was born—six months after her parents were hastily married in the sub-registrar's office—with no one to celebrate her entry into the world except Jessy, the hospital nurse; her mother was too tired to care and her father overwhelmed by the fact that she had survived.

January was the month that Shrinivas Moorty had set off on his honeymoon—bliss for three days and then disaster when it started raining in the hills and they were shut indoors in a small cold room with each other, and his hands turned heavy and inert.

January for Balaji Brahmendra was good. He loved the bracing air and the blue skies, and his sweaters hung well on him. He usually spent the Christmas and New Year week in Goa, partying with friends and swimming in the cold sea, which he found exhilarating—a great way to begin the new year.

January was a revelation for Pushpa Rani, for she discovered the new year. Till then, on 1 January, she had just shouted 'happynewyear' at everybody and they had shouted it back at her. But that year she attended her first new year party and danced through the night and, there, she and Ranjit had definitely been an 'item'.

2

Later, Balaji Brahmendra would say he had a presentiment after his meeting with the programme director. If not he would not have been so insistent on clearing all the traces from the computer. He had lightened the load in his inbox and cleaned up his personal folder well before three o' clock. The rate at which he received messages every day, he should have had a whole website to himself. Other than the hundreds of responses to the questions he routinely asked on the show, there was always the odd one that sneaked up on him. An offer from Tricia Frey to make his penis grow two inches longer; one from the director of the Central Bank of Nigeria who had written to him in absolute secrecy to say that a sum of 25 million dollars, left over from an over-invoiced deal that had been paid out already, was lying unnoticed in the bank and he had reason to believe that he, Balaji Brahmendra, was a trustworthy partner for the receipt of those funds—all that Balaji had to do in return was reveal the address, phone and fax numbers of his bank, as well as his own, and his account number, for which he would get ten percent of the 25 million dollars. And then there was the persistent Nelly. He had had to open a separate folder to house her messages; together, they traced the tortuous course of her love life with a man who seemed to have promised her eternal passion and then reneged. He was cautious while dealing with such breast-beating types, careful to send back their more-than-token gifts, and made it a point not to meet them or invite them to his show, as they begged him. The trick was to deal with the most agonized confession with a light touch, reassuring but just a tad flippant, even mocking if he felt he could carry it off. And these were tactics he had figured out for himself. The course they had been put through when he had joined as RJ had certainly not taught him the finer points of dealing with people on air.

He went through some of the old messages he had saved—some of the genuinely complimentary ones he could not bear to delete. Those from some of the students of National Trust College, for instance. He had met them months ago, but some of them still wrote to him—students and teachers—women all.

A few months ago he had received a letter from the head of the Centre for Inter-Disciplinary Studies at National Trust College, inviting him to conduct a seminar on the 'Opportunities in the Media, with specific reference to the Radio Professional'. The letter had come on bond paper, with a printed letter head, complete with crest and motto and the usual typing mistakes. Balaji Brahmendra had been highly tickled. Respectability and legitimacy had come seeking him out. He told his mother about the invitation at once, hoping she would relay it to his father. No seminar, he wrote back to National Trust College, though he was open to an interactive session. But in the event it turned out to be a gladiatorial contest, and he had truly enjoyed himself. The students had launched themselves at him like fans in a rock concert and the teachers, well, like rocks.

He was recognized as soon as he arrived at the gates of the college where a small crowd of students was waiting. One student had been posted to look out for him, but soon the number swelled. From the gate he was borne aloft by the students, who expressed their delight in his show and in him and then one of the girls was asking him why he never played her requests and another as to whether he really was an engineering college dropout, by which time they had traversed the field and arrived at the rather grubby looking college building. After a low-voiced, uncertain discussion as to where he should be taken, the students led him to the office of the 'Head' in preference to that of the 'Princy'.

'Dr H.R. Jairam, head of the Centre for Inter-Disciplinary Studies.' A small-made man but trim, muscular, with a strong handshake, welcomed him into his office. Balaji noted the upholstered sofa set and the fresh flowers arranged in a vase. 'Glad to have you with us Bali Brums.' Dr Jairam had a hearty manner and a sinewy voice, with just a hint of an American twang, that inspired confidence, which to Balaji was a good beginning. 'Shall we—'

Balaji Brahmendra was flattered to find that he was being taken round by the head on a tour of the sights, as if he were a proper dignitary, like a philanthropist or a head of state. The college, he learnt as they walked on the grounds, was more than a hundred years old, established 'to uphold Indian values . . . provide education to our people to bring them on par with people trained in the colleges of the British presidencies. Of course, the building is not a hundred years old, despite the way it looks; it was built in nineteen sixty-four . . .' Dr Jairam laughed.

When Balaji was looking for a college to do his pre-university, before joining the engineering course—it was decided by his father early on that he would be an engineer—National Trust College had figured on the list. His father had wanted it for its traditional values and Balaji had shot it down for the very same reason. 'Traditional' values would mean plastering your hair with coconut oil, wearing long sleeves so as not to show your arms, walking with downcast eyes and speaking softly, and singing the national anthem everyday—and those would be the rules just for the boys, it would be worse for the girls. He wanted to have a blast in those two years of pre-university and decided to go to a college in the centre of town, close to M.G. Road—named after the Mahatma but with nothing of his spirit, thank god—and Brigade Road, where all the shops and the pubs and the girls were. And it was not as if National Trust College was his father's alma mater or something—he hadn't even gone to college, having plunged straight into the family business after school.

As they walked across the grounds, Dr Jairam told him about himself, and the walk was long enough for an extended life history. He was an alumnus of this college he said, and Balaji tried to spot the note of pride that should rightly have been there. After his graduation here he went on to do a 'double MA' at the university and then, as a teacher in National Trust College he was given the opportunity to travel, to go abroad and study further and see a bit of the world—a truly transformational experience. Though the opportunity to travel and study in the US, which students seemed to take for granted now, had come a little late—considering that they

USHA K.R.

had grown up on European literature and Western ideology—he was grateful for it, and it had been an eye opener. All his ideas, his pet theories of life that had been rock-solid in his protected state had taken a beating.

'Those of us who grew up in the sixties and seventies cannot help but believe in a fair, equitable world . . .' Dr Jairam threw him a sideways glance, as if faulting Balaji and his generation for not thinking so and at the same time hinting that such a belief was a weakness, and that Balaji and Co. were not thankful enough that they no longer had to fight that battle.

His deep-rooted faith in the heroism and natural sense of justice of the Communist state, where he believed that each would give according to his ability and take according to his need, was shaken when, as a backpacking senior student passing through Rumania he was arrested, 'for nothing at all really—all my papers were in order'. In his cold jail cell he recalled Arthur Koestler's *Darkness at Noon* and Orwell's *1984* and realized that there was a very real possibility that he would never get out and that his wife and newborn son who were waiting for him to finish his trip and join them would not even know where he was, and even as he shook with the fear of this realization he was let out, quite miraculously. After that he went onward to the wide open spaces of the US, to Rightwyn for his research and to pursue a doctorate and the five years there helped him recover his balance and review things with an open mind. He experienced for himself some of the complexity of the world and saw that pre-decided ways of looking at things were misleading. Ideologies could be straitjackets if not seen as systematic attempts to codify knowledge into digestible bites. They were best treated as points of view and not ways of seeing.

And there at Rightwyn, he had met B.N. Swamy. Did Balaji know who B.N. Swamy was? Bennehalli Nagasimha Swamy? Balaji confessed he did not, and then added quickly, recalling the invitation to the seminar, that he must be the founder of this centre for it was called the B.N. Swamy Centre of Inter-Disciplinary Studies. Dr Jairam nodded approvingly and said that there was a B.N. Swamy Centre of the Sciences as well, endowed by the same man. B.N. Swamy, who was on the board of academic advisors of Rightwyn College, was another alumnus of National Trust College, a senior who had succeeded as an entrepreneur in Silicon Valley, USA, with a burning desire to turn 'angel' and pay back his dues to the institution that had given him such a good start in life. And he, Jairam, was now the instrument of that enterprise. The onus of setting up the B.N. Swamy Centre of Inter-Disciplinary Studies was on him.

'Sam and I—BNS is known as Sam, I call him Ben sometimes—' Dr Jairam said with charming self-deprecation, 'we spent hours at Rightwyn, weeks together, working out a blueprint for the Centre. You see now . . . you see that the crux lies in . . . in the management of knowledge and we have to *codify*—' the word catapulted from his rounded lips, plangent, emphatic '—codify the interconnection of human experience in all the relevant fields of study—economics, society, politics, the sciences, the environment, business, the arts—in working out the key conceptual assumptions of each and connecting it with life.' Clearly, he had made this point many times before, to a committee of important people perhaps, or he could even be quoting from a brochure.

'And we did it, Sam and I, in consultation with the best minds, trained in the best universities. We devised a blueprint for making knowledge relevant to our times. There's no point being hung up on the "classical"; how I hate that word, an excuse for purists and fuddy duddies, as if tagging it even on straw can turn it into gold! When I came back and presented it on a platter to the people here—they would have had to pay a consulting firm lakhs and lakhs for the model, I can tell you—you'd think they'd welcome it with open arms, but no!' Dr Jairam threw out his arms, widened his eyes and stopped suddenly in his tracks and Balaji, who almost fell over him, noticed that the man was a good twelve inches shorter than he was. 'Anyone would think that a college that complained of chronic lack of funds, with no money even . . . even to change the fused light bulbs in their classrooms, would be glad of getting that kind of corpus—of course, Sam had made the conditions of its use very clear—but no, they insisted on looking the gift horse in the mouth!'

'People here still behave as if they are living in the last century . . . and everything . . . *every thing* is treated like the spoils of war!'

Balaji checked his immediate impulse to egg Dr Jairam on and returned a bland smile to this open invitation to probe, signalling that he was at best a concerned observer, a guest, and not a curious meddler and did not want to be drawn into the politics of the institution. His natural disposition was to provoke, to play devil's advocate but this had got him into trouble with his programme director several times. Besides, experience told him that Dr Jairam would get it off his chest without much encouragement; he seemed to be on the look-out for a sympathetic ear.

'But it must be easier, now that colleges have been granted autonomy, to set up the new centre . . . no red tape . . .' Balaji said evenly, ready with the information he had. In keeping with the new unfastening of policy rules, the state government had, very recently, granted permission to select colleges to start their own post-graduation and even doctoral courses. He knew that for it had been the subject of one of his shows and the education minister had given him some good sound bytes.

Dr Jairam shook his head and clicked his tongue. 'Theoretically speaking, it should be, it should be . . . but it is easier to cut through red tape than the clutter in the minds of people too set in their ways. They just can't see that even while holding on to your values, you can and must progress. They do not understand that the world has changed, we have to get much more done in much less time and the same size does not fit all. The same old BA, MA, they make no sense now. We have to be nimble—change even as we are changing. Besides, people have the strangest fears, do you know, some of us here are scared of the Internet, they think it's evil!'

'No!'

'Yes! And there are some who will not work on computers, who refuse to touch a keyboard; they think it is beneath their dignity, that they are being demoted to typists.'

'We must realize—' Dr Jairam was addressing his imaginary committee, his voice had turned plummy again '—that we have a responsibility to our students. We have to teach them how to think clearly, and that's a matter of training you know, to teach them how to say exactly what they mean . . . the huge difference between correspondence and communication. Do you know,' he challenged Balaji, 'what the two most commonly misused terms in the English language are?'

Balaji shook his head.

'Yes and No!' Dr Jairam pronounced triumphantly. 'Our students say "yes" when they mean "no", "perhaps" and "possibly". And they *never* say "no".'

Dr Jairam had presumed that Balaji was on his side, which did not surprise Balaji. He was not even surprised that in the space of twenty minutes Dr Jairam had told him the story of his life. Notwithstanding the fact that middle-aged men tended to trot out précis of wisdom garnered from their experiences, he, Balaji, had a sympathetic effect on people. Since they heard his voice every morning, in the intimate space of their homes, people were inclined to treat him as an old friend.

They had reached the other end of the grounds, where the land was dug up into deep pits, preliminary to laying the foundations of another building. Dr Jairam walked away from Balaji to survey the half-filled pits and kicked the dislodged clods of earth about quite moodily. 'Work on this new building has stopped, for the present that is. I'll see to it that it is resumed as soon as possible . . .'

The Centre for Inter-Disciplinary Studies seemed beset with neo-natal problems. For once funds were in plenty, policy was on their side, but the teachers in the college seemed set against it. From what Balaji deduced, they had not taken well to Dr Jairam's recommendation that the new centre hire new faculty to teach the courses: 'We need people with a completely new approach, not the same old hackneyed class notes business. The profile of students must change too. We have to be in a position to attract the best talent.'

In retaliation the teachers on the committee set up to vet the proposal for the centre had vetoed a new building for it. 'Typical Indian mentality—when you can't get something, make sure

USHA K.R.

the other guy doesn't either,' Dr Jairam said. '. . . the half-dug foundations there . . . such a pity, we have so much space—soon these same people will be selling out to a shopping complex. Look at this place—' Dr Jairam gestured to the building across the grounds. 'Do you see how grimy it is? It hasn't had a lick of paint since I was a student here . . . so many parts of it are falling down . . . the cycle shed and the canteen have zinc sheet roofs. And now that we have the funds, they don't want it repaired—something to do with not finding the right architects for the restoration job, restoration if you please, as if this were a historical monument . . .' he forced a smile.

'Tell me Bali, do you think it is ennobling to live in squalor? When you can have bright buildings full of sunshine and fresh air, designed by the best architects and not some PWD contractor . . . is it consumerist to want to be healthy and live well? Do you think it does the soul good to be covered with cobwebs and rust?'

Before Balaji Brahmendra could decide whether this flow of rhetoric required an answer, the phone in Dr Jairam's pocket went off.

'Excuse me. Hi Ben! Hello!' he beamed into the phone and walked a distance away from Balaji. 'I was just talking about you and our centre to a young visitor here—'

Balaji listened as best as he could but was able to make out little except for the drawling Yesss and Nooo and the hearty laughs in between.

Dr Jairam came back from his conversation with B.N. Swamy a new man. 'Come now, enough of listening to problems,' he said briskly, shaking Balaji by the hand as if he had been doing all the complaining. 'I'll introduce you to the others. The done thing is for the seminar guest to have tea with the faculty, spend some time with them and then go on to address the students. Today,' he looked at his watch, 'we have made time for a long tea. The teachers are as keen to talk to you as the students. You may expect a grilling,' he reached up to chuff Balaji on the shoulder. 'I must tell you frankly, I had to fight to get you—you are truly a wild card entry.'

As soon as they entered the staff room, Balaji Brahmendra knew that he had walked into a fight. Dr Jairam's office, with its sofa and fresh flowers and a melamine tea set with matching coasters, was plush compared to this: bare wooden chairs, some with sagging plastic netting on their seats, and a row of metal almirahs looming on one side. A vase full of dusty plastic flowers tried to add some cheer to the room. Dr Jairam's office also had more lights and ventilators.

He introduced Balaji formally to the staff: 'Mr Shrinivas Moorty, our history lecturer; Dr Mohan Paul, chemistry; Ms Bela Bose, sociology and women's studies; Dr Cheluvamba, Sanskrit; and Dr Basavaraj, Kannada—' stressing the misters and doctors, making the pecking order clear. Dr Jairam left after making the introductions, and Balaji was on his own.

Tea was a guarded affair. They looked him over with reluctant curiosity. He knew then, what Dr J had meant when he said he had to fight to get him. The room too was quite oppressive. It was not the dark walls that crowded in—there was nothing that a few brush strokes of whitewash would not relieve—but the people. Balaji Brahmendra could feel their hostility as if it were a physical thing. Somebody handed him a paper plate and he looked down at the standard public function mix—SKC: sweet, khara, coffee—and he winced at the stuff, the orange kesari bhaat sliding about on its greasy bottom, the green chillies standing up at right angles in the mass of quickly congealing khara bhaat and the coffee in the thick dull white regulation 'railway station' cup, which he had to wedge against his mouth.

His college dropout story did not charm them. Too late he realized that it was not likely to be viewed in the right vein by a group of college teachers. 'I hope you are not planning to share it with the students,' the sociology teacher, a fat woman with greying hair and footwear so clunky that he had mistaken them first for prostheses, said severely.

'So, what are you planning to tell us this afternoon?' He turned, relieved to hear the flute-like tones and was rewarded to find a well-preserved lady in a chiffon sari and long hennaed ringlets by his side. The English teacher.

'The prospects in radio . . . what my job involves. I'm keeping my presentation short. That works best. I find that the questions are the most interesting part, things can get really scorching . . .'

The prospect of scorching questions seemed to have few takers. They looked at him with little enthusiasm.

'Well, since this is also a centre for media studies . . .' the history teacher, the man in a batik shirt that strained round his middle, whose head his sculptor friend would no doubt have pronounced 'fine', began with the discursive air and the precise intonation of one who was used to standing on a dais and commanding a class with his bare voice. 'Radio, traditionally and more so in a country like India, has been the instrument of social change, a means of reaching far flung neglected corners with information, entertainment, a message of hope . . . What is the purpose of your radio station?'

Such a sitting duck. He waited for a while. 'To make money,' he said with a straight face. 'Our purpose is to make money.'

The English teacher gasped and clicked her tongue as if he had said something naughty, and there were a few titters.

'Of course, of course—' he held up his hand and there was silence. 'Our mandate is to become part of the city, part of its collective unconscious,' he relented.

'But does the city want you?' Bela Bose of sociology, of the greying head and prosthetic footwear, and Shrinivas Moorty, history—neither of their names had been prefixed with a 'doctor', he remembered—exchanged conspiratorial smiles.

'Well, at any given time, one tenth of the people in and around Bangalore, almost five lakh of them are listening to our station, so our survey tells us, and at peak times it's ten lakh . . . On a normal day I get sixty SMSes per hour—'

'Now, when you play a cassette—'

'Music is not played off cassettes or even CDs. It is ripped and burnt on to hard discs and stored on servers.'

'The language, if you notice . . . so indicative . . .' Sociology murmured to History, speaking across him, 'ripped . . . burnt . . . hard . . . stored . . .'

'How do you have such a fund of small talk? Do you find it easy to prattle?'

The best way to answer such a question, he had decided long back, was to take it seriously.

'We have very strict rules of "prattle" as you call it. There is a certain amount of factual information that we have to impart—updates on current events, the weather, traffic snarls, sound bytes from the authorities—and we have to maintain a distinct tempo for each phase of the programme. In the beginning, I used to write everything down, working it down to the nanosecond. We have dry runs with live content. And there is a ticker at the bottom of the log editor—it's a small green light flickering at the bottom of the screen that tells me how much time I have to finish my "prattle". There are no second chances on radio; the spoken word cannot be taken back. If you goof up once, you're gone. I must admit, I have a lot of help; we'd be nowhere without technology.'

He saw Sociology's eyes flicker at the word, and knew that if he explained the detailed working of the machine, she would go completely blank, as most humanities or touchy-feely people did when they encountered the very basic technology. She must be one of those whom Dr Jairam was talking about, who thought of the Internet as the work of the devil.

'Why do you play so much Hindi film music? You claim to be part of Bangalore city yet you make fun of our Kannada language—'

Easy, easy here, he told himself. This man, on whose forehead the vermilion blazed in a bed of sandalwood paste to match his two angry eyes, must be the Kannada teacher. The other teachers had given up all pretence of indifference and were now gathered round him in a circle.

'Let me take the first part of your question first, sir. I don't decide what music to play on the station, the programme director does. And he decides based on what people want. Bangalore city *wants* the latest Bollywood songs. And every single song and jingle is coded and programmed into the log editor—the rotation policy for a song is decided for the week, sometime even for the month and that is done by the computer—to make doubly sure that I *don't* play what I want.'

'Besides Basavaraj,' History, in the loud batik shirt turned his back on Balaji, 'the whole point is that this is a city of migrants, you can't ignore the historical pattern of the city—'

'And as for making fun of our language,' he raised his voice a little and three of the lecturers who were about to make a private circle turned, broke up and came back to being part of the semicircle around him, 'surely, that's unfair.' He paused and smiled, expressing just the right amount of regret at the small mindedness in high places. 'We come to it from a position of strength, we believe that our language is confident of itself and rooted enough for us to take some liberties with it, make light of it. It is only the immature who are prickly about such things; we haven't lost our sense of humour and others will be more receptive to our language when they see it as funny—'

'So you dropped out of engineering college in the fourth year, a private college, you said. Your father must have paid a hefty capitation fee to get you in in the first place—'

A silence fell over the company and the hallowed trinity—Physics, Chemistry and Maths, two men and a woman—looked him over, coldly speculative.

'I have the option to go back,' he mumbled.

'What do you do the rest of the time?'

'I keep getting asked that all the time,' he sighed and smiled what he was sure was a disarming smile. 'It's a full time job, and a very demanding one. I face a live environment every day—just like a teacher in fact, but without your advantage of a captive audience. I have to persuade my audience to listen to me. I take few vacations, don't have much of a social life, never go partying over the weekend; I have to make sure I don't wake up with a hangover—ever! I can't get into fights either. I've had people ringing me up and saying, Hey Bali, what's the matter with you, you sound terrible!'

He had made a mistake. He knew immediately from the stony expressions of the women that he shouldn't have said 'hangover'.

'It must get very boring—' Batik shirt again, silky, dismissive, preparing to walk away.

'On the contrary,' Balaji Brahmendra held on to his temper, 'I find it very fulfilling. We get to meet a lot of people—positive minded achievers, who have done something with their lives, made a difference to others. Besides, I have my finger on the pulse of the youth of the city. They listen to me, I know that. I also know I have the power to influence their mindsets. Personally I find it very stimulating—I have to be quick witted, sharp with repartee, good at multitasking and above all know how to deal with people, the kind of things kids say to me . . . boys and girls in their teens. Why, your son or your daughter may be calling me—' he smiled at Batik shirt and saw his face go stiff and dead pan.

'Don't you think that's a little far fetched,' the man's voice was dry and stretched with anger, 'thinking you make a difference. Those achievers you are talking about, what is the "difference" they've made? Are they leaders of movements, purveyors of ideas, have they moved the masses? Are they true agents of social change? Tell me Mr Bali Brums, whom do you admire, who are your heroes?'

'I don't know about movements, Mr—?'

'Shrinivas Moorty.'

'I'm not into movements Mr Shrinivas Moorty. Individuals make sense to me. History may be your bread and butter, but it's the present that talks to me. An individual working for a winning cause. Now. Today. Touching the people he comes into contact with. A man like Bill Gates, say, or closer home, someone like Bindeshwar Pathak.'

'Who?'

'Haven't you heard of him? More relevant than any historical figure to me today. The man who has single-handedly tried to revolutionize the shit-hauling system in our country—' He was not dissatisfied with the outraged stares of some of them, and a smothered laugh from the chiffon-clad English teacher.

'For instance, do you know that this country generates nine hundred million litres of urine and hundred and thirty-five million kilograms of the other stuff every day and we do not have the technology to deal with it; we still have people to cart it away manually. Ninety per cent of our people do not have a toilet to which they can close the door—most of them do it in the open; I believe it would be like the whole of Europe, from the Elbe to the Pyrenees, squatting on its haunches.'

'You seem to know a lot about—'

'And here comes a man,' he swept Batik shirt and Third eye aside and gave his undivided attention to Chiffon sari, 'who did not stop with condemning the system, but came up instead with a win-win proposal, an alternative—a toilet that can be flushed with one mug of water, a pit system by which the solid matter turns in time into manure and finally an effluent treatment plant that can generate biogas—'

'Oh yes, their pay-and-use toilets—it's been used as an illustration of NGO–community partnership. I've used it in my class,' the sociology teacher came up on his left. But the rest of them were looking a little shocked at the turn the conversation had taken.

'I must say—' the history teacher began but was interrupted.

'Bali, the students are ready for you now,' Dr Jairam called out from the door. 'Sorry about the delay, but we had to change the venue from a classroom to the auditorium. Such a large gathering—I believe students from other colleges have also come.'

'How did you take such an interest in . . . this . . . the . . .' the English teacher fluted from his right.

'. . . in the scatological?' the history man sneered.

'In all this muck, you mean,' Balaji flashed his smile at the English teacher, ignoring the other. 'The last thing I did before leaving engineering college—almost made me reconsider—was this project on urban waste management. I travelled to Gujarat to meet—'

'Bali, the students are waiting—'

'Bali, please Bali,' the sociology teacher he realized was tugging at his left sleeve. 'Could I have your autograph, please? Now? Before you go into the hall to address the students. After that I'll never find you; it's for my daughter,' she looked guiltily at Batik shirt. 'She's such a fan of your show. And Bali, will you take her call the next time on your show? She's called so many times and she's never put through. Her name is Kirtana—'

'Bali!' Dr Jairam made an exaggerated show of pointing to his watch.

He ambled across the field, with the English teacher on one arm and the sociology teacher on the other, while the others followed like a lengthening trail of dust behind him. 'You know there was a doctor in China who did the same thing. And guess what he was called. Simply, Mr Latrine. He changed the hygiene of a whole province . . . actually convinced the peasants that their apples would taste a lot sweeter, fed on their own manure . . .'

'Could we visit your studio?'

'Sure, sign up for the RJ for a Day with Bali Brums but I must warn you the show is booked for a year in advance for the weekends—'

'Is it open to us as well, the offer?'

'Oh yes, to all of Bangalore. Welcome to my show!'

After that session, there had been a slew of emails from the students of the college and a few from the teachers as well; he couldn't connect them with their faces, and knew only that they had all been women. They loved his show and praised him to the skies. Most of them wanted to be invited to the studio. Some had told him all about themselves, their likes and dislikes and their tastes in music. Some had complained about the teachers: We heard that the history sir was rude to you, one wrote, but he's like that. An okay teacher; shows us some good films in his film club, but oh man, he thinks no end of himself and doesn't know what's what, lost in his own world.

His watch showed ten minutes to three. If he could quickly clear the rest of his mail, he would have time for a cup of coffee and a breath of air in the happy January sunshine, before beginning his preparation for the evening slot. There was an invitation from yet another college to participate in a panel discussion; word must have got round that Bali Brums was available and willing.

Someone wanted him to judge a fashion show—no more of that he decided, unless it was the Femina Miss India show, leading to Miss World. Even as he deleted that, a new one popped up from Nelly. You haven't replied to my morning's question, she said. Really, Nuisance Nelly.

'Hey Nelly, hey hey girl,' he wrote, 'drop that baggage, I can see it's bothering you. Make that your new year resolution—float as free as a bird in the sky. Drop all the old petty hatreds and resentments, the bad bad things that keep you from feeling good—'

And once that was done, he hit the delete button, sending them all into e-oblivion—Nelly, Tricia Frey, the Nigerian banker, the students who wanted him to judge their fashion show, and the hundred plus correct answers to the previous day's quiz.

nine

~

1

Neela returned to the office in the stillness of the afternoon. Her first feeling was one of relief; relief at being back in the safe, cool environs of the campus, out of reach of the snarling city. MTR was not the place for a workday lunch—the food was so good that the meal always turned out to be very heavy, and she was sure she would feel sleepy all afternoon. Besides it took too long. As soon as you entered you were herded into a waiting room and given chits to wait your turn by an attendant who behaved as if he was supervising the queue to a free kitchen. When you finally went in you had to sit on cold metal chairs and get up as soon as you finished, for you could see, all along, the beseeching eyes of those who were waiting their turn in the hallway beyond. But the food, when it came, was heavenly and both Dr Larson and Alka Gupta had fallen on the rasam and the rava idli as soon as they set eyes on it. They had insisted on dessert—fruit salad and ice cream drenched in vanilla, which gave it a curiously homely flavour, but Neela was not in a mood to enjoy it. After lunch, Dr Larson and Alka Gupta had gone off to meet someone instead of returning to the office, and she was annoyed that they hadn't told her earlier.

She hurried down the corridor, faintly guilty: taking visiting researchers to temples or shopping or on long leisurely lunches in the office car meant strictly for Dr Subramanyam was not quite done, but at the same time she composed the magnificent put downs with which she would crush anyone who dared to bring it up.

As soon as she entered her wing of the building she paused, waiting to catch an unwary snatch of conversation, a sound even, and was rewarded. From Daisy's cubicle she heard sharp repetitive 'kha-tacks'—Daisy was cutting her nails in the office again. Neela had warned her many times, saying that one did not attend to one's toilet in the office—it was as bad as shaving one's underarm in public—but it had little effect on Daisy. Next, she would proceed to paint her nails and the smell of acetone would spread through their open office. Daisy, Neela would call out, Daisy Dee, after a popular brand of brassieres but that just seemed to amuse Daisy more.

The door to her section of the office was standing open and the grey stone floor was messy with wet footprints. How Sukhiya Ram got the soles of his slippers wet in the men's bathroom was something she did not understand, but chose not to dwell upon either. There was a small pile of letters on her table. She settled into her chair and turned to them, ready to get on with her routine chores. Systematic by nature, she liked to get things done in order. Out of the pile of letters, she picked out the most colourful envelopes first. These generally contained promotional material that could be thrown out straightaway. Dr Subramanyam received a variety of letters—there was an invitation to inaugurate an exhibition of office furniture, a quotation from shamiana renters, and the usual official letters, which she accorded degrees of importance. Those which she thought did not merit his attention, she dealt with herself. The one from the astrologer in Chamarajpet giving him feedback on his son's horoscope she put right on top of his pile. National Trust College, she thought, had become very ambitious of late—there were two proposals from them. One from a film studies person, a Shrinivas Moorty, asking for funds to upgrade their equipment—which she threw into the dustbin without a second thought—and another from the head of their Centre for Inter-Disciplinary Studies suggesting a collaborative workshop—which was a cleverer way of asking for money—that she put into the Important pile. The last letter was a promotional leaflet from a certain Rajitha Group of Hotels promising a 'naver befor experiance'. The name seemed familiar and she paused. When she recognized the name—it had been plain Rajitha Lodge some months ago—a needletrack of shame coursed all over her, causing her to look over her shoulder to see if anyone was watching. Sure enough, when she looked again at the address on the envelope she saw that it was addressed to Prithvi Kumar. She tore up the leaflet and stuffed the pieces into her handbag; she did not want to leave any evidence of it in the office.

Sukhiya Ram came in with the tea, which she took without comment, and then opened her email. There was just one message; Dr Subramanyam had written to say that he was cutting his trip short by two weeks and returning in two days' time. The man had a right to come and go as he liked—it was his office and he was the boss—but immediately it filled her with anxiety. She ran through all the things she had to get done before he came: the accounts, a list of the funding proposals, the visitors over the last two months and their cards, a progress report on all his projects . . . And then she remembered the letter she had not sent.

She fumbled with her keys, scratching against the keyhole, but the key would not turn. In a panic she wrenched the key out of the keyhole and, as the drawer slid open along with the bunch of keys, she understood why. The letter was gone. As was Alka's cheque.

'Sukhiya! Daisy!'

Daisy came running in first, her eyes wide, her blood-red fingernails pressed against her face. 'What happened madam?'

'My drawer has been opened!'

Sukhiya rushed in then, rubber chappals flapping, holding a dripping mug and a washcloth. 'Madam, I could hear you at the other end of the corridor—'

'There was a . . . important documents in the drawer. They are missing now.'

'Oh, that letter. Prithvi sir came and took it,' Daisy smiled.

Neela choked her words back but a small growl escaped.

'I knew his letter was in your drawer madam,' Sukhiya said simply, 'and your drawer was unlocked, so I gave it to him.'

'Never mind whether my drawer was locked or not, you had no business opening it—'

'But the letter was two months old madam; Subramanyam sir signed it before he went—'

They looked puzzled, unable to understand why she was so angry.

'Anyway, Prithvi sir said it was too late. He's already got another job. In Hyderabad. Reported there even. In fact he came to give us sweets. I've put Dr Subramanyam's box in his room.'

Daisy held out a small cardboard box with two round white globs and half of a third, its soft insides squished out on the floor of the box.

'Still, you should not have opened my drawer,' Neela said lamely, making a face at the box, as she tried to think, to anticipate what the repercussions of this could be and how she could circumvent them.

'Prithvi sir said that if he had got it in time he might have reconsidered the Hyderabad offer.'

'What Prithvi Kumar says or does is none of our concern. He no longer works here. What you must remember is that whatever the compulsions, however urgent the matter,' she heard the customary authority return to her voice, 'unless I instruct otherwise, nothing in my room is to be touched, much less, given away. And the cheque? There was a cheque there too.'

'On your table madam. Below paperweight.'

Neela saw it then, under her very nose.

'Shall I send it to Alka madam?' Daisy reached out for it before Neela could say anything. 'It is also three weeks old—'

'Right, get going both of you. Dr Subramanyam is returning day after tomorrow. He has sent me mail.'

'I know madam. He sent me mail too.'

After they left Neela sat at her desk, the keys to the drawer still in her hand. They must have known about it all along, both of them. If the matter ever came up she could always say that it had slipped her mind. What with Dr Subramanyam not being there, she had so many things to do; she practically had to run the place. And neither Sukhiya nor Daisy would dare bring it up on their own.

She sat still for a while, thinking. She looked out of the window, at the bright winter afternoon sunshine, listening to the sounds around her—she could hear the faint hum of the traffic, the clinking of spoons as someone made tea in a nearby cubicle, and then she became aware of the bird calls—the insistent coo of a cuckoo close by and the answering, faraway whoop of the crow pheasant. Sukhiya and Daisy had given her a way out. Her dilemma—what to do with the letter—had been solved by them. Perhaps they had even saved her skin for if Dr Subramanyam had found out about the letter first, it might have meant a memo or a delayed promotion or worse, and there were people in the Centre who would love to see her humbled, even humiliated. But now, things had taken their own course, propelled by their own momentum.

And then she turned, as she had done so often in the past, to the disembodied voice at the other end of her email query and tried to school her chaotic thoughts into a semblance of order, into information that could be communicated.

After a while she realized that the corridor had turned quiet. There was no sound from Daisy's cubicle, neither could she hear the slap of Sukhiya's slippers. Some time later, she heard them in the corridor, Alka and Daisy.

'But Daisy,' Alka was protesting in her high pitched voice, its diction sharp and clear, 'this cheque is dated three weeks back—'

'Yes, I know Alka,' she heard Daisy reply. 'What to do? Sometimes the accounts office makes mistakes.'

2

One magical term in school, when Neela was twelve, she had topped her class in all subjects. For a few weeks she was the most popular girl in class, she had friends, and on her thirteenth birthday, her small drawing room was full and her mother had served cake and chips, beaming from ear to ear. 'Our Neeli will be a doctor, what do you say Mani,' her father had said, half-seriously. But that was merely a flash in the pan and Neela had slid from excellent to good and finally to average by the time she finished school. Of her friends, only Jessy's daughter Molly, the old faithful, remained. While her father still continued to hope she would be a doctor, her mother came up with a scheme that would take the shortest route to a government job, and her aunts started pressing eligible boys upon her. Neela enrolled for a degree in commerce in an evening college. In the mornings, on alternate days she attended a course in computers and one in typing and short-hand. As for her aunts' eligible boys, she swatted them away impatiently, knowing that they would not come up to scratch. Of Lakshmi aunty's candidates only one had resulted in a meeting—the one-armed engineer, as Lakshmi aunty herself referred to him. His credentials were impeccable—he belonged to a renowned old Mysore Smartha Brahmin family, well known to theirs, he had done his graduation and his post-graduation from an Indian Institute of Technology, one of the premier engineering institutions not just in the country but in the world—and except for his obvious 'physical defect', the result of his mother taking the wrong medication while he was still in her womb, he was as good as perfect. He said he would like to meet the girl first, before the families met, which gave Neela hope. They met in a place of his choosing, which turned out to be a small smoky restaurant, its laminated table-tops greasy, the tables placed so close to each other that if you sat back in your chair you could easily join the conversation at another table. He told her that he was a broad-minded person and caste and creed did not matter to him. He was ready to overlook many imperfections in an alliance that was otherwise congenial. He asked her no questions about herself, her plans, what she wanted out of life or even who her favourite film star was and volunteered no information about himself either. To be fair to him, he looked a little doubtful in the course of the evening, even anxious as he searched her face, trying to read her response, and all along his left hand in its long sleeved shirt sat quietly in his lap, tucked between his thighs. She had been very angry with Lakshmi aunty after that and not spoken to her for days. And then, she refused to meet any of Lakshmi aunty's other boys.

After getting her degree, Neela duly applied for the post of executive assistant in the Centre for Socio-Economic Studies, one of the many organizations directly under the ministry for human resources development, which, she had learnt, combined the promise of tenure as in a government job with some of the comforts of the private sector—staircases without paan spittle staining the corners, no end-of-the-corridor water dispenser standing in a puddle of stagnant water, clean rooms with curtains, and lounges with sofas and flower arrangements on the table.

Dr Subramanyam had picked her from an exacting list of candidates and his judgement had proved right. She was the perfect fit for the job—a trained secretary who could manage office accounts, even read a balance sheet, handle computers independently, knew enough English to write a letter without glaring mistakes of spelling and grammar, and above all, one whose ambitions did not override her capability. He had seen that young people these days had an eye only on what they could get; everything was just fodder for their resumés and they were out of the door the minute they spotted something more attractive. But Neela had just enough skill at everything to be competent at her job, without aspiring for something bigger, without aspiring to replace *him* some day. Moreover, she was a woman and belonged technically to a minority community—twin feathers in his administerial cap—which met the considerations of equitable justice that his quasi-government institution specified.

For Neela, for the first time there was no ambiguity about her position and standing. She did not have to speculate about what the other person was thinking about her, under what slots she was being pigeon-holed, what signals her name, her address and her parentage were sending out, what concessions and adjustments the other person was making, or what she would have to do to match the impressions she imagined they had acquired of her. She was neither being asked, however tacitly, to stand tall and proud and unapologetic nor play down certain 'awkward' facts—the pieces of the jigsaw that did not fit when she was a child, however hard she tried, which she just shoved under the mattress or crammed into the space between the balcony and its wooden railing after trying for some time. Here, everything about her was put down on paper. There was no room for speculation. Her curriculum vitae was her advance guard, her passport to the new world. Neela's curriculum vitae—all of it, her middle-of-the-road aspirations, her middling marks, her mixed parentage, the confluence of communities—represented in a way the nation's tryst with destiny, that its first prime minister had so grandiosely proclaimed from the ramparts of the Red Fort when the country became independent, the nation's tryst with modernity, not so much a break from the past but a correction of it, a hope that the baggage of the old would be left behind. Ambitious, watchful, pushing herself hard with what little she had, Neela was the hope of the nation.

In the Centre for Socio-Economic Studies, in the vast sea of heads, deputies, directors, supervisors, executives, incharges, chairpersons and convenors, she knew where she stood; she was no longer a creature of uncertain provenance. In the labyrinthine structure, her place was known and secure. And once she was on a sure footing there, she learnt to use the space that it provided to her advantage. From her position of strength, she saw herself as unique, a hybrid, and learnt to harness it. In time, she could say casually to an Antonia Larson that she felt equally at home in a temple and a church, and invite her home to subject her parents to close scrutiny. Along with the promise of permanent employment, there was the actual power she wielded as an efficient executive attached to an influential and glamorous but largely absent boss; it was almost like running a mafia operation.

And into this careful scheme there had been introduced of late the irresponsible element, those who did not play by the rules of the game. People like Alka Gupta and even Prithvi Kumar—with no roots and no loyalties, with no hankerings for permanence, flitting like bees from flower to flower, intent on building private honeycombs.

An Alka Gupta she could handle. But Prithvi Kumar had brought in an unexpected twist by being . . . well, a man. Dr Subramanyam had hired him as a consultant to conduct an audit of the department, to put the house in order since the department's activities were getting so varied that they were getting out of hand—there were so many projects going on simultaneously, so many reports being generated, so many people coming and going. He needed someone to give him an outsider's perspective, the mother of all reports, a bulleted view of what was going on in his kingdom.

Neela began by treating the newcomer—the tall young man with lips like full, perfectly shaped bows turning a little in on themselves at the edges—with the same circumspect coldness with which she greeted anything new, but he just ignored her. Her standard methods of hedging and prevaricating did not seem to bother him: 'I'll wait for the report till Dr S returns,' he'd say easily or 'Why don't you and I go look for it in the library together?' When he first invited her to have coffee with him—at the office canteen—she declined from force of habit; moreover, she never stepped into the canteen, always getting Sukhiya to fetch her coffee in a flask, which she drank out of a cup and saucer. 'It's too much of a bother to go to the canteen, too noisy, and they serve in steel tumblers,' she said. 'Then I will have coffee with you in your room,' he said, 'and we can discuss the report while we enjoy ourselves, it'll be fun,' without hesitation, without thinking for a moment that it could be anything other than fun for her. And thus their daily twenty-minute morning meetings began for which Sukhiya brought on a tray two china cups of coffee that Neela paid for; Prithvi never offered to.

Without realizing it and without meaning to she found herself cooperating with him, and making sure everyone else did. 'Sukhiya,' she would say, 'see that Prithvi sir's computer is dusted and all six of the pencils on his table are sharpened.' Like water, she gave way. Her standard five-point ignore-meter, her instinct to stall things till she was sure she was in control, her habitual way of working—she surrendered it all, turning almost coy in her loyalty.

One evening, when they were in the parking lot together, as

his Japanese-collaboration motorbike sputtered and choked and her desi moped purred to life, he told her what a useless vehicle she had. 'Time to go for a new one,' he smiled. 'This model has long been eased out of the market; you won't get any spares. What were you thinking when you bought this one—or maybe you weren't? This machine guzzles petrol.' And instead of pointing out the obvious, she had laughed happily, taken by his lopsided logic. Another day, during their morning coffee ritual, he stopped suddenly, smiled and said: 'You shouldn't wear orange, you know, makes you look darker. Yellow, that's more your colour.' They so startled her, these audacious comments of his, like squibs suddenly going off underfoot, that she forgot to take umbrage at their personal tone, forgot too that she had a reputation as a martinet to protect. Instead, she looked forward to them, relaxing in his mischief, looking for further temerity, ready even to grant him license. Neelu, he'd slip in suddenly or even Neeli, and at that she was close to tears because it reminded her so much of her father's 'My Mani' and 'Kanmani', the only evidence of his love for her mother.

So disarming was Prithvi Kumar that he could draw out trivia and confidences in the same breath, almost as if they were the same thing. She hated, she told him, beetroot curry with Bengal gram seasoning and coconut, the staple of all canteens, which was why she would not eat in the canteen, admitting in the same breath that Dr S could be a pompous bore at times and that there was a certain tree near the gate that she never walked under because it reminded her of her grandfather who had fallen in the bathroom one day.

They started going home together in the evenings since they both had to travel in the same direction, and Neela's Indian-made khatara tried heroically to keep up with his 'foreign collaboration' power machine. It was also natural that they should stop on the way for a snack or fruit juice, and that most of the time Neela should foot the bill. It was a small thing, she told herself, for the amount of pleasure he was giving her. 'Do you like music? Would you like to go to a fusion concert? An Indian band is playing with a jazz group,' he asked her one evening when they had stopped for fruit juice. 'Yes,' she said immediately, 'when?', though she was unfamiliar with fusion and associated jazz with a dissonance of instruments, punctuated by sharp blasts from a trumpet-like creature. Her own taste veered towards Kannada film music and the Tamil hymns in her church. The only musical programmes she had been to so far were the film hit countdown 'nites', where local singers belted out popular film songs and the programme ended in a raffle—she had won a water cooler in such a lucky dip once.

But at that fusion concert, nothing had mattered—not the music, nor her carefully chosen butter-cup yellow salwar-kameez—other than the fact that Pushpa Rani and Alka Gupta were also there, that Alka had greeted Prithvi Kumar with a casual hug, and that both women were on terms of easy familiarity with him.

'Your friends,' she started referring to them loftily thereafter. 'I must applaud your democratic spirit,' she said, 'mixing equally with all kinds of people; best friends with both a typist and a research scholar.' Every day, a fresh remark would wrench itself out from her: 'I bet you liked that dress that madam wore—' she would make an elaborate play of not making clear which of them she was talking about. 'Tell her please not to stitch all the mirrors and sequins of India on to one dress. It may cause a traffic accident if she glitters so much.' Or, 'Why do your friends look like refugees from a drought-stricken land? Don't they eat? Look at them. That other one, how can she sit? She has no bums to sit on—see how thin she is. Aren't they fed at home?' And he would laugh, enjoying her sharp comments, adding a few rejoinders of his own, never letting her know what they said about her.

Then had come the invitation. To go out with him for the weekend. On work, he added, quickly looking away. He had an assignment in Mysore, he explained, and he could do with some assistance, some one who could look after the paper work. She would be paid, of course. Will Pushpa Rani and Alka be going too, she asked tartly. No, he replied seriously. You. Only you.

This then was the moment of truth. She trembled at how clearly,

USHA K.R.

how unambiguously she had recognized it. A weekend business trip. They would stay in Mysore. They would leave on Friday evening and return on Sunday. In between somewhere, she would risk her one chance at love. All her years of magazine reading were finally paying off. She was trusting in her convictions and following her heart. Every single tip, every caution, every reminder, she summoned. The rest of the week was spent in a feverish drill of shampooing, blow drying, plucking, waxing, massaging, firming, supporting and finally, relaxing in a bath of aromatic oils—she spent a month's salary in preparation. In a further burst of recklessness she went into the women's wear shop that had come up in the newly constructed mall, and from its hushed, perfumed and lime-lit Funwear section, bought herself a black lace negligee, and some cute baby doll pyjamas—just in case.

That Friday evening she left work early and as she was leaving, Prithvi, who was standing with Alka and the others, came towards her and said in an undertone: Slight change of plans, I won't be able to get away for some time from here; Dr S wants to see me. I'll meet you there directly, around eight. Don't be late. Oh, she had said, oh. But that had not disconcerted her. She had to get off on Mysore road on the stop after Ramanagaram. The bus stop was named after the hotel—Rajitha Lodge.

The lodge, to her surprise, was a little seedy. Hardly the venue for a business meeting. The large garden that seemed to have been laid out initially with care had now become a large bare field, its lawn bald, its paths overgrown and the ornamental shrubs overtaken by weeds and discarded rubber tyres. The place seemed deserted but there was a booking in the name of Prithvi and Party. A very young boy in a stained shirt stood at the reception counter and he came out from behind the counter and led her to her room, whistling all the way down the corridor. The room itself was quite large and had both a TV set and a phone. But it smelt musty and she could see the dust in cobwebby swathes under the beds. It was, she noticed, a room with a double bed—two singles joined together. But the TV was working and there was hot water in the bathroom.

She allowed herself a long, luxurious bath, anointing herself with Ever Youth, after which, as the magazines had advised her, she popped a cardamom in her mouth and a small ball of cotton wool soaked in her favourite perfume into her bra, switched on the television, and waited.

A loud blast of music from the TV woke her up. For a few minutes she lay stupefied till she realized where she was. It was past eleven o' clock. Her eyes trailed the bare walls of the room, the plywood table and chair in the corner, the curtains with jagged holes in them as if they had been attacked by rats, the water jug and the two steel tumblers next to it and came to rest on her black lace negligee spreadeagled expectantly on the bed and her new fluffly bedroom slippers laid out on the floor. In the bathroom, when she was having her bath earlier in the evening, she had noticed, stuck at random on the mirror, several felt-tipped stick-on bindis, large and small, black and red, and had thought of the women, fully unclothed, even wet perhaps and in the middle of their bath, coming upon these vital but everyday brands upon their foreheads, without which they did not feel fully dressed, and taking them off, with a click of impatience perhaps, with amusement or tenderness or resignation; perhaps they had reflected on the small creature that sat between their forefinger and thumb for a moment, before slapping it on to the mirror, their fingers quick and dripping. And now, she wondered about the nameless women who had passed through this room, each leaving an anonymous but very personal mark upon the mirror, a gesture of intimacy made instinctively but amounting merely to the violation of a minor rule of bathroom etiquette, women whose beings were coded in a dot which only added to the spots rapidly collecting dirt on the blackening mirror.

She knew then, without a doubt, that he was not coming. She reached for the phone and called the reception. Where is the rest of the party, she asked. What party, he asked back. Prithvi and Party of the New Generation Office is headed for a business meeting, she said imperiously. What business meeting, he said and she knew that he was smiling into the receiver.

USHA K.R.

Two things struck her immediately—it was amazing how clear headed she became at once. She could not spend the night in that room. She had to get back and show her face at work the next day. Her presence had to be registered. The office worked half-days on Saturdays and she had applied for leave that Saturday. Instinctively she knew that she would find Prithvi Kumar in the office the next day.

The last bus leaves in five minutes, Reception told her. It has already left Mysore and it should stop over here briefly. Get me a seat on it, she replied, even as she bundled her negligee and pyjamas into her bag. It is a government bus, you have to wait at the bus stop on the road, Reception replied.

Nonchalance. That was the key. She slipped into the office in the morning, as unobtrusively as possible, gritting her teeth at Sukhiya's bright 'Madam has not taken leave today, she has come to work!' She thought she saw Alka and Pushpa Rani eye her doubtfully but could not be sure. But it was Prithvi's reaction that she waited to see.

He came towards her as soon as he saw her. 'Oh, you're here!' he exclaimed, walking in through the open door. 'I'm sorry,' he tried to whisper confidentially, 'I was held up—'

'Did you really think I'd turn up?' she said loudly, not caring who heard. 'You must be mad if you did,' her laugh broke into a harsh cackle. 'What do you take me for?'

For days after that, she ruminated over her behaviour, growing breathless at her stupidity. How could she have agreed to such a tryst? A lodge on a highway—even a child knew what that meant. A stop-over for trucks and truck drivers. How he must be laughing at her with Pushpa Rani and Alka. She couldn't tell from their behaviour but she was being fierce with them to pre-empt any sly remarks. To Prithvi, she stopped talking. Showing up at work the next day had saved her. She was lucky she had not been spotted by someone she knew and she had been careful enough not to put her real name and address in the register at the lodge. The whole thing could easily have blown up in her face. In a gush of relief, she said a special novena in the name of the

Mother, and kept repeating it in her mind whenever she could. The days of routine lessened her agitation and her behaviour in the office returned to a semblance of normalcy. But that was not enough. She needed to talk to someone. She needed a friend, a dispassionate, objective voice of reason she could confide in but one who would ask no questions, demand no explanations and pass no judgement. Molly would not do; in fact her docility was a hindrance. She could be shocked so easily.

Being in love was a state of mind that did not suit her, Neela realized. It made her pliable and stupid. She was more comfortable hissing and cackling. Prithvi Kumar would now know what it meant to cross her.

The opportunity, when it presented itself, was so simple that at first she was sure there was a hidden snag in it, something very obvious that she could not see and which would trip her up and give her away. But the more she thought about it, the simpler it seemed. Only, the timing had to be right. Her faith in the system, this saurian creature of checks and balances, as always would stand her in good stead.

Twice a year, once in December and once in June, the two section heads—the head of research and the head of higher education—went through the grand ritual of issuing and renewing contracts. Over the last few years, in keeping with the trends, the Centre had stopped hiring staff on a 'permanent' basis and the number of employees on contract had risen. The rules governing their employment were nebulous, which rendered the process of employing them and renewing their contracts complicated, with the Centre doing its best to plug all the loopholes through which a claim for permanence or perks could be made. It was a labyrinthine administrative process, one that called for approvals, checks, verifications and validations, and much to-ing and fro-ing between section heads and central administration. There had been instances when contracts had got lost in the involved process—an errant clerk, an indifferent peon, a missing file—and though they were recovered in the end, it usually took time and much depended on the cooperation of the administrative staff. There were some anxious days of waiting for the contractees but mostly things ended well as those whose tenures would not be extended usually knew about it and were given the opportunity to leave. This was of course, in the ordinary course of things. If one intended mischief, things could go differently.

That year, the day the contracts came from the administrative section, brought in a bag with self-conscious importance by Sukhiya, for Dr Subramanyam to countersign, he was in the throes of leaving for his three-month long fund-raising sojourn. The stack of envelopes lay casually on his desk for two days but he did not have a minute to spare for them. On the morning of his departure, with the receiver of the phone stuck to his left ear, he signed them all and called Neela in. He hadn't the time to hand them out personally, shaking each person by the hand and making the small speech that he had composed for each of them. It was a nuisance, really, he said. He wished admin had thought of a simpler way of doing these things. She just had to see that Sukhiya Ram delivered all the envelopes to the right people. 'It's a pain, but it's important. See that it's done at the earliest,' Dr Subramanyam said as he stepped into his car and signalled to the chauffer to drive off.

Dr Subramanyam left for his trip. The letters shifted from his desk to her drawer where she let them stay. The contractees hovered anxiously round Dr Subramanyam's door. She let them stew for a few days more before sending the letters out with Sukhiya. All except one. She saw an anxious Alka fumble with the envelope in the corridor, too impatient to go to her desk, and her face relaxing in relief. She watched the temporary office accountant run to the phone to inform her mother that her job was secure for another year. She saw Prithvi Kumar the following week looking down the corridor many times, at the closed door of Dr Subramanyam's office, puzzled, resentful and then angry. She saw him start towards it determinedly, as if he intended to search the room, and then come to a halt just outside the door. In a week, if he did not get that letter, he would have to leave.

In that week, Prithvi Kumar tried all his tact and charm to find out what had happened, but nobody could tell him for sure. Some of the assistants in the administrative block swore that they had seen the letter, others smiled and said they were sorry, they didn't remember, there were so many contracts that went out at one time, and no, the woman in charge of the accounts copies was away on maternity leave. He wouldn't have the courage to come out and ask her, Neela knew, and there was no way he could ask Dr Subramanyam because when Dr Subramanyam was travelling she was the official conduit of communication between him and the office.

One letter gone missing out of so many—well, she wasn't responsible for routine administrative glitches. And now three months were almost up and she had other things to think about. She had to prepare for Dr Subramanyam's homecoming. She was glad she hadn't been there that morning when Prithvi Kumar had come, glad too that the letter had finally gone. As her favourite person had said that morning, she was ready to drop all her baggage and move on. How did he know, she wondered. How could he divine her thoughts and moods so accurately? Some people, she had read somewhere, just had the gift of pre-science.

3

Pushpa Rani had been waiting for over an hour but the doctor had not yet come. The small lobby was over-crowded; there was a bench out in the corridor as well, crammed with people, equally hopeful and resigned. At the end of the lobby was a tiny cabin, separated from the rest of the space by a glass door with black film stuck patchily on it—it was torn in two places and people had no qualms about putting their eye to these naked spots to see if the doctor was in—and inside sat one of the best homeopathic doctors in the city. He had been recommended to her by Philomena, who worked with her at the call centre, and whose headaches he had successfully brought under control. His medicines had given her father so much relief that Pushpa Rani put her visits to him on par with her visits to the temple—if god moved in mysterious ways, so did he. The doctor was always late—a speciality, Pushpa Rani discovered, of homeopathic doctors—and he was as inscrutable as the powders he dispensed in small folded-up packets. He usually said nothing as he listened to the litany of her father's symptoms, taking notes now and then, and then at the end of her recital, scribbled a prescription down on a postage-stamp-sized square of paper, which his compounder translated into several packets of fine white powder. But these strange potions seemed to do her father good.

Outside, the bright winter evening light turned milky as the sun began to set, and yet again an impatient man asked the attendant when the doctor would be coming. Soon, the attendant said soothingly, very soon. And that last 'soon, very soon' was said in so mechanical and perfunctory a manner that Pushpa Rani realized the doctor would not come that evening. At that very moment it struck her that her visit to the temple too had been fruitless. She had gone to give thanks to Him for the many good things He had done for her—her promotion and the bank loan and the new friends, but His door had been closed. It was a sign she could not ignore. Her mind sallied further—not just a sign, it was a bad omen. It had begun with the locket. That morning the gold locket with the red stone at its heart, whose 'golden waters' had nursed her to health and which she had never taken off since the day she had first worn it, broke. The chain snapped into two and fell by the bucket when she was taking a bath. She had taken it to the jeweller to be repaired immediately, but all day her hand travelled to her neck in an unconscious gesture, to caress the unaccustomed hollow between her collar bones where she should have encountered the reassuring hardness of stone. But her silver friendship ring, with two hands interlocked, which Ranjit had given her, was safe on her finger and she was growing quite attached to it.

A few months ago, just after she met Ranjit, some of them went out together after the evening shift. It was not the same as having pizza and Coke after work, or even eating out of knives and forks in a restaurant with tablecloths; they had gone to a place called a lounge bar where the lighting was dim, where there were no proper chairs but a lot of squishy shapeless leather sofas that sunk low when you sat on them and no waiters came to take their order as soon as they sat down. Other than a man and a woman who were dressed in identical black suits and who stood behind the counter minding their own business, there seemed to be no staff around, and very few customers. It was only when she saw a boy about their age walking across to a group of people—a mix, she noticed, of Indians and foreigners, some of whom looked either Chinese or Japanese, but it was very difficult to tell these days when everybody coloured and streaked their hair and dressed the same—with a tray of differently coloured drinks that she realized he was a waiter.

Ranjit ordered beer, Philomena said she wanted something called shandy, and the others ordered what they wanted and when it was her turn she said, 'I want that blue-coloured drink that I saw you carrying just now, in a tall glass with something red floating on it.'

'You must mean a Blue Curacao. And that something red is a cherry.'

'Whatever,' she said. After all, she was paying for it.

The menu too was very different. She did not expect to see the thali meal listed on it, but she was surprised by the absence even of naan and palak paneer and kalmi kabab. Instead they had served little eats, small pieces of bread with different toppings, things she had never eaten before.

The place started to fill up after some time, a boy started strumming a guitar all by himself in one corner, and their own conversation, which was always loud, was muted, like the lights and the sounds and the furniture.

'I like it,' she told Ranjit when they left. 'Let's come here again.'

Ranjit laughed and said, 'Not too soon. The prices are too steep, even for us.'

'Pam hasn't been to a disco yet,' Philomena, whose work-name was Phil, said. 'We must take her dancing.'

For New Year, their Qualis, instead of taking them to work, took them to Coorg. Surprise, Ranjit said, just for one day. We'll be back tomorrow. You are crazy, Philomena said, you want to drive two hundred kilometres, just like that. Besides it will be so cold in the hills. That's the whole point, Ranjit replied. The river will be beautiful and I want you all to taste pandi-curry. Pushpa Rani was thrilled actually that he had sprung the surprise. That was what she liked about him—he was always coming up with something different. In the morning, on Ranjit's farm they went fishing in the stream and roasted the fish they caught on the banks and in the evening, they strung up lights in the garage and borrowed a huge music system. The noise it produced was terrific and the music blasted into the night. Pushpa Rani danced her way into the new year, the first time ever to western music, but she was not unprepared or fazed by it for she had seen it on TV and in films all her life. She and Philomena turned out a biryani as best as they could. People went in and out of the shed all night long—Ranjit's brothers and cousins, his parents and friends—and they all complimented her on her cooking, but she did not really care for her mind was only on the dancing and the throb of the music.

In the cold soft night, they were warm in the hot shed. If it grew to be too much all they had to do was step out and take a few turns on the path, with the hills and the forests looming around them and the clear star-scrunched sky spread above. The gyrating strobe lights threw shadows on the walls and splashes of colour on the people, reflecting off a face there or an arm here, catching the dazzle of a sequinned shirt or the glitter of an earring. The lights fell on her and Ranjit dancing together, on her calves and ankles—braced to meet her new high heeled shoes—and on Ranjit's arms—lean and veined and changing colour—and at that moment she felt something urgent leap within her; the music stopped, her body fell away from her, she was pure heartbeat. Somewhere beyond the horizon of her mind she heard a distant conch resonating.

The day she returned from Coorg, she was disoriented and snappy—she was even curt with her father when he asked her why she had stayed out all night without letting them know. This is what happens, her mother remarked, if you make too much of your daughters. They start to think that they are the same as men. She should listen to her brother now. After all, he too is earning.

Pushpa Rani had immediately sought the temple out. She realized that lately she had been visiting the temple more often, to pray, to offer her apologies to the Lord, to keep her faith. Perhaps it was after she met Ranjit, or perhaps it was because her friend Philomena was going away to Dubai or perhaps she was more tired of late and her back was hurting, but she found herself growing more impatient, and bickering with her family. She was afraid she would be rude to a caller one of these days and that would never do for she would lose her advantage. She, who had kept her temper and good sense under extreme provocation, could not afford to give in now. Whenever she could, she went to the temple, for the still face of the idol, lit up in the dark sanctum by the smoky lamps, quietened her fluttering heart and the stone pillars, cool against her skin when she rested her head on them, helped restore her equanimity, her good spirits.

Today, a darshan of the deity had been denied to her. She did not even get to peep at Him through the small open square in His door, or even get as far as the tray with the vermilion and the vibhuti and the flowers. She was forestalled by those three women from the Centre for Socio-Economic Studies. She had barely recognized them at first and then memories of that place came flooding back, far more copiously than she cared. The other two women looked the same and welcomed her warmly, but Neela Gopalrao looked more sour than she remembered—sour of heart and sour of face, that was what she was. The last time she had seen that sour look on Neela Gopalrao's face was when she had caught Prithvi Kumar talking to Alka or to her. The 'lick of lime look' Prithvi Kumar would say wickedly when he saw Neela approaching, her sari pleats abustle with disapproval. Prithvi Kumar had been one of the good things about the Centre.

USHA K.R.

In fact Ranjit reminded her of him. He had had the gift of making a humdrum day come alive with nothing at all, by reading the headlines of the newspaper aloud in a funny voice or imitating somebody's gestures or even pretending to read your palm. And what a monkey he had made of Neela Gopalrao! Anyone could see that she was besotted with him.

Now, Pushpa Rani would have handled a person like Neela very differently, now that she knew the power of compassion, now that she knew that most people were like worms in their underground holes afraid to put their heads out into the sunlight. For everyone, she knew, had a story, a path down which they had walked, a journey that had formed them, that they were indistinguishable from. That story, she also realized, could change; it depended on how you told it to yourself. The same events could be seen very differently, the same people could become better or worse, kinder or harsher; a person you had not noticed before could become a friend. You could weave yourself into your story with the threads of providence or make a hole in its side to let some air in and perhaps, climb out on an unravelling skein.

When she thought of her own story, when she imagined herself telling it to others, as she had to the reporter from *Nation Today*, she saw it as a saga of grace and deliverance. Her father had given her the precious gift of health and Lord Mallikarjuna had showered her with the right opportunities. In return, she could not presume to give the Lord anything other than her undying devotion, but for her father, she had a pithy story in return. When a quarrel had broken out in Mount Kailash, the abode of Lord Shiva as to which of his two sons loved him more and what each could do for his parents, each had offered to circumambulate the world to prove his devotion. Subramanya, the older son had set off on his peacock to do just that, while Ganesha, the younger had just gone round the bench on which his parents were seated, saying that they were his entire world.

So she was the Ganesha to her father's Emperor Babur, and he was her world. Or so she told herself.

When Pushpa Rani woke up, she found that it had turned dark outside and there was no one else in the waiting room. You were fast asleep, the attendant said, and I did not want to wake you. The doctor will not be coming today. She checked her mobile phone to find several missed calls, two from Ranjit but there was no point calling now, his phone would be switched off; he was in the middle of his shift. As she stumbled out of the doorway on to the street, she realized that her day had been wasted. She would have to go home empty handed. No prasada and no medicines either.

'Ammanagudi street,' she told the auto man, wincing at the shooting pain in her back as she climbed in.

ten

~

1

'So madamma, all set to make a fiery speech today at the meeting ...' Basavaraj said in his usual suggestive, bantering tone.

'I'm going to roar like a Royal Bengal tigress.'

'I hope you will Bela, we need all the support we can get,' Shrinivas Moorty said, with a hint of admonition.

Shrinivas Moorty bridled at Basavaraj's ingratiating tone and Bela's indulgent reply. As always, he wondered how she could demonstrate such a fondness for the man. When he himself tried that cajoling tone with her, she usually cut him short. 'Stop it,' she had said to him once. 'Basavaraj is old fashioned. He thinks it is charming to talk to a woman that way. You should know better.' He was flattered, but it was not an unmixed feeling. Even when he made digs at his wife's experiments at exotic cooking in an attempt to entertain the ladies, Preeti enjoyed them and would giggle away but Bela frowned impatiently at him.

'A mouse has come into the room ...' Preeti Vaidya had said, all those years ago—had it been fifteen years—with a frisson of spite in her voice.

'A mouse? I thought it was a nymph ...' he returned, to annoy her. In truth, he had scarcely noticed the new entrant. He thought it was a student who had come in to talk to one of the staff.

'And did you see what she is *wearing*!'

'What?' He made a song and dance of it, shooting bolt upright, narrowing his eyes and craning his neck to look at the unexceptionally clad figure sitting at the far end of the room, reading the newspaper studiously. 'Oh!' he clapped his hand to his head, 'I was hoping she'd be dressed like Helen, all set to do a cabaret.'

And Preeti had gratified him by giggling like a schoolgirl.

Those were his hamming days, when he played the gallant, especially with Preeti Vaidya. The other women lecturers then had been Girijamma, who taught chemistry and Nasreen Banu, Hindi, and his conversation with them was limited to listening to their complaints about the students and polite enquiries about their families. Preeti Vaidya, the English lecturer was a different kind altogether. Her husband was the head of a multinational company, whose photograph and pithy comments appeared almost every other day in the business section of the newspapers, and Preeti made it quite clear that she didn't need the job; her house did not run on her salary. She was there only for her love of English literature. Which didn't make her any less attentive to her entitlements of dearness allowance, and scale and seniority, but it edged her dealings with her colleagues with a mild condescension. She drove to work in a large red car which was parked conspicuously in the parking lot, next to the physics lecturer's second hand Fiat. The disgruntled gossip from the women's camp was that she was never known to repeat a sari. In deference to her silks, perfumes, leather hand bags and her groomed hands and feet, Basavaraj treated her with an elaborate courtesy, as if she were minor royalty. To avoid discussing literature with her, of which he thought she knew nothing, Shrinivas Moorty spoke to her about trivial things—like whether Bangalore weather was really becoming warmer, or what certain streets were called before their names were changed either in a rabid effort to wipe out traces of a 'shameful colonial past' or to accommodate the present. They had set up a playful tenor in which one teased the other about supposed aspects of their personalities or their tastes—her discriminating knowledge of continental cuisine and his dislike of a certain film star—blowing up mild likes and dislikes into fetishes, which each knew was a gambit, a conversation piece, relevant only when they spoke to each other.

A few days after his conversation with Preeti, as he was riding out of college, he had seen the mouse at the gates, struggling with an assortment of odds and ends, trying to hail an autorickshaw.

He stopped. She had just moved house to be nearer the college and needed help to shift her things. In an inspired spurt, he parked his scooter back in the college, put her in an auto with a few things, hailed one himself and, loading some more of her stuff into it, said, 'Lead the way, I'll follow.'

Manfully, he bore the buckets and brooms and boxes up the stairs to her second-floor flat while she scampered up and down. Finally they were done and after he wiped his dusty hands on the rag that she brought out from somewhere, he stood in the middle of the empty room, hands hanging down his sides, feeling awkward. Now that the burst of gallantry was spent, he did not know what to do. He was also feeling a little tired, a little out of breath.

'Would you like a drink?' Bela said.

'A drink?'

'A drink.'

'A drink?' he repeated, thinking she must mean water.

'A *drink* drink. I know beer would be nice. But I don't have a fridge, haven't unpacked it yet. I have whisky though. Indian. Single malt or so it claims on the bottle. I know it's a little early in the evening—'

Why not, he thought, *why nought* . . .

They drank out of paper cups, he sitting on the only chair in the room, and she on an upturned cardboard carton for she was light enough for that.

So there he was, drinking with a strange woman, at her invitation. He looked at her, properly for the first time—from her hair, unevenly cropped and standing up like a child's who has just woken up, her eyes, regarding him with friendly interest, waiting for him to say something, passing over her nose and mouth and chin, all small, and the mousy brown stuff she wore, to her foot from which dangled an insouciant slipper. The tendons in her neck, hands and feet were prominent; from the top of her shorn head to the end of her sinewy foot, she curved in a tensile arc. He straightened his shirt, conscious of the buttons already sitting too trim across his midriff and patted his hair noting how readily his scalp came up to meet his fingers. He recognized that look in her eyes—bright, unshy—and met it reluctantly; he was no longer used to women like her, Geeta having receded into a distant vault in his mind.

'Tell me Shrinivas,' she said with a forthrightness, a sense of self-consequence that he was to grow familiar with and which sat so oddly, so endearingly, with her small frame. 'Tell me about this college—'

Again he was reluctant. As he went through the paces, telling her when the college was established, its place in Gandhi's Non Cooperation movement, its luminaries—the list of scholar-administrators who had headed the institution, including a Jnanpith winner—he could sense how dull it sounded, how impersonal. 'I studied here and returned as a teacher. There are three of us who did that—Jairam, Basavaraj and I. You can make what you want of yourself here, the place has all the opportunities and it's up to you to make the most of them,' he ended in apology, in defiance. She said nothing but smiled quickly and looked down into her paper cup, running her finger along the rim. His words hung in the air, a confession of his stodginess, of his state of stasis, the confirmation of his *mama*-hood. He was well settled in his groove then, eight years as a lecturer in National Trust College, tenured, unshakable, quite satisfied with himself.

'I would like another drink,' he said loudly.

'Yes, yes of course,' she said, jumping off the carton lightly.

When she came back with two more paper cups they spoke of other things, moving on easily, through the fading afternoon.

A child had come home from school and interrupted the evening. But he had left feeling man again, back in the hunt, a certain predatorial secretion beginning to make its way through his veins, the air a-tingle with possibilities, with the faint whiff of prey even; he felt the shadow of his former self stirring, coming back to life.

She had made him recognize and recover something in himself, something that was just slipping over the edge, that he could not name but had a faint memory of. In return he supported her in every one of the fights she launched into against the college. It began with the salwar kameez—known as the 'Punjabi dress', a garment that he had only just begun to recognize and had immediately classified as graceless and fit only for students. Perhaps that was why he had thought she was a student when she first came into the staff room. Bela's first gesture of protest against the college was her refusal to wear a sari; she would come to work in a salwar-kameez, in coarse hand-spun khadi. There was an unwritten rule, a tacit understanding about what was sartorially appropriate for the women—whether they wore nylon saris like Girijamma, or silks like Preeti or pulled a burkha over it when they stepped out of the college compound like Nasreen Banu—and it was they who were most offended by Bela Bose's violation, and she had to depend on the support of the men. Shrinivas Moorty signed a petition saying he found nothing 'offensive' in the salwar-kameez even as he wondered how Bela would look in a sari but he would never know for she had forsworn saris. It led to a falling out with Preeti Vaidya but he did not care, it was Bela he wanted. 'Look at her,' Preeti hissed into his ear, 'so shameless, that *bodamma!*' lapsing in a weak moment to her primeval, vernacular self.

Next, Bela mooted a Feminism and Women's Studies elective as part of the sociology course and asked for funds. She is aggrandizing the syllabus, the part-timer, worried about her job, said. And cornering the benefits, added the head of the sociology department, who had taken on the part-timer unlawfully, passing on the more dreary bits of his course to her. You must understand that academic trends are changing, the world is changing, Shrinivas Moorty argued in the academic council meeting. And who will teach this new elective? We cannot hire extra staff, the head of the department who had been teaching the same paper for the past twenty years and was on the university syllabus committee, said. I will, was Bela's impatient reply. There will be no question of your foregoing your normal load of classes, the department head said, as if issuing a warning. Then, the establishment, goaded by Girijamma and Basavaraj, had struck on the 'outsider' issue: Bela was a non-Kannadiga and the college had not adhered to the norms of recruitment in employing her. But their jubilation was short-lived for it was discovered that Bela met the requirements of domicile—she had been a resident of the state for the required number of years. On this point too Shrinivas Moorty had been one of Bela's most vociferous supporters.

Their burgeoning friendship had been grist for the staff-room gossip mill, but he turned a deaf ear to the insinuations and whispers. It helped that Bela did not care about silly niceties either; she was spontaneous enough to take what she wanted, reach forward and grasp it with both hands, unhampered by what people would say and make of her motives. She made it clear to him too that she wanted neither his indulgence nor his condescension, no smoke screen of any sort. If happiness was a spontaneous, everyday feeling, untainted by what was to come, he would say those were the happiest days in his life. He wanted only to savour each day, the jubilation of each morning when the weather and the traffic and the other pinpricks did not matter, when even the humdrum became enjoyable.

They paired off for college duties and worked on projects together, they planned joint study tours with their students and in time he toyed with the idea of suggesting to her that they work out a way to extend a college trip, just the two of them together. He selected films that mirrored her course work to show in his film club and they prolonged their discussions at the club by the poolside, where for once he was not distracted by the other women. He did not know what he liked better: when she agreed with him, lacing his arguments, his observations and his witticisms with her own, or when she disagreed with him and they clashed delightfully. They skirted the inconvenient areas of their lives in the process of getting to know each other. He was careful not to invite Bela home; he could not expose her to Lily, and Balu and Suppi, or rather, he could not bear to stand exposed in their company. After that first day when he helped her move, he did not visit her at home again either. Of her attachments outside, he knew the bare minimum. She had two small daughters and a husband in the merchant navy who spent six months at sea and the rest on land. He had no wish to know any more either. Why tempt fate he thought, why pre-empt what would happen in the natural course of time?

It was Basavaraj who nicknamed her the Royal Bengal Tigress. 'So, Shrinivas Moorty,' he said in his inimitable way one day, when both of them were retrieving their scooters from the parking lot, 'the Royal Bengal Tigress has you purring like a Karnataka Cat or should I say, a *Bengalur Bekku*. Enjoy, enjoy I say.'

There were old slights with Basavaraj, old fights, past scores he had to settle, for Shrinivas Moorty had met Basavaraj in college and knew him, since, to be brash to the point of being vulgar. There was his obvious statement, his flaunting of his identity, the red and yellow kumkum and the stripes of vibhuti on his forehead. But one could not interpret sheer bad taste as an unvaunted flaunting of religious or cultural symbols, Shrinivas Moorty conceded; that was his own prejudice speaking. But Basavaraj, apart from his vulgarity, habitually reduced any matter to its meanest component—a matter of who benefited at the expense of whom, of victim and perpetrator—always to suit his purpose. In the early eighties, just after both of them had been confirmed in their jobs (and Jairam was still teaching budding secretaries the basics of English grammar at the Ramnarayan College of Secretarial Practice), Basavaraj had jumped into the fray, joining the movement to make the language of the state—the language he taught and not too well by all accounts—the compulsory medium of education at the primary level and the language of administration, and that a percentage of jobs be reserved for locals. Shrinivas Moorty remembered the many sessions that Basavaraj had with him then, in an effort to enlist his sympathies and his involvement. What we are asking, Basavaraj said, easily appropriating ownership of the cause that had only recently become his, is that we must not be reduced to the status of outsiders in our own home. That's not much to ask, is it? Basavaraj's appeal to his fellow-Kannadiga failed. Shrinivas Moorty said that he had no sympathy for such a chauvinistic movement. 'One day Shrinivas Moorty,' Basavaraj had said then, 'you will have to climb down from the fence you are sitting on, and you will choose to land on my side of it. Mark my words.'

It had taken a long time—twenty years in fact—for circumstances to be extenuating enough for him to see eye-to-eye with Basavaraj, but his ardent flush for Bela had cooled abruptly, in a matter of months. It had started out as a trivial issue. There was a medium-sized room at the end of the corridor of the administrative section—or the beginning of it, for the corridor could be accessed from both ends. It was known as the Sundry Purposes room. Meetings with parents or students were held there, sometimes even departmental meetings, in order to avoid disturbing the others in the staff room. On film club days Shrinivas Moorty held the screenings there. It was a tedious process, putting up black curtains against the windows to keep out the light, bringing in and then laying out the heavy, cold, uncomfortable metal chairs, and the durrie in front to seat people as there were never enough chairs. But where space was at a premium and funds not to be had, these were but pinpricks and the film club had prospered, and there was a time when even standing room was not to be had at the back.

Bela suggested that the room be turned into a crèche so that all the women who worked at National Trust College could bring their children to work. The administrative section that contained the room was far off from the teaching section where the classrooms were, and they would not be in anybody's way. She mooted the idea casually in the staff room and even as Shrinivas Moorty made his joking protests, he saw how it galvanized the other women. It was open to the men too, Bela added generously. The women showed a surprising unity over the matter, resisting all attempts to drive assorted cleavages between them. By the time Bela appeared on the scene the number of women on the staff had grown significantly from the Girijamma–Nasreen Banu–Preeti Vaidya days to make up two thirds of the teaching and non-teaching staff and most of them were young with small children. The proposal meant that the room would be lost to the film club since the college ran evening classes as well and the working hours overlapped. Shrinivas Moorty, who had been asking in vain for funds for a projector of their own and for rudimentary sound-proofing of the room, was shocked into heart-felt protest. To the others, it mattered little what the room was used for. Moreover the film club was seen as an affectation on Shrinivas Moorty's part by the other staff members, an unnecessary non-curricular fuss from the point of view of the administration, a ploy to attract the loyalty of the students, according to the principal, who also felt it was a rather lascivious activity—boys and girls sitting in close proximity in a darkened room, with suggestive stuff being shown on the screen—and the attendants who had to arrange and dismantle the chairs thought it a weekly nuisance. So, Shrinivas Moorty stood alone against a phalanx of women, and a principal who was sympathetic to them.

His arguments with Bela had been playfully edgy at first, then vociferous and had finally turned vicious. As a clincher, she had thrown at him scornfully, in the staff room, within everyone's hearing, 'How would you *know* Shrinivas how important it is to feel that your children are close at hand and safe? You don't even *have* children of your own!'

And he who had not been unduly bothered about his childlessness till then had been cut to his manhood. He found it impossible to even speak to Bela for a while after that. Even Basavaraj had known not to make capital of that but not Preeti Vaidya. 'So all over?' she mocked when she found that the two of them no longer sought each other out in the staff room. 'Thoo bitbitra? Katti kya?' In Bela's next battle, when she proposed to make the staff room a no-smoking zone, he supported the smokers, though he did not smoke himself and would otherwise have joined the no-smoking side. Eventually, the crèche idea was dropped and the staff room did indeed become a no-smoking zone, leading the men to dart into the open space at the end of the corridor for a few furtive puffs. And in time too the edge of their animosity wore off and he and Bela became friends again.

But of late, Basavaraj's Royal Bengal Tigress had become rather toothless, even her roar seemed congested with catarrh, thought as he cast a fond, regretful eye over her dumpy f[...] her limp khadi kurta and the terracotta beads that clutter[...] her neck. The vast red bindi stuck in the middle of her for[...] only drew attention to her tired eyes. Bela's kurtas and short hair were hardly radical any more, they had become the norm and now she looked distinctly staid; she was, in fact, on the committee to prescribe a dress code for the female students, the principal having preferred her to one of the long haired, business-suit clad younger teachers.

In the new Centre for Inter-Disciplinary Studies that was being proposed, the fund-flush, 'globalized' model, which came with strings attached—one of them being that Jairam would head it, just as another of the funding alumnus's friends would head the Centre for Science—all three of them had been sidelined. Bela would have a very small part to play and Shrinivas Moorty and Basavaraj, none at all. The fall in registrations for Bela's Women's Studies elective was cited as the reason for her diminished role. The course had been very successful for many years but of late the number of registrations had fallen. Girls no longer vied with each other for a seat in the course. Basavaraj and Nasreen Banu, who probably hadn't spoken to each other for twenty years, could be seen now, heads bent together in one corner of the staff room; neither Kannada nor Hindi, no languages other than English, and that too of the 'communicative' variety, were required by the new module. And Shrinivas Moorty had lost both film studies and history. They were getting 'foreign-trained' experts, as the principal put it, for film studies, as part of the larger approach to media and as for history, the subject itself had disappeared, bits of it having been sucked into various multi-disciplinary compartments. Besides, he was not qualified to teach in the new module; he did not have a PhD and so was not considered expert enough.

That afternoon's meeting would be a fight to the finish. They would truly get to know what the staff room thought through their representatives on the academic council. His only regret though, and he cringed at the thought, was that Basavaraj had been proved right. The two of them had finally arrived on the same side of the fence.

2

Shrinivas Moorty had always believed, until recently, when the doubts began to creep in, that he had a good life; he would even go so far as to say the best. He woke up to an excellent breakfast, liked his job, was one of the best—if not the very best—teacher in his college and popular too, ran a film club that won him the adoration of many students—some of whom thought that *he* had made the films he showed—and after college, when he did not have a tutorial class or work in the library he had time for a beer by the poolside in his club before going home to an excellent dinner and a quiet wife, thanks to Balu and Suppi.

It was either idli or dosa for breakfast; he had established that as soon as they were married—no uppittu, either ravé or avalakki for him—and there was both sambar and chutney to go with the idli or the dosa, and home-made butter. All said and done, his wife was a good cook—her idlis, even on the coldest of winter days, fluffed out like jasmine flowers, and there was just enough menthya in her dosas to underscore the blandness of the rice and the stodginess of the dal, and lend it that slightly-bitter after taste. (She also had at least one full-time servant to help her, but that was another matter.) She had the knack for it, an intuitive nimbleness at the tips of her fingers, kaiguna as they called it, which his mother, for all her elaborate cooking, had not had. Of late, though, she had begun to slack off; on the mornings she had her massage he had to make do with cornflakes and milk, which he tried to relieve with bananas, but perhaps that was a good thing for his paunch. And to be fair to her, she made up for it with her dinners.

For several years in a row he had won the best teacher award—this was not a formal ranking but an informal award which the students had instituted, announcing it in their magazine. It was a big thing with his fellow teachers, he knew, though they pretended it did not matter; Jairam used to get quite caustic over the fact that Shrinivas Moorty's name figured in it every year and his, not even once. The students had stopped the honours roll recently, for there were too many teachers and too many courses and things had grown too complicated for them to establish the common ground. It would not be an exaggeration to say that he was a legend in his own right, in his circle. His classes on the Russian Revolution and the Second World War were attended by students from the sciences, he had heard, and others who did not take history. The fact that he always showed a film or recommended a work of fiction was part of the attraction—a tradition that he had carried down from SVK's days. It was so important to put a human face to every movement, every event, even an idea. When he did the Russian Revolution he went back often to his childhood reading of the beautifully illustrated and incredibly inexpensive retellings of the Russian classics, and other books that he could now see as attempts at romancing the Soviet Union—lives of young boys named Alexei and Vassily who followed the Red Army and dreamt of becoming soldiers or were farm boys who larked among ducks and tractors on wide expanses of green and under blue skies, As a teacher he had never repeated his choices. There was no chance that a second-year student would tell a new entrant: 'Oh him, don't bother. Every time he does the First World War he screens *Paths of Glory*.' Or, 'If it's *Battle of Algiers* at the film club he must be doing Imperialism, if it's *Garam Hawa*, it must be the Partition.' He still remembered how a girl had come to him in tears after reading *The Diary of Anne Frank* when he had recommended it to the all-girls class one year. That class, in particular, had looked upon him with a reverence that was heart warming.

For his evenings of beer by the poolside in the club he had to thank his father. Every morning, when his father had set out to catch the factory bus to work in his brown and beige uniform, one could not have guessed that here was a man in whose breast there seethed irreconcilable, even irrational desires. Once a week Vasudev Moorty got dressed in his suit, a present from his father-in-law when he had got married and which he could still get into, brushed with reverential care and laid out on the bed as if it were a holy relic by his wife, and set off to attend lectures and discussions on the maxims of good citizenship or what democracy means today, at the Gokhale Institute of Public Affairs, a place that aimed at keeping alive and alert and involved the civic consciousness of the decent, educated middle-class man, so that the public space would not be overwhelmed by politicians and lumpen elements. In Jairam's words, it was a place for stuffy old geezers who still read Mill and Bentham. At the same time, some quirk, some contrary desire, a streak of snobbery too perhaps, had led his strictly vegetarian, non-smoking, non-drinking, non-athletic, non-cards playing father to seek the membership of the upper crust Bangalore City Club, whose members at one time had largely been Englishmen. It was the same strain that made it impossible for him to resist the 'super fine' tag, Shrinivas Moorty's mother used to say. If the shopkeeper said, about anything, 'Try this sir, the super fine variety, just ten rupees more', he'd fall for it immediately. Your father should never be sent to the shops, was his mother's dictum. His father had gone to the Bangalore City Club, whose membership he had moved mountains for, just once, in the same tight suit, ready to talk about the issues of the day in a spirit of respectably jousting conviviality, and had felt so out of place among the smooth-talking hard-drinking men there that he had never gone back. But he had left to his son the legacy of his membership, for which Shrinivas Moorty was ever grateful; he just couldn't dream of becoming a member of a place like that on his own steam and neither could he afford the membership rates. The club's 'personality' tests and membership 'culture match' checks were so demanding that he was certain that it was easier indeed for a camel to pass through the eye of a needle.

He looked forward every evening to sipping his beer between mouthfuls of steak and watching the girls by the poolside at the club. It had begun as a dare in college. We must break out of our Brahmin shackles, Jairam had said, and alcohol and beef had been the obvious initiators. But their furtive experiments with marijuana, after they passed out of college and were in the university doing their post graduation, in Ammanagudi's wood depot did not last beyond one glorious summer. That they would court girls from outside their caste and community did not seem so urgent then.

What had mattered was the two of them. Jairam himself had reneged—he was after all essentially a kootu-lover—and had gone back to vegetarianism and non-smoking and non-drinking; he even gave up tea and coffee, while Shrinivas Moorty learned to enjoy his beer and his beef.

In the last few years, his routine visits to the club were shot through with a new excitement. The place seemed suddenly to have come to life. It was always full of people, young and old, in spandex and lycra, and branded sports shoes, working out or playing tennis. The courts had been refurbished, the gym had expanded and the regulars in the swimming pool were heard complaining that they couldn't swim the length in peace without getting entangled with another swimmer. Pool tables had been set up in the basement and the menu changed to include a variety of sandwiches and pizzas along with the stock-in-trade peanut masala and pakoras. There was also a special counter for salads and 'diet' foods. Sometimes he noticed that the only people who sat in the poolside bar for hours at a stretch, downing the drinks, were men like himself, mature, in no hurry to leave and go anywhere. But he too had felt that new age spirit, that crackle in the air and had responded to it. He had bought, for the first time in his life, an expensive pair of Bermudas and t-shirts to go with them, which he reserved for his weekend marathon pool-side beer drinking sessions with the regulars at the club.

He had also become quite friendly with some of the young women who came for a swim or played tennis regularly, and sometimes they sat with him for a drink. Their constant peals of laughter and amused shrieks often attracted glances from the other tables. One of them, an events manager called Priyanka, he particularly liked and much to his gratification she greeted him now with a full-body hug. Your t-shirts are really cool, he had told her. His favourite was one that said 'Narasimha rocks' and had a picture of a lion wearing a dhoti—the Prahalad–Hiranyakashipu–Vishnu legend had been transformed into a print on a t-shirt with such remarkable ease. He liked the way young people straddled different worlds, not making heavy weather of their holy cows, accommodating them with humour instead. It was easy to engage them—after all he had years of practice grabbing and keeping the attention of a classroom full of reluctant students, and once caught, they were like fish on a hook. He loved the girls—their hair, their skin, their unbumpy bodies and the uncomplicated way they gave themselves up completely to the moment, to being there with him without the foreshadow of the past or the hanging cloud of the future. He felt himself grow in their presence, become handsomer, wittier and sharper than ever, and they were always in splits or open-mouthed at his aphorisms. The pleasure he felt at their proximity, at their unblemished physicality, the tingle in his sluggish veins was akin to the thrill of first contact, but from a position of strength, without the reciprocal, helpless confusion; he could take all without being rendered vulnerable. He was sure he was better equipped now to recover the ideal of love—that state of unblemished body and tabula rasa mind—his own to imprint and savour but with none of the excruciating anxieties and uncertainties of youth.

One evening, he was just settling down by the poolside, when Priyanka and another girl got up to leave. The other girl said something in an undertone as she was leaving, something about getting away before 'F2C L2G' caught her but he had not got the joke. All the other new acronyms of the technology jargon—B2B, B2C, C2B—he was familiar with. It was the stuff of banter between him and Priyanka. Surely this is taking binary relations too literally he had said and she had laughed heartily. He forgot to ask her what this new combination F2C L2G meant, till it came up casually in a conversation with one of the others. 'Oh, that just means First to Come, Last to Go,' she said with an embarrassed laugh. After that Shrinivas Moorty shed his shorts and t-shirts for shirts with ethnic prints and khadi kurtas and full-length cotton trousers. He also grew a little wary, and was careful not to appear too eager to join the girls at their table.

When he had had his fill of the club, he would leave for home, grateful for Balu and Suppi, his constant dwarapalas. A few minutes of bright talk made those two happy, and they went away satisfied, while his wife went to heat his dinner. If Balu or Suppi were not around, she was usually asleep by the time he came, leaving his food in a casserole, and he let himself in and ate in peace; he preferred, actually, to let himself in. At that hour even the few minutes of interaction with her he found fatiguing.

But of late, he had begun to feel that things were not quite the way he perceived them to be. For one, he got the impression that people had started speaking 'soothingly' to him. Was he imagining it, or were more people trying to humour him, the way he and his mother had started treating his father after his retirement. Dwelling on it, he would say perhaps that it had all started with the way things changed with Jairam. In his mind there had been no doubt about the trajectory of their friendship, 'where they stood on the learning curve' as Priyanka would put it. Jairam was his oldest friend, his closest buddy, who had set the lead in college, but he, Shrinivas Moorty, was now his senior colleague, even mentor, having rescued him from imminent dissipation and a lifetime of Leftist theatre by recommending his case strongly to the board of National Trust College, which had been reluctant to hire him though he had been an alumnus. Unlike Shrinivas Moorty, Jairam had been an indifferent performer and his teachers still sighed in memory of his volatile personality. But then, he had forgotten the opportunistic streak in Jairam.

After putting in the required number of years of teaching, before being considered for promotion to the grade of reader, National Trust College permitted its lecturers a study sabbatical. The college had a tie-up with a few foreign universities—this international opportunity had come their way with the opening of the doors of the economy—to sponsor their lecturers for refresher courses or doctoral programmes. A few years ago, Shrinivas Moorty was offered a chance to take a break and do a course, even register for a PhD with a Canadian university. His immediate reaction had been one of suspicion. Was he being told his teaching skills had become rusty? Perhaps the college was trying to get rid of him; the study hiatus had been used before to ease out people they no longer wanted. Moreover, the Canadian university on offer was unheard of and had been chosen, he suspected, only because a college alumnus was on the donor list and the governing council of the university. So he met the principal and told him that he would rather do a full fledged course in film studies from the Film Institute in Poona, in the country itself, so that he could offer an undergraduate course on the subject in college. It was some time later that he casually mentioned to Lily that he had refused the offer to go to Canada, expecting her to say nothing.

They were sitting in the drawing room, on the cane chairs, watching TV, with Balu and Suppi flanking them like two protective gorgons—by then he had got used to those two—and he said, 'Guess what, the college is trying to send me away to the wilderness, pretending they're giving me an opportunity to do a course.'

A statement like that, about his doings in college, which had no immediate implications, no effect on the functioning of their household, was usually met with a blank stare from Lily or a nod from Balu who perhaps felt that he had to show an interest in his host. That evening, Lily looked up from her embroidery and said, 'Send you away? Where?' But before he could tell her she held her embroidery frame across to Suppi and said, 'It's the wrong colour, look. I suspected it in the shop but both of you said it matched.'

Balu, though, was still looking at him enquiringly, so he said, 'To a remote place in Canada, a university whose name I can't even recollect. I told them I'd rather go to the Film Institute in Poona—'

'What?' Lily said, putting down her embroidery and sitting up straight. 'You said you'd rather go to Poona when the college is sending you to Canada?'

'It's not like that, Lily, not as straightforward. It's not as if they are asking me to choose between Harvard and Stanford. Canada is not the US. Besides, there is just one university I can go to, in some godforsaken corner, and the subjects I can do there are of no use to me. I know someone who went there some years ago and he came running back in two months. He said it's so cold that your breath turns to ice even inside your nose, and there is no one, absolutely no one, to speak to. His wife said she'd go mad if they stayed there—'

'You gave up a chance to go abroad?'

'Abroad? Abroad is not heaven, Lily.'

She said nothing but continued to stare at him, her mouth a little agape, the sheen of her teeth catching his eye.

'It's not as if I've refused the opportunity of a lifetime, Lily,' he tried to keep his voice from rising, 'the allowance is barely enough for one person to live on, forget two. And where will I get the airfare for you; the college will only fund my ticket.'

She turned to Balu in appeal, but Balu had the sense to say nothing, not even by gesture, so she returned to her embroidery, pulling at the needle in quick flying motions.

'Lily,' he said, his exasperation now edged with a plea, 'I know my interests best—'

'*My* interests?' her voice rose so high that it was almost a squeak. Then, abruptly, she bundled her embroidery together, wincing as the needle pricked her, and got up.

'Come,' she said to the other two, sucking on the ball of her thumb, 'we were planning to go to the market.' They got up with alacrity, Suppi reaching out for Lily's hand with a worried expression.

That night was the first time his sphinx-like wife actually spoke her mind; they had their first fight.

'Did you ask me? Did you care about what I wanted?' she flung at him.

'Are you not happy here?' he asked her, bewildered by her vehemence.

'As for the money, Balu said he would have paid for my ticket.'

What will you do there, you who cannot make friends, with no Balu and Suppi there to keep you constantly amused, he wanted to ask her.

'And my people told me you were brilliant, that you had a bright future ahead of you,' she said bitterly, lying rigid next to him on their bed.

216   USHA K.R.

Immediately, he had reconsidered his decision, discussed it with friends, and changed his mind. But it was too late. The council had made the same offer to Jairam and he had grabbed it with both hands. He had even managed to switch universities, and was going to the US instead.

Once the viscous mix of his mind had been stirred, several bubbles floated to the surface. For the first time he sensed that his wife might have had expectations that he had not lived up to, that she might have been *ambitious* about her marriage. Perhaps Lily, with her Ikebana, her Chinese cooking and ivory skin had considered herself the perfect trophy bride for a man-with-promise. On paper he had suited—the only son in line to inherit a large ancestral house (she could not have known that only a measly flat would result from it), a bright student, a well spoken-of teacher in a government aided college—till he had refused the one chance to make his future. Perhaps she had dreamt of a future in a foreign land, where she could set up an exotic home and charm strangers, and she would have succeeded for it was only acquaintances who felt her power most.

The opportunity passed Shrinivas Moorty by completely—he was promoted to reader the next year and was no longer eligible for the scheme. There was a whole set of younger people waiting for their turn. Jairam returned a few years later from the US with a doctorate in an esoteric subject that stood at the crossroads (the graveyard, Shrinivas Moorty preferred) of many disciplines. But more importantly he came back with an endowment fund from B.N. Swamy, their senior at National Trust College, to start a new centre to teach the new disciplines of the new world, provided he, Jairam, be responsible for the funds and the centre. Thereafter, Shrinivas Moorty began to witness a remarkable turnaround in the fortunes of his friend. The management turned craven and conferred on Jairam the unmistakable authority of the man who holds the future in his hands, of one who would take the right road forward while he, Shrinivas Moorty was condemned to the road not taken. Jairam was nominated to committees and councils, not just in the college but across the state and by the end of the year, he was recommended to the National Education Think Tank and the Human Resource Commission, chaired by none other than the prime minister himself. The local press interviewed him, praising his skills and resourcefulness, his vision and reach. But as far as Shrinivas Moorty could see the only 'skill' Jairam had exhibited after his return, apart from his new accent, was the knack of the powerpoint presentation. He brought his own laptop to class and flashed on the wall his lecture condensed to twenty slides with five bullet points in each and soon all the teachers were vying to do the same. In time the students too had caught on and now in the new centre it was officially recognized that given the urgency of the times and the vast amounts of knowledge that had to be absorbed and conveyed, the old notes and 'essay writing' method was a waste of time. In the new Centre for Inter-Disciplinary Studies there would be computers for all, powerpoint presentations galore.

And there was Lily. She, who had disdained to take an interest in his affairs till then started following every turn in Jairam's new fortunes with an interest he found baffling. It was she who first told him that Jairam was buying a flat. Where is he getting the money from, she asked. I believe his wife bought herself a lot of gold in Dubai on their way back. Though the subject did not come up between them again, he knew that Jairam's new flat had burnt a hole in her heart. She had connected his missed opportunity with the flat he did not have. If he had gone to the US instead of Jairam, he would have bought her the gorgeous new flat, Lily had decided, and he did not have the patience to explain that it was Jairam's gambling instinct, his readiness to stake all he had, even the future well being of his wife and children that had bought him the flat, and which could easily have left him penniless. What does it matter how much gold his wife wears, he had started on glibly, it makes no difference to the way she looks. But you, you look like a queen even in paste necklaces and glass bangles. But she had not waited for him to finish.

It was Jairam's return that had done it. Ever since he came back from that third rung American university, armed with a doctorate in a new fangled subject, set to attack the temperate roots of the

National Trust Institutions, all these doubts had arisen, like debris in an unclogged drain. Shrinivas Moorty had become an unsettled creature. For he had thought till then that all disappointment was his. It had not occurred to him to consult his wife on any of his affairs, as she had nothing to do with them. Just as she had so little to do with most things that mattered to him. Lately, he even found himself speculating on a Lily-less life; total freedom from the one fetter that bound him but after giving it some thought decided that Lily, even in her minimal role had her uses. She was the salt that sharpened his sweet-loving tongue, the slightly-bitter menthya in his dosa that refreshed his mouth and massaged his liver, the not-noticeable drag in his foot that made his gait brisker and thus better, the ghost at his elbow whose breath he felt on his neck, which prevented him from becoming completely complacent, from lapsing into anarchy.

It had not been like this when they had started out together; he had given themselves a fair chance. When they were newly married, he was beset with anxiety, that he must be worthy of the goddess he had married. On the day they arrived at the hotel in the hills on their honeymoon, he was worried sick that the room was too mean, too cold, just not good enough. Her radiant beauty made everything look small, even sordid. But their mutual inexperience made them comfortable with each other. He could well believe, like the wall hanging that someone had given them as a wedding gift, that this was the first day of the rest of his life. Naked in body they faced each other, and so, naked in soul—a feeling that passed as soon as they clothed themselves by daylight, but the strength of whose memory persisted. Nothing that he had read, seen or fierily imagined, no amount of pleasuring himself had prepared him for the real thing, of how transfiguring skin and mouth could be. He believed her to be as entranced as he was, as completely in love. She had pranced round the room wearing his t-shirt and nothing else, he had combed her long hair and made her promise never to cut it; they had come down hand-in-hand to the dining hall in the hotel and so compelling must have been their glow of satiation and anticipation that the others had parted to make way for them, as if they were walking down a red carpet. They had been the centre of attention in that government-run hotel, where most of the holidayers were middle aged family people with growing children. Perhaps those people in the dining room had looked at them with nostalgia, thinking back upon their own newly wed state or with disbelief even, that two people could be so happy, so wrapped up in each other that they had no eyes for anyone else. Together, they had trekked the trails in the hills; he had even lifted her across a stream or two that crossed their path. When it started raining unexpectedly, they both decided by common consent to go back home sooner than planned.

Back home, the feeling, the easy tenor of their bliss, had bled away even without his realizing it. Her family, only two streets away, were always at hand and then Balu and Suppi started making their regular evening appearances. And right through the day there was a servant, a legacy from Lily's childhood, a square, buck-toothed woman with a long grey plait and a limp, who dressed like a pre-pubescent schoolgirl in a long skirt and a short blouse, lurching about their small flat. She sat on the floor of the kitchen all day, looking grim, and at night she sat in the passage outside their bedroom, the first line of defence in his siege of Mt Pubus. And as he entered his room she gave him a look that said quite clearly: Be careful with my girl, she's fragile; don't hurt her you big rough beast, slave to your senses. Once inside the room he waited for Lily to finish her unending ablutions in the bathroom, intrigued by the sounds—he would never be privy to the secrets of aloe vera or of the magic potion that produced the milk-like fragrance of her skin—as the fire of his ardour was gradually dulled by sleep. Sometimes he stood on the balcony and smoked—these were times when he felt that a cigar was a man's best friend.

Long after, when the maid was pensioned off and the fire of his ardour had relocated from his loins to his mind, he was still intrigued by the paraphernalia of her sensuality—the many curvaceous and voluptuous bottles on her dressing table on one side and her hair brushes on the other, strong and handsome, like an array of gods, the lemony zephyr that trailed her as she went in and out of the bathroom, a lace-edged, silky petticoat draped on the head of the bed, a just-discarded sari-blouse still inhabited by the ghost of her breasts.

Casting his mind back on the juncture when things had started to drift, he knew that the sari-blouse had a definite role to play. He would even say that it was symptomatic of the failure of his efforts to get to know her when they were newly married. Their evening entertainment, after he returned from work, consisted of one or all of three things—a trip to the shops in the nearby bazaar, visiting one of her innumerable relatives or an outing to the tailor's. It was the tailor who finally made him decide. After walking down to the tailor's shop at the end of Ammanagudi Street, he was expected to stand on the footpath and watch while Lily entered the box-like room—windowless, with two men whirring away on their sewing machines in a further recess—and the master tailor, a professorial-looking man in gold rimmed glasses, took intricate measurements of her shoulders, back and chest. The thumb of his left hand holding the measuring tape would press lightly into the hollow at the base of her neck, while the other rested on her shoulder or traversed her back as he measured the distance from the top of her arm where her shoulder blades began to the elbow, the length of her collar bone, the space between her shoulders and the small of her back, all the time calling out the measurements right down to quarter inch adjustments over his shoulder to a boy who sat on the floor and took them down, while Lily stood like an obedient schoolgirl in front of him, the master, turning round, lifting her chin or her armpits as he bid her—all this so he could produce a blouse that would mould her bosom perfectly.

That man is a pervert, he told her later. No he is not, she replied, he is a tailor.

After that, he gave up. He found himself defeated. She had come to him completely unformed, with few of her own resources, expecting everything of him, offering little in return other than her urge towards domesticity. When her cousins Balu and Suppi started appearing in the evenings, he was glad; willingly he handed her over to them, to take shopping and visiting and tailor groping.

He still made the effort on their wedding anniversary, buying her a gift, taking her out to dinner—thankfully she had the sense to leave her two faithfuls behind—where most of the evening was spent watching the décor or the door to see what interesting faces would appear.

Sometimes he wondered whether she missed having a child, whether her progressive infantilism was a reflexive act of withdrawal. Not that they ever spoke about it, nor did her behaviour show it. It was she who had stopped going to the gynaecologist, refusing to go through the prescribed tests and examinations—they are too painful, she declared. Pain was another thing she abhorred—for five days in the month, she would stuff herself with pain killers and take to her bed. He had never seen his mother or sister ever do such a thing; his mother joked constantly about the low pain threshold of men and the infinite amount of pain that women could endure and did, without thinking about it. They never did find out whether it was his sperm that was grudging or her womb that was inhospitable and, to tell the truth, he did not mind not having a child; he had never consciously longed for one. The only time he had been bruised beyond healing was when Bela had challenged him, so crudely, all those years ago, but that too had grown less painful and the memory of the incident evoked no emotion at all now, not even a twinge of anger. Lily's near obsession with her cat too he put down to her childlessness. Few pregnant cats would get the kind of fuss and diet that hers did and when the animal finally littered in an alcove in the balcony, Lily and her maid-of-the-moment would get into a frenzy about making the balcony tom cat-proof, but the tom cat usually broke through and once it managed to kill the whole litter. All his hints about getting the cat spayed, she had ignored, going through the painful drama every few months. Cats are used to it, she would say in a matter-of-fact way.

There was a hard streak in her that surfaced when she wasn't watchful and of late she had stopped bothering completely, especially with him. Of her cousins Suppi and Balu for instance, whose evenings were given to fulfilling her whims, she often spoke slightingly, and all his jokes, his rather cruel asides about her humble servant Balu or the gargantuan oil-yielding sponge Suppi, she enjoyed, without even the token protest—But they are good people . . . my friends . . . my family.

The first time he noticed it was at a family dinner a few years after they were married. She had stationed herself in the middle of the room, like a deity in a shrine, waiting for people to come up and worship her, which they all did unfailingly. She had looked wholly worthy of homage, in a deep red silk sari and a perfectly fitting blouse of the same material, with cream coloured piping at the seams and a mesmerising bindi flashing in the centre of her forehead—by then though, Bela Bose's khadi kurtas had taught him to doubt his wife's taste. The talk turned predictably to whether it was better to fall in love and then marry or find love within marriage. An older couple were arguing strenuously for love after marriage and he was thinking how unappetizing they looked—she with a moustache and he without—when one of Lily's younger cousins asked her whether she had married for love. He had not been able to catch what she said but he had seen the look on the cousin's face and remembered still how Lily had laughed, her small frame shaking, a blue vein moving in her throat, her perfect teeth glinting, an aberrant thread of green stuck invitingly in the crevasse of an upper canine.

She was quite strong too, despite her small size and delicate manner. He was surprised to find how with one stroke of the kitchen knife she could heft a red pumpkin in two and how effortlessly she pushed and pulled the chairs around when she took it into her head to rearrange the furniture. Once, in the early days of their marriage, in an attempt at being masterful, he had held her in a tight embrace. He had imagined, in true film fashion, she would beat ineffectually against his chest with her fists and fall forward, her hair covering her face, in the time-honoured gesture of surrender. But she had merely flexed her shoulders to gain some purchase and hefted her knee into his groin, not too hard but still . . . and walked away without even making a joke of it. After that he had learned to leave her alone till he received unmistakable signs that his attentions would not be unwelcome.

Perhaps he had also done her an injustice. He could not presume she was unintelligent just because she had no sense of humour. She ran the house well, even if she was a little slovenly. She did not ask for more money than he gave her. She had brought no dowry but she took care of herself—all those shimmering saris and their matching piped blouses, and those shining trinkets and the array of mysterious bottles, she paid for herself from what her father had settled on her. The household chores too were divided satisfactorily between them and they had worked out a good system for the keys and the messages. 'Don't wait for me. I'll be late today' and 'Leave my dinner on the table' were his standard lines to her on the blackboard that he had rigged up on the dining room wall. Hers would read 'Satyanarayana pooja in Sarasi aunty's house today' or 'Gandhi Bazar with Suppi'. They were much like two planets each with its own moons and constellations, mindful of the other's orbit, making sure their paths did not cross. He could say now that there was harmony between them, of a workable kind. Of course, it would be such a bonus if they liked each other.

3

He walked across the dimming playground, noticing how the light failed even as he covered it. He could barely read the dial of his watch. It was a little past six-thirty. Everyone else seemed to have left. The meeting had gone on for three hours and he could say that it had been a fateful day. The third day of the new year. Now he could claim that the year had begun well for him. Deliberately, he took a detour to the parking lot, to take a look at the trenches being dug on the southern side of the playground. So, they were all set to build the new building, were they? That would stop now, he thought, with satisfaction. He would see that the trenches were covered. 'Would you rather see a shopping complex or a mall come up?' Jairam had shouted. 'Can't you see the Trust can't hang on to so much land anymore?' But he had been unmoved. We can develop it into a garden or have a proper cricket pitch or courts for tennis and basketball, he had replied.

The afternoon's meeting was such a success that he himself was taken aback. His faction—for it boiled down to just that—had ousted Jairam's in the academic council meeting quite roundly. He was surprised by the margin; clearly many more people were threatened than they cared to admit. Their motives may have been mixed, confused, or even plain self-serving, but whatever they were, they had been of use to him. The proposal for the new buildings at the other end of the field with the state-of-the-art rooms, audio visual equipment—Jairam had even tried bribing him with a projector for his film club—was struck down. There was no point using the endowment fund towards accumulating more brick and mortar. They could juggle the timetable to accommodate the classes in the present building, perhaps add a few more rooms on top or as an annexe to the administrative corridor. They had allowed for the building to be painted and the toilets to be renovated. As for the courses, there was no need for new faculty, either guest or visiting, it was decided. The present staff could be retrained; they needed to be given a chance to prove themselves—after all the endowment fund included a generous measure for faculty development. These, and many of Jairam's pet schemes were also put into cold storage.

After the meeting, Shrinivas Moorty was surrounded by the others, effectively keeping him back in the staff room longer than he wanted.

'That was a good move. Wanting the faculty development fund to be opened up,' Basavaraj nodded, as if in acknowledgement of craftiness superior to his own. Shrinivas Moorty looked at him sharply, and at Bela next to him, all smiles. Of course, they would expect to be 'rewarded' for their support: first in line in the faculty development queue, with himself leading, that much they would grant him.

Out of the corner of his eye he saw Jairam waiting, so he signalled to Basavaraj and Bela that they would celebrate at the club another day. 'Tomorrow,' he mouthed, keeping an eye on

Jairam who waited across the room for the others to leave before confronting him. The confrontation was inevitable, Shrinivas Moorty knew that. They had been putting it off for months, allowing the acid to accumulate. And as he walked to cover the few feet of floor space between them, he was assailed again by the odd mix of feeling—confusion, anger and affection—that Jairam was so adept at arousing.

'Look Jairam,' he began softly, and he thought, reasonably, 'I don't want it to be like this. It's nothing personal but—'

'Do you think it's over?' Jairam voice was low and harsh with fury. 'That you've won? Of course it isn't personal. It's the way things are headed you fool. Even I couldn't vote against it if I wanted to. If you had it your way, you and your chamchas, you'd keep this place chained to the past forever, have the students grinding away at noble, low-skilled jobs, like yourselves. Do you think we can sit in a room, on aluminium chairs and discuss what is to be done forever? You have to get up and *do* things—'

'Now look Jairam—'

'No! You look Shrinvas. Do you think your precious academic council cannot be overruled? That your decision even matters?'

'We can make the management think again—'

'Management? What management?' Jairam exhaled impatiently, and then took a turn in the room, as if to get a hold over himself, while Shrinivas Moorty waited. 'Do you remember Shrinivas, when we were in college—the errands we were made to run? Collecting firewood from the depot, waiting at the ration shop for the rice and kerosene, waiting for the kalai wala and the plastic wala—'

It had been the most enduring chore of his boyhood, even his youth, waiting in a variety of queues and to catch an assortment of repairmen—waiting at the post office, the bank and the corporation office, waiting at the ration shop where the clerk would not answer his extra-polite questions for their quota of subsidized rice and their allotted one-bottle of kerosene for the wick stove they used when they ran out of gas and a second cylinder was not to be had, waiting with his mother's blackened thick aeroplane-guage aluminium-sheet woks to get them re-silvered, waiting with a bucket that had a hole in its bottom for the seconds-plastics man who would choose a piece to match the colour of his bucket from his carefully culled bits of discarded plastic before melting it over a flame and fusing it with the hole.

'A plastic bucket, Shrinivas, get it into your head, is not a consumer durable. Those days are gone. Even a beggar would throw a broken bucket away, even if he couldn't afford a new one.'

And before he could reply, even as he reached out to clasp his shoulder, Jairam had turned his back on him and had walked away rapidly, as if he could not bear to talk to him anymore.

His scooter was the only vehicle left in the parking lot—last man standing. As he strapped his helmet on, he looked round the empty playground thinking how desolate it looked, like a battlefield at dusk, only recently cleared of the debris of battle but feeling keenly still the clash of steel, the heat of hooves, the thud of each fallen head—a battle in which all had been vanquished, even the victors. The college building at the far end looked grim, with a few lights flickering weakly in the porch and in the corridors. There was another light at the gate and in the watchman's shed, and a few along the periphery where the compound wall ran—the management maintained that it was too expensive to have lights all along the wall, and unnecessary too. But now there would be lights enough.

His scooter would not start. He turned it over on its side as far as he could without toppling it over to get the petrol flowing, grunting as the morning's spasm renewed itself. He must stop for the antacid, he told himself. And it was also time to get rid of the scooter, he reluctantly admitted to himself. The old warhorse had served him well. He had bought it the year he had got married. He remembered the way Lily had wrinkled her nose at it the first time she had seen it. I've never sat on a two-wheeler before, she said. I hope it's safe. Her cousin Balu used to take her round in his car, which he still did. Stubbornly, Shrinivas Moorty refused to buy one, even though he could easily raise a loan to buy a second-hand car now. There was no need for one when there were just the two of them, and for the kind of travelling he did.

Her name is Leelavati, his mother had said. She pestered him for weeks. These people are very insistent. They are related to Raji, I can't put them off, his mother said. I told them you don't want to get married now but they are pressing me. Why don't you just see the girl? Raji says she is very beautiful. I know, she added, you prefer brains to beauty, but why don't you see her, just to help keep my word?

No, he had said impatiently, no. He had been teaching for two years at National Trust College then, confirmed and one could say, settled. Though they had never discussed it, it was understood that eventually he would ask Geeta to marry him. Apart from Jairam she was his oldest friend, the one who was best used to him. They read the same books and saw the same films. Whenever he came across anything new that excited or amused him, his first instinct was, I must tell Jairam, but as Jairam became less accessible, it became I must tell Geeta. They would have to break the news to each other's parents. This was another thing that was making him postpone it indefinitely. His parents would make a fuss for she belonged to a different caste, a *lower* caste, and she was not Kannada-speaking, but that she was the daughter of a rich, socially prominent father would be in her favour. Rumour had it that Geeta's parents were so distracted over their son—a drug addict whom they were trying to rehabilitate—that they would be relieved their daughter had chosen a safe man.

He agreed to 'see' this Leelavati more as a way to tell his parents about Geeta. This was as good a time as any since Geeta had started dropping pointed hints as well. She was twenty-six and though she had started working on her doctorate, she could not stave off her parents, however preoccupied they were, much longer. For days his mother would bring home bits and pieces of news about Leelavati. Of her looks—they say she is like Sita. Which Sita, he had asked. Rama's wife, of course, his mother had said. And would you believe it, they live just two streets away from Ammanagudi Street, and I hadn't even heard of them till Raji came all the way from Madras to tell me. I wonder why she isn't married though, at twenty-six. Her father was a retired government official, an honest one, so he may not have had too much money, enough to attract a boy good enough for his daughter. She was his only daughter. They lived in a large joint family, so she was used to people. She had done her BA. She could paint. She went for flower arrangement classes. Each piece of information was served up with his dinner, like a tit bit to placate his sweet tooth, and he could tell that his mother had been planning it all day. He received it all calmly; his mind was made up. After all the 'seeing' was just a formality. He was doing it to please his mother.

When he walked across to her house with his parents one evening, at an hour carefully selected to evade rahukala, he was buoyed by the sense of the absurd; it kept him afloat and amused enough to go through the introductions with a roomful of assorted relatives, whose eyes rested on him with deferential expectation.

'Bring the girl in,' the girl's father commanded.

Bring the girl in ... bring the girl in ... the command went down to the antapura of the house, where the girl, no doubt, was waiting. He watched the doorway with no more than normal curiosity to see the girl.

After several minutes the girl was escorted into the room. Till then there had been no women from the girl's family in the room and then suddenly there was a crowd of girls and women in the doorway, a rustling of pleats, sibilant instructions hushed hastily, much giggling too and from his family whispers of Which is the girl, How on earth are we to know if so many come in at the same time. But he knew at once which the girl was. She paused briefly in the doorway and looked up, straight at him. Their eyes met for an infinitesimal second, and that was it. He felt the blood rush through him like a dam-burst, sending the heat through his limbs and his face, setting him on fire, rendering him numb, his whole being concentrated in an acute confused consciousness. It took several minutes for the shafts to subside, for him to collect himself and sit down, for without realizing it he had risen to his feet. Her uncle who was sitting next to him asked him several questions but they did not register and he answered them, not knowing what he said, relying on the residuum of urbanity, of instinctive good manners and breeding to tide him over. She was made to sit directly in front of him and for the rest of the evening, he couldn't, he wouldn't take his eyes off her. Again and again, in the crush of women who surrounded her, he could see only her face and form, as if it was lit up by a spotlight, as if her very soul was calling to him across the room. His mother had forewarned him about her beauty but clearly she knew nothing about her allure. Once the girl sat in front of him, she would not look at him again. She looked down and sometimes up, her lips moved, sometimes in a smile and sometimes in speech, in reply to a question someone asked her, but she did not look or smile at him. She was small, fragile almost, and carefully formed, like a doll that was hand crafted and custom-made. Her sari fluffed around her, a confection in orange organza, and here and there, from beneath its semi-transparent folds her skin glowed, luminous and full of promise. But he kept coming back to the trick of her eyes. She had a way of lifting her eyelids, slowly, as if she were bringing to bear a deep mysterious inner resource, a boon, a blessing upon the person or object on whom her eyes would rest. He sat there, abjectly longing all evening, for those eyelids to lift and for her eyes to fix themselves on him.

Finally someone suggested that 'the boy and the girl should speak to each other alone'. As they walked into the balcony, he knew he had to seize the moment—say something deep and mesmerizing, something worthy of the man he was, something that would stun her speechless, or something that would at least make her laugh.

'What,' he said 'is your name?'

She leaned across to him like a flower on a stem. 'Lily,' she said.

'*Lily*?' he repeated '*Perfect*.'

When they came home, even his mother, who could be depended upon to chisel out a serious flaw in the most perfect of things could only declare that the girl was a 'dantada bombe'—an ivory doll—the ultimate praise.

'Well,' she turned on him with a challenge in her voice, 'What do you say? What do we tell them?'

'Tell them,' he said, blushing, 'tell them I said yes.'

'Just as I thought,' his mother nodded in satisfaction. 'I'll tell them tomorrow.'

'No, tell them today. Now!' For he was sure that she would not last till the next day. Someone else might snatch her away. In fact, he wondered how she had not been taken for so long.

Much later, he remembered Geeta; he remembered also his avowed preference for dark complexioned women. Much later it also emerged that Lily was older than he was, that she had a younger brother, not quite right in the head, hidden away, who was not brought out of the closet on such occasions, lest he spoil her chances. But none of these things mattered. However, he had to think of some way of breaking the news to Geeta. He called up Jairam. Jairam, he said, I have some good news. Then he added, Will you tell Geeta? Please do me this favour—

Three months later, Jairam and Geeta were married. Shrinivas Moorty was on his honeymoon then and could not attend the wedding.

PART V

eleven

~

Monday, 3 January 2000

There are no trees on Ammanagudi Street in James Hunter's late eighteenth century sketch of the Pagoda of the Amma. You could even say it is not the same street, except for the temple. There is a lone palm tree behind the temple, and the street is empty of people and buildings, even stray dogs. Ammanagudi Street, narrow though it is today, has many trees—old, full grown trees that burst into flower in summer and shelter sleeping dogs and cows, and vendors of sundry wares all the year round. The trees also house birds and proffer a helpful limb to passing creatures who may not want to stay the night but just rest awhile. The trees look lopsided, for the telephone department comes from time to time with its high ladder to cut off the branches which tangle with the overhead telephone wires. The roots of the trees too are trimmed often to widen the street or tile the footpath or when they puncture the underground drains. But roots are stubborn things and the roots of the Ammanagudi Street trees rise to the surface in a matter of months, making large cracks in the newly cemented footpath and the cement slowly collapses along those cracks, breaking up the smooth surface, causing people to trip. There is one Cassia, generous of canopy and flower, whose roots are particularly errant, and its single exposed root almost caused Neela Gopalrao, Pushpa Rani and Shrinivas Moorty to come to grief that evening. The next ferocious bout of unseasonal rain would see the Cassia, roots ripped out, fallen across Ammanagudi Street, much to the bewilderment of the birds nesting in it, but that was still to come and none of them would be there to see it. But on that day, 3 January 2000, the tree and its roots were hale and hearty and determined; the one exposed root lying in wait in the darkness, gleaming slick like the coil of a giant's intestine, to trip Neela up and send her flying, to her eternal undying shame, into Sukhiya Ram's arms, to bring Shrinivas Moorty back to earth from his reverie with a neck-displacing jerk and to give Pushpa Rani a premonition of death.

That evening, the evening of 3 January, a Monday, the bus set Neela and Sukhiya Ram down far away from Ammanagudi Street, because of the obstruction caused by the debris of the flyover, which meant Neela had a longer walk with Sukhiya and she was not quite sure of the way home.

'Don't worry madam,' Sukhiya said, 'I know the way. When the flyover started, two years ago, I was supposed to work on it, madam, along with the others from my village—'

Neela stepped up her pace to stop him from talking, secretly relieved at his offer for this side of Ammanagudi Street seemed to have far more narrow alleys than her side. Besides, there was a power cut and the evening was strangely eerie. The sky looked ghostly, the last grey light lifted high into the heavens, leaving the creatures below to fend for themselves in the darkness. They were walking down a broad street with large houses and deep compounds. The street was deserted and the branches of the trees were the only things they could see clearly outlined against the unresisting sky. She smelt the strong, fetid, powdery rush in the air and even as she was trying to guess, something swooped past her ear, causing her to start and move closer to Sukhiya Ram.

'A bat madam, harmless,' Sukhiya said soothingly. 'In my village madam—'

'Once we turn into Ammanagudi Street I will know my way,' she said but could not summon her usual hauteur.

They walked on in silence, into the grey evening that was descending rapidly into blackness, when Sukhiya Ram said, 'Madam, Prithvi Sir's letter—you knew it was in the drawer?'

It was the darkness. And the bat. And her own behaviour. Instinctively, she had moved towards him in the darkness. He would not have dared otherwise.

'It doesn't matter, madam,' he said reading her silence. 'Whatever happened was for the good.'

Yes, she echoed silently in her mind, whatever happened was for the good. God moves in strange ways, she told herself. He had saved her from discovery, from exposure, and from the thing she dreaded most—loss of face. She thought briefly of Prithvi Kumar, with more comfort now, not with fresh, blinding anger but as if he were an unpleasant memory which would be exorcised soon, and so allowed herself some regret. In the darkness, before she could help it, a tear rolled down her cheek and she hoped that Sukhiya had not seen it.

They turned into Ammanagudi Street and she felt a little better. The emergency lamps in a few shops relieved the darkness. She was still trying to locate the familiar shops and other landmarks by the faint light when something caught her foot and she lost her balance, lurched forward and fell straight into Sukhiya's arms. And even as she was torn between the pain in her wrenched ankle and her shame, there was a rush against her right ear and she sensed a shadowy figure dashing past. She must have screamed for the next thing she knew was that she was firmly, unambiguously clasped in Sukhiya Ram's embrace.

'I thought it was a giant bat,' she said later in the evening to the reporter who questioned her, 'a huge grey vampire bat.'

The autorickshaw man dropped Pushpa Rani on the wrong side of Ammanagudi Street because it was in complete darkness. I can't go in there, he said, pointing to the hulk of the flyover that loomed above them. She hesitated, still sitting in the auto but got off hastily when he started the vehicle again and raised the engine to a questing screech. It meant a shorter walk for Pushpa Rani, but she was not familiar with this side of Ammanagudi Street. She made her way tentatively down the left side of the street, where the pavement would have been had it not been dug up, weaving past the cars parked on the wrong side of the road, trying to avoid the two wheelers with no headlights. And just as the outlines of the buildings were beginning to take shape in the light of the shops, just as she could see the shoulders of people walking on the street, and just as she had identified the turn she should take to go home, her foot got wedged securely under what she thought was a hose pipe and she went sprawling. Even as she got up, her elbows grazed and burning, feeling for her purse amidst the rubble and grasping instead the protruding root of the Cassia, she saw a face framed above her, in the full light of the headlamp of a motorcycle, huge eyes, teeth bared in a snarl, and behind the face . . . No! She thought with a clutch of agony. It couldn't be, surely it couldn't be . . .

She ran home, as quickly as the darkness would allow her, and even before she entered the narrow passage leading to her house, she knew her worst fears would be realized—and sure enough, her mother's blue rubber flip-flops were missing and her father's brand new leather slippers that she had bought him for his birthday the previous week, were there, exactly where they had been when she left in the morning.

We were waiting for you, her sister said, we couldn't get you on your phone. He fell when he was getting down from the bed. They have taken him to Modern Nursing Home. Mani Nurse was here.

There was a funny taste in Pushpa Rani's mouth and she suddenly felt dizzy; it was such a bad feeling that she slumped against the door jamb and sank to the floor.

'I know,' she said, 'I saw him.'

'Saw whom?'

She knew then that she had not been mistaken. She had not imagined it. When she had fallen on the ground in Ammanagudi Street and was trying to pick herself up, distinctly, behind the snarling face, framed against the light, she had seen the horns and the bulk of a buffalo.

'My goodness,' her sister said, holding the candle up. 'Look at you, there's blood on your face. And on your arms too. Why Pushpakka, what happened?'

How had it come to this, this quicksilver life, decreed by fate to be played out in such narrow environs, within a radius of three kilometres to be precise. He had not travelled, had not seen the world, yet he knew it well. So much had changed even as it remained unchanging—his parents were gone, SVK would go any moment, his friendships were a chimera and his wife an enigma—and still he remained, solid, of the flesh. He could see them all, their cores, still pure, illuminated, shimmering, and also the layers that had thickened around them—dense, impervious, impenetrable, wilful in self-absorption.

When Shrinivas Moorty turned into Ammanagudi Street that evening, between the crossroad and the exposed root of the Cassia that lay in wait for him, he had traversed his whole life. But these were not his thoughts. He was lamenting several things—that the meeting was over and that he had won so decisively, leaving no ground for rapprochement with Jairam, that he could no longer see his wife as he had first seen her, that he had not been able to take Basavaraj and Bela to the club. In fact he was lamenting Bela Bose's now thickened neck when the scooter hit the root and even as his neck whiplashed into place, jerking him back painfully into the present, he braked and steadied himself, and the lights went off on Ammanagudi Street, plunging the whole place instantly into deep darkness.

For a few minutes, till the shops that had generators turned on their lights, he was aware of the intense darkness and the street that had suddenly turned quiet. And then the welder's torch scattered beads of light and a corner of the street turned festive for a minute, and Shrinivas Moorty was relieved. The headlight of his scooter, pale, yellow and weak, showed him the way home. The sound of his scooter, as he manoeuvred the narrow stretch of unbroken land connecting the street to his house, seemed unnaturally loud. He revved up the engine before switching it off so that anyone emerging from the pitch-dark parking basement would know that there was a vehicle in their path. Deciding against parking his scooter in the basement, he stood it against the wall and was locking it when something fell next to him with a thump. He looked up to see the something, a creature of some sort, scurrying off on all fours towards the gate. Intrigued but not alarmed, he felt his way up the two flights of stairs and waited at the door. His knuckles grew sore from knocking and, when she finally opened the door, he found his wife quite incoherent and in tears. She had not had the presence of mind to switch on the emergency lamp, which he too could not find. It was only when he lit a candle that he saw the blood on her clothes—a fetching gown in purple lace he noted absently—and the scratches on her right forearm. They did not seem too deep but they were bleeding profusely and she could not say how she got them. She had been sleeping and a noise in the balcony had woken her up. She had gone out to see what it was when whatever it was had attacked her and jumped off the balcony. All she could do was cry and hold out her forearm, like a child. He cleaned her wounds with Dettol and bandaged her arm, and then stepped out onto the balcony.

'Don't come here,' he told his wife. 'Stay indoors.' For even in the flickering light of the candle he could see the blood on the floor and when he moved the candle closer to the 'safe alcove', the torn bodies of the kittens, born just the other day, their eyes not yet open.

'I want Mani Nurse,' his wife said, sinking back into the rumpled bed. 'Fetch Mani Nurse. She is the only one who is good to me.'

In the corridor, outside his flat, he could hear people talking. The powerful beam of his torch caught Singhania, his neighbour, full in the face, distorting his features, making him unrecognizable almost.

'Have they caught him?' Singhania asked, putting his hand out to ward off the light as if it were a physical blow.

'Caught whom?'

'The thief. There was a thief in the compound. Some one shouted from the second floor balcony. A woman. He must have jumped in from the building next door.'

'No, not a thief, I mean it did not seem like a man,' Shrinivas Moorty said slowly. 'More like some kind of animal, a creature of some sort.'

'Is that so? Did you see it? Do you hear?' Singhania called out to his wife. 'Moortyji here saw the thief.'

'I saw him—it—run off.'

'Can you hear the voices in the street? They must have caught him. Must have wanted to rob the place, or snatch that woman's chain, the one who screamed. Are you going out?'

'Yes,' Shrinivas Moorty said, suddenly remembering the errand he was on. 'My wife, I have to get some medicines for her. She's hurt herself in the dark. Something seems to have scratched her.'

Back on the street, on the way to Mani Nurse's house, he found the men standing about in knots. There was a nip of excitement in the air—the kind that came with rumours of a riot. The electricity had still not come back, but the generators had brought some lights on here and there.

'A strange creature was seen on the street,' the man at the chemist's said.

'What? Oh! A bottle of Dettol and a roll of gauze bandage . . . and Milk of Magnesia if you have it,' he said to the waiting chemist as he tried to recall the form he had seen scurrying away in the darkness. 'I know, I saw it,' he said. 'A monkey, I think, or some such thing. Oh!' It occurred to Shrinivas Moorty even as he spoke that it must be the same creature that had killed the kittens and scratched Lily before making off. 'It was there, in my house in the balcony. I almost caught it—'

'Really? Some people say it was a man—'

'My neighbour was quite sure it was a thief.'

'—or a man-like creature, like those pictures of primitive men in my son's textbook. What are those names—'

'Neanderthal man. Cro-Magnon man.'

There was a hubbub as more men crowded into the shop.

'Have you heard—'

'Did you see—'

'The TV people are here—'

'And a journalist from a newspaper too. The boys at the fast food joint, they are talking to the reporter.'

'Already? The newspapers don't waste much time, I must say.'

He made his way through the small groups that had gathered, people who were hailing each other, in excitement, in nervousness, still standing in the darkness. Mani Nurse too was agog with the news. Apparently her daughter had had a brush with the creature. Only, she thought it was more bird-like, a giant bird whose wings scraped the floor. The girl had rung up the local radio station for she knew the RJ.

Later in the evening, after Lily had been taken to Modern Nursing Home and had the first of her rabies shots and Mani Nurse had settled her down for the night with a mild sedative and news of a patient who had had much worse luck—a very nice man who had slipped and fallen from his bed and broken his hip and who had to be operated upon immediately—he got a call from Bali Brums, the RJ, to appear on his live interview show the next day.

Shrinivas Moorty's instinct was to say no and bang the phone down.

'Yes,' he said instead. 'Yes, I'd like to share what I saw, my impressions with your listeners.'

twelve

~

Tuesday, 4 January 2000

The Morning After

Neela woke up that morning to the state of besieged calm that follows great excitement. She was going to be interviewed by Bali Brums on Voices from Heaven. Bali Brums, her friend, her soulmate, the voice in her heart, her spur, her conscience keeper, had spoken to her the previous evening and said, Neela, will you be mine? Yes, she had said, a hundred times over, yes.

She chose her clothes with care, and for a long time caressed the fine-textured cloth, revelling in the strong colours. Wear the colours that speak to you, the columnist in *City Lights* had said, never mind what is fashionable, you must feel good in whatever you wear. Then, your aura will be bright and will send out positive vibes. Her earrings, her bangles, her rings, her hair clips and her shoes too she laid out, and surveyed the ensemble, imagining the effect when they all became part of her. She would reveal all that day, she would tell Bali Brums and the whole of Bangalore what she owed him.

But, it was getting late. She had to get ready on time. The taxi, specially arranged by Bali, would be coming soon. The only irritant was that Sukhiya Ram was also coming with her. She just could not avoid that inconvenient bit. For Bali Brums, clever man, had unearthed Sukhiya too from the slum he lived in and invited him to the show. She was in the bathroom when her mother, another innocent, called to her in great excitement that Sukhiya Ram had arrived. Tell him to wait then, she said through gritted teeth. By the time the taxi came, Sukhiya Ram had finished drinking two cups of tea and telling her mother all about his village and his cows, and also that Antonia Larson and Alka Gupta were going to visit.

In the back seat of the taxi, something was bothering Shrinivas Moorty. It was not the overwhelming perfume that Mani Nurse's daughter had doused herself in, nor the incessant chatter in Hindi by the boy in the front seat. It was not even the fact that Balaji Brahmendra had not recognized him when he had identified himself over the phone the previous evening; obviously he was one of these new fangled morons who had a brain like a sieve. Take that other reporter for instance. The young man from the first newspaper that had got in touch with him. What did the creature look like sir, tell us, he had said, scribbling in his pad. Shrinivas Moorty was very pleased with his reply, which he thought was spontaneous, urbane, succinct and of course, educated. 'Nasty, brutish and short,' he had said. But the reporter had not caught on. He had made him repeat it and asked him to spell 'brutish'. But that was not it either. It was something else, something that had bothered him all night and all morning, which he couldn't put a finger on. But it would come to him.

There had been a sudden shower of rain in the morning and the weather had gone from bright and sunny to muggy in the space of two hours. In the first week of January! That was Bangalore weather for you—never too hot and never too cold, nor rainy either. He looked at the trees on either side of the road, shorn of all leaves, damp, holding out their bare arms to the sky, like barrels of smoking guns. He shifted in his new shirt, still stiff with starch and smelling of shop, and thought glumly that he shouldn't have come.

He was being harassed by reporters since last evening. He had kept them away from Lily, though. She had been resting all day. Mani Nurse had faithfully reported in the morning, to look her up. He had repeated his story ad nauseum to several reporters, till he knew his account by heart—the same words, only with successive reportings his enthusiasm waned, till he became impatient. Refer notes of previous class, he wanted to snap at them as he did with his students. And now, as he tried going over the events of the previous evening, he was surprised to find how hazy they were. He could get no further from the welder's torch and the light from it. He tried deliberately to recall the creature he had glimpsed in the gloaming—had there been a flash of white?

Balaji Brahmendra was nervous. He wondered if he had been a little over-enthusiastic in going in for a live interview. Though he had done them before these things were always chancy. But then he liked taking that risk. That was what made his interviews so great, so different from the others'; that was what got the fan mail rolling in in an adoring gush and the acknowledging nod from the older listeners. He was known for his chemistry with the people he interviewed, irrespective of their age and sex. He could draw people out, get them to say unexpected things about themselves, admissions they would not have dreamt of making perhaps. The trick was to lull them into trusting you, and then take them by surprise, go for the jugular by throwing their own words back at them. Ultimately what mattered was that the interview should be interesting, that the listeners be entertained, and of course, that he remain master of his show. But today it looked as if it would not quite gel. For one, the three of them seemed slightly hostile to each other, rather the woman and the teacher were. Perhaps these three were nervous, which was usually the case. It was their big moment. He would have to try harder to put them at their ease. In a way, this was his final test. He had been making too many mistakes, small trip-ups, but any more and the programme director would have his scalp. Too much personality, he had told him. Hold yourself back a little. Don't put so much of yourself in the show. Remember, it's not about you. But it was about him; if not they would have got someone else to run the show.

He had taken care to send a taxi to pick up all three of them. Now he felt three were too many. He should have dropped the babbler. He had brought him on to outdo Chantal, the only other RJ at the station to rival him in fan span and intensity, and all because she imitated a rustic, speaking a cutely inventive mixture of English and Kannada. He had got Sukhiya Ram just to be one up on her; so much better to get an actual performer rather than imitate one—the man's quaint Hindi in an English programme would tickle people no end. Besides, he would not be speaking in Kannada, so the prickly brigade, the self-appointed watchdogs of the Kannada language, who were just waiting for someone to offend their sensibilities, would not take umbrage. But now he felt he should have dropped him; even before the programme had begun he had become unbearable, talking non-stop, asking questions all the time. The oldish teacher, who was now beginning to look vaguely familiar, seemed ill at ease; in fact he looked as if he were in pain. He had been difficult right from the beginning, asking for the questions in advance. From the woman he expected no trouble. She had been looking at him out of the corner of her eyes, with suppressed excitement from the time she came, but that was not unusual. He wished Pushpa Rani had been able to come. She was the other person who had spotted the creature and had phoned in to his show to say so, and nothing was more gratifying than having a regular listener in the studio—it made them so happy—and the Flower Queen would have been face to face with him at last, but there had been an accident at home. Her father had fallen down and had to be taken to hospital. He made a mental note to mention the old man on the show and wish him well.

The conducted tour of the studio was over. He had explained to them how the recording would work, the system of cues and signals, and what they were expected to do. He had got the woman to remove her jangling bangles and earrings, explaining that the sound would carry and added that she looked equally great without them, and she had removed them coquettishly, with many a pout and moue. So when they went into the studio, they were all in a good mood and he felt that things would go off smoothly.

USHA K.R.

'Remember,' he smiled one last time, 'when the red light comes on, we are on air. Everything you say can be heard—by the five million people in our city.'

The moment he wore his head phones and the red light came on, Balaji Brahmendra was on song. The introduction went off like a dream.

'—a plane? A bird? A monkey? A man? The whole of the city has been waiting to know since last evening, when an unusual creature was spotted on Ammanagudi Street in south Bangalore. And right now, here on Voices from Heaven, on the Bali Brums show, I bring you the first three people, yes the first three, to spot that . . . THING . . . and they will tell you, in their own words, what they saw with their own eyes—'

First, he thought, he would bring on the rustic. Keep the older man for the last; he was still looking a bit ill.

'Sukhiya Ram, the man from Lord Krishna's village no less, and like Him, he loves cows—'

'I'll tell you what I saw,' Sukhiya Ram boomed into the mike. Balaji winced and reached for the console to tweak the knob. 'I saw a rakshas.'

'Tell our listeners what it looked like—'

'Like a rakshas of course. What do rakshases look like? Big, black, hairy, with fangs for teeth and fire coming out of its eyes.'

'Is that what you saw?' Balaji interjected a little sharply.

'That's what a rakshas is like, isn't it, and I saw a rakshas. Besides they are experts at changing their form. They are not like you and me; they change shape from minute to minute, second to—'

'No, no. When the creature went past you . . . when you saw it—'

'At that exact moment I was concentrating on comforting madam. She was very frightened—'

Balaji immediately switched to the woman. 'Neela—'

'Bali,' she said huskily and he could see her eyes shimmering,

'I am here to let you and the whole of Bangalore know what a wonderful support you have been to me, how much your good spirits, your music and your advice have meant to me—'

'Thank you so much Neela, that's really sweet of you but—'

'No, you don't understand. You see, I am Nelly.'

He stared at her, his mind absolutely blank.

'*I* am Nelly.'

Still nothing.

'I want to thank you for holding my hand and leading me through the difficult moments, for helping me connect with my inner self. You taught me to be a real person. I have followed all your cues: "Go for it girl," you said and I did. "All is fair in love and war"—you never spoke a truer word. And the other day you said, "Let go of that baggage and float free," and that's exactly what I did. That was so right. It was so me—'

For the first time in his life, Balaji Brahmendra was completely at a loss. For a moment he forgot where he was and what he was doing; desperately he floated free of his body, searching for a clue, while she babbled on and on. And then it struck him. Of course. Nelly! Nuisance Nelly. The creature who plagued him with emails and SMSes and phone calls. With flowers that he had to ask her not to send and chocolates that he had had to return. He remembered her telling him something about a man—

'That's good, we do our best to help our listeners,' he managed, knowing how inadequate that was, 'but if you could come back to yesterday evening. Ammanagudi Street, when you got down from the bus—'

'The monster does not matter—' she gestured grandly, hitting the microphone next to hers, 'what matters is that we are here and we are all connecting. Isn't that what the show is all about, isn't that what you say every evening? So many thousands of us, maybe millions feel the spark light up within us at the same time—'

'Of course, of course Neela—'

'Call me Nelly, Bali. To you I am Nelly; my name sounds so beautiful on your lips—'

And then, just as he felt the waters closing in above his head, he was saved most unexpectedly. Shrinivas Moorty, the reader from National Trust College, whom he had just recognized as the balding man in the batik shirt who had given him a bad time at that seminar he had gone to attend and whose turn it was to speak next, pitched headlong into his microphone, struck the console sharply, sprawled across it and lay still.

Then, only then, did Balaji Brahmendra have the presence of mind to press the red button and set the programme into auto mode.

It was the red studio light. When the door closed and the red light came on, Shrinivas Moorty saw again the welder's torch of the previous evening on Ammanagudi Street. He saw the welder's protective visor and his naked hands on which the sparks fell, he saw the torch lighting up everything around it momentarily with a fiery, devouring radiance, even the yellow plastic box with the STD/ISD sign that hung on a branch of the stunted honge tree seemed on fire, and he saw silhouetted against that light, something under the STD/ISD sign that he had not seen before and he knew then what it was that had been eluding him all the time.

And then the first doubt crept in, bringing others in its wake, weaving a trail of thought, of memories, of associations so quick, so fantastic, so improbable and so heartbreaking that it could only be true.

Ever since he sat in the taxi, he had been feeling uneasy, and in the studio the feeling had grown into a heart-pounding anxiety. He wondered whether the others were feeling as hot as he was, despite the air-conditioning. He had reached to unbutton his collar several times, only to find it already unbuttoned. He knew he'd feel better once the waiting was over and the recording began. And then the door closed and the red light came on.

He thought then, of Lily. He remembered the look of dazed stillness on her face, the purple, blood-stained lace at her throat. Licking her lips nervously. Eyes wide with fear. The breath rasping in her throat. Clammy hands. Constricted chest. As cold as ice.

As still as water. As silent as a grave. As cunning as a fox. Vixen. Vamp. Witch. Every old cliché, every worn illustration of idiomatic English from the standard middle school text book came back to him, filled with new sense-making meaning.

What he had seen last evening on Ammanagudi Street, by the light of the arched scattering of golden sparks, was the back of a car, a red Maruti 800. In the darkness he had first hit something hard on the road and had almost been thrown off his scooter and then by the lucky light of those sparks he had also fatefully swerved to avoid the vehicle parked almost halfway into the street—the driver could not have helped it for the footpath where he would have otherwise parked had been dug up to accommodate their new fibre optic cable.

A red Maruti 800. Could it be Balu's car?

He had not seen the number and the Maruti 800 was not the most distinctive of cars but it could well have been Balu's. But Balu was out of town. Lily had told him so when she called him during the day asking him to pick up her medicines. The phone call had delayed him and he had gone to class a good ten minutes late but he remembered she had said quite clearly that Balu could not pick up the medicines as he would not be coming that day. He was away, in Coimbatore. But Balu could have changed his mind and stayed back. And then, as he stared at the red light above the studio door, he made a leap, of reason or perhaps of bizarre illogic.

Could it be Balu who had dropped out of his first floor balcony, almost crushing him to death?

But why would Balu want to shin down the drainpipe in the dark? Why? Because something must have taken him by surprise. Something unexpected must have occurred. But Balu was not supposed to be there at all. But then, neither was he. He had told Lily that morning that he would be late, and he rarely came home earlier than he said he would. He had changed his mind after the meeting. Balu too could have changed his plans. But why had he not walked out of the front door like he had every right to?

This was ridiculous, he chided himself. The mind was a monkey, a creature of untamed instinct. It could run in several directions at the same time if not held back. The Maruti 800, especially the red Maruti 800—he couldn't even be sure of the colour—was the most common car in Bangalore. On Ammanagudi Street alone there were at least ten of them parked at the same time. And there *had* been a creature; he had seen it scrambling away. Others had seen it too. By now the whole city was talking about it. And there had been the scratches on Lily's forearm—so deep and vicious—like the claw marks of an angry cat. Cat! The scat cat. The tom cat. Eternal prowler. Relentless predator. Seeker of warm new blood even if it were his own. How many litters had he devoured, all of which he had sired. The tom cat had been lurking around since morning. He himself had chased it away when he set off for work. Could it be that his wife and Balu had surprised the tom cat in the act of killing the kittens? But what had they been disturbed by? By the sound of his scooter of course, loud for he had had to rev it up to negotiate that bit of dug-up ground. He thought of the cat, cornered, hissing and in his hurry to get away, hitting out at whatever came his way. Balu, simultaneously in a panic that his bhava would catch him in the act, that he could not chance meeting him on the stairs, had got away, much like the tom cat, through the only exit route available to him—the drain pipe.

This was just too far fetched. What was he thinking? That Balu had run all the way home, in his chaddis, impersonating a monster, a monkey? But Balu *was* the original nasty, brutish and short creature. He himself had said so. He thought of all the times he had teased Lily about her 'devoted servant', her Hanumanta to his Rama and her reaction—that startled look, the short gasp of outrage turning to delight, the watchful stillness of her face, as if any moment he would turn the corner and find out. Those inexplicable short black trousers in his cupboard that were the dhobi's mistake, the multiple bottles of pickle which neither Lily nor he liked. When had it all started? The brief period when Suppi was absent after she had married the widower? Did Suppi know at all? Was it possible that she was abetting them—?

He laughed again at his stupidity, at the delusions of his mind. Just pluck the whole thing out by its cancer-spreading roots and throw it out, he told himself. If he watered the seed of doubt with his imagination it would grow into a monster of certainty. And then, just as he had settled the matter, there was that little prick of uncertainty again, ballooning through his chest so quickly, growing sharper and sharper and knifing through his heart with a pain so intense that he had to scrabble at the buttons of his shirt to tear his chest open . . .

PART VI
~

Postscript

~

The 'simian terror' stayed in the city for a month or so. After exhibiting itself first on Ammanagudi Street the creature travelled to the north of the city where it turned playful, even sadistic and then it broke free of all bounds—of geography and biology, of man-made states, of form and structure and DNA—shedding its anthropomorphic skin, and reaching for the sky in a simpler, more atavistic avatar. It mutated, not just into different beings but increased in number, appearing simultaneously in the north, south, east and west of the country.

From Bangalore it seemed to have approached Madras—recently renamed Chennai—cautiously, restricting its attentions to animals alone. It entered the Arignar Anna Zoo in Vandalur, and killed three locked and caged animals in the dead of night, before moving into the surrounding reserve forest where its next victims were a couple of spotted deer and a porcupine, and then, apparently becoming bolder, the creature ventured into the environs of the famed Madras Christian College where it did in a goat and a piglet. There was no evidence that it had tried to eat any of its kills. The principal conservator of forests was unable to identify the animal. The director of the zoo appealed to the central government to release funds for the completion of the compound wall round the zoo.

By the time it reached Delhi, the creature was no longer shy. It now had a name. It was definitely the Monkey-man that cavorted in the electricity-less gullies of Delhi's lower middle-class areas for days in the sweltering summer, till the police issued shoot-at-sight orders. The creature appeared in the west, in the Khanpur Darwaza slum in Ahmedabad, around the same time. The two men who saw it and fainted immediately, on recovering described it as dark-skinned, curly haired and remarkably nimble, and were reportedly behaving 'abnormally' since—the local maulvi, strenuously denying that the creature could be a drug addict, a prankster or a madman, was treating them for hypnosis. And right then, even as the creature hopped from tree to tree in Ahmedabad, a man in Russalgaon in Guna district, Madhya Pradesh, woke up in the middle of the night to find a peculiar animal sitting on his chest, watching him calmly. It had the face of a dog, or perhaps it was a cat, he said, he couldn't be sure, but it was quite small, not more than two feet. The man was taken to the local veterinary hospital and administered a series of shots.

On the coast of Orissa the creature rose into the sky after sunset, a huge ball of fire, turning night into day, causing birds to chirp in the middle of the night and men to cower under their beds, before falling out of the sky and gutting scores of thatched houses in Mayurbhanj district. The director of the observatory at Nainatal, holding a stone that reportedly fell out of the fireball on to a rooftop, said that it was in all possibility a meteor and that the stone he was holding had distinct magnetic properties, and that his people were still studying the phenomenon.

In the villages of Uttar Pradesh and Madhya Pradesh—the heartland of the country—reflecting the fabled forthrightness of the rural people, the creature simply went for the eyes and was named, with equal lack of ado, the muhnochwa or face scratcher. Village after village reportedly was attacked by a small creature, a winged blistering orange-sized thing that emitted a red light when it attacked and a green light from under its uplifted tail before departing. It left deep scratches round its victim's eyes and mouth. A newspaper carried a photograph of one such victim—a young man whose eyes stared wildly through his bandaged face with the women folk gathered round him. While the deputy inspector general of police, Faizabad district, described the muhnochwa as a 'technologically-developed, man-made insect' brought into the country by anti-national elements to create panic in villages and towns, the weary chief of police of Lucknow dismissed it as 'just people's imagination'. By now, an All-India Expert Committee, constituted of members of the National Institute of Human Behaviour and the Central Forensic Laboratory, concluded that the phenomenon could be attributed to 'socio-economic deprivation, stress, psychiatric disorders, alcohol-related illness and mental retardation of the people'.

Meanwhile, a professor of the premier Indian Institute of Technology, Kanpur, a specialist in high voltage electricity, ascribed all such mysterious flying objects, big, small, fiery, furry, blue, green, red or yellow, to lightning: 'Balls of lightning, ranging from the size of a tennis ball to a football, that abound in the dry season.' The scratches on the victims' faces were burn injuries caused by the lightning, he added. There was nothing new about these travelling balls of lightning. They were commonly reported in Europe and the US as well.

Not to be outdone—as if taking umbrage at the good professor's dismissal—the creature resurfaced briefly, in its monkey avatar, in the Varanasi, Mirzapur and Chandauli districts of Uttar Pradesh and then, a year after its first appearance, it disappeared from the pages of every newspaper in the country. That is, not counting a wolf-like Bear-man who appeared in the Nalbari district of Assam, which the Assam Science Society was investigating and the neem tree in Calcutta that started bleeding—drops of real blood—when someone tried to chop it down with an axe. The local people believed that the tree was an avatar of Sheetala Devi.

Meanwhile, back in Ammanagudi Street, life resumed its sedate lull-and-minor-disruption routine that was its usual rhythm. The flyover was completed but it made little difference to the traffic on the street for the cars and scooters preferred to use the road they had grown accustomed to. The welding shop and the flour mill, the last two that were still holding out, made way for a medium-rise lifestyle store. The Cassia tree fell one morning after a night of heavy rain, ripping itself from its moorings, falling partly on the footpath and partly on the street, prising open the freshly done road into wedges of tar cake, patterning the footpath to resemble the parched, drought-stricken, monsoon-less landscape, so favoured by photographers, and blocking traffic for a whole day—but harming no one. The Mother reigned undisturbed at her end, equally immune to the crowds that jammed her street on festival days and the sewage pipe that burst next to her shrine and threatened to engulf her sanctum sanctorum.

For Bali Brums it was the end. Nemesis had caught up with him, he acknowledged, as he prepared to go back to engineering college and being Balaji Brahmendra again. He quit before the programme director asked him to leave. He could not believe he had made such a mistake, he who was so good with people. To think that Nelly whom he imagined to be a sweet sixteen-year old had turned out to be almost thirty-something and dressed in those garish colours. (Moreover, he *never* spoke to women who wore salwar-kameez if he could help it.) He made up his mind decisively, not in the studio, after the programme was over, but later, in the house of the dead man, when he accompanied the body to the small flat in a narrow street, where reportedly the creature was first spotted, and met the man's widow. There, he was moved beyond words at the sight of the still, delicate figure, her eyes dazed with grief and disbelief, her face perversely glowing—but then how could she help it if her oil glands worked perfectly—her small forearm wrapped in a big bandage. Right then, when he was struck speechless confronted by her, he decided that his RJing days were over; he had to get serious.

As for Neela, she never for a moment doubted the wisdom of Bali Brums and it was with regret that she heard that he was leaving Voices from Heaven. Meeting Bali Brums was cathartic for her—it cured her of her need for him and, as he had advised, she was leaving the baggage of her past behind. She was seriously considering Antonia Larson's offer to travel to China, the Philippines and Mauritius with her for a year on a new project—connected with women and IT—as a sort of assistant-cum-manager. It would do her good; Sukhiya Ram would have to learn to live without her.

Pushpa Rani's father came home from Modern Nursing Home and began recovering very well, till one evening three months after the operation, he had a massive seizure and died in his bed at night, with all his family members asleep around him. A little after that, Pushpa Rani married Ranjit, the boy from tech support, and moved out of Ammanagudi Street.

At National Trust College, the condolence meeting for Shrinivas Moorty was held in the auditorium, since there were so many people. Jairam announced that the Centre for Inter-Disciplinary Studies, under its media studies wing, would continue with the film club that Shrinivas Moorty had started and institute a prize in his name for the best short film made each year by the students. He also proposed compulsory yoga classes for the faculty and a new medical plan that included an annual health check-up; it was high time they all became health-conscious. He had known Shrinivas Moorty for thirty years, he said, and would never have suspected that there was something the matter with his heart . . .

Lily sold the flat on Ammanagudi Street and went back to her parental home, two streets away. Her cousin Balu handled all the transactions for her. Suppi and Mani Nurse kept a round-the-clock vigil on Lily, taking turns, for Lily could just not be left alone after that bizarre and ghastly sequence of events. Moving to the parental home was a good thing for Lily. It was easier now for Mani Nurse to come to her for they lived on the same street, and what with Suppi's advancing knee problem, Mani Nurse and Lily were fast becoming inseparable.

Acknowledgements

~

To all those—friends and family—who unstintingly shared their memories of growing up and working in the city, thank you for your generosity.

The quotations used in this book are from the sources cited below, which I gratefully acknowledge:

1. 'Palanquin Bearers' by Sarojini Naidu, http://www.poetry-archive.com/n/palanquin_bearers.html, reprinted from *The Golden Threshold*, Sarojini Naidu, New York: John Lane Company, 1916. (last accessed 20 August 2009)
2. 'Saviraru Nadigalu' by Siddalingaiah, from *Saviraru Nadigalu: A Collection of Poems*, by Siddalingaiah, published by C.G. Krishna Swamy for the Karnataka Rajya Samudaya Samanvaya Samithi (Regd), Bangalore; 1979; 1981; Samudaya Prakashana. (The free translations of the lines quoted are mine.)